OUT OF TIME

Michael Stewart

COPYRIGHT

DEDICATION

This book is dedicated to my wonderful wife Kath who is my support, my rock and my soul mate.

THE BOMBER BOYS

There are times when military force, even brute force is necessary to overcome great evil.

From 1940, Britain, assisted by young men from the far flung reaches of the then empire; Canada, Australia, New Zealand, India, and South Africa, stood alone against the tyranny of Nazi Germany. The war had to be won and for four long years the lone responsibility for taking the war to the enemy homeland fell to the brave young men of Bomber Command and the USAAF's Eighth & Fifteenth Air Force.

The strategic bombing offensive against Germany was the longest and most costly of all WW2 campaigns and expensive in both human and economic terms, but it measurably shortened the war and saved tens of thousands of allied lives.

Of the 125,000 British and Commonwealth volunteers who served with Bomber Command, more than 55,000 lost their lives and 8,403 were wounded during the six years of conflict.

It required sustained and supreme courage for the young aircrews to take off time and again, night after night in the face of deadly and almost un-survivable odds. The airmen who began their tour of thirty operations realised it was unlikely they would get more than one third of the way through, and it wasn't just the likelihood of death but the method of dying that kept the young men of the RAF awake at night in their billets. Their choices were stark; perishing from fire, flack, fighter bullets or falling without parachutes from suddenly disintegrating aircraft.

Many of those who survived the terrible strain of answering without question the needs of their nation are either no longer with us or in failing health, and squadron associations are being wound up. They have had little thanks since the war and in recent years much criticism from some of those who, like us, enjoy the luxury of freedom and the right to free speech as a direct result of the sacrifices of those brave young men and women of Bomber Command. Surely there is no better time for us to say thank you to them all for bravely bearing the flame for later generations.

The Royal Air Force Bomber Command Memorial, Green Park, London.

CONTENTS

Chapter One

Philosophers and Psychologists will argue about what's real and what isn't, but I think you'll agree most of us tend simply to accept the reality of our day-to-day lives and everything we see about us. Or at least we think we do.

I view everything a little different now. Reality for me has become merely a thin skin of ice over a deep dark lake; easily broken if you're not careful and a whole new, unexplored and frightening world awaits you should you have the misfortune to fall through.

There were no warning bells to tip me off on the approaching danger that winter's afternoon when I fell through the ice; no sense at all my life was about to change so dramatically. Why would there be?

Do I wish I hadn't gone to work on that particular day? Should I have thrown a sickie and stayed in bed with a good book? For certain it would have spared me the pain and the horror of what was to come, but I didn't know that then. None of us ever do, do we? As they so often say, life turns on a sixpence.

Or maybe some things are just meant to be and can't be avoided no matter what you do or what actions you try to take. After that day I first broke through the thin ice of reality - as the magnificent Stephen King once quoted – I have come to believe something is at work. Somewhere in the universe (or behind it), a great machine is ticking and turning its fabulous gears.

Chapter Two - Bedford, Dec 12ᵗʰ 2015

I stood outside the old Corn Exchange building glancing up at the ornate but solid stonework, as I did every morning at that time. I'm no architect but I've always been deeply fascinated by our old buildings and the detail that went into their construction. Our ancestors knew how to build and it's so sad to think that the skills to construct anything like it again probably don't even exist nowadays.

Gazing up at the high arched windows I realised I had always loved the history of this particular place too. The BBC relocated to this very building during the Second World War when London became far too dangerous for the stars of the day. It must have been an amazing time here in Bedford back during those war years; the centre of broadcasting, the big band sound and British and American military uniforms on display everywhere. I glanced around at the people rushing past, focussed on getting to work and clearly annoyed at the idiot standing in the middle of the sidewalk gazing at up an old building.

Ah well, it was too cold to hang around for long anyway. November had been bitterly cold and December didn't look like it was going to fair much better. I pulled the collar of my old brown corduroy jacket up and stuffed my hands deeper inside my pockets to try and bring some warmth back into my numb fingers. I can't think why I didn't put my coat on this morning...although if I'm honest I do really. My one and only coat is bright emerald green and canary yellow, which is a little embarrassing, even for me. Most other guys of my age would own a trendy pad, a fast car and have a beautiful girl on their arm by now. They'd possess more than one coat too, and most likely not one in emerald green and canary yellow picked up at the local 'help the aged' shop (unless of course they were a Norwich City supporter). I have none of those things. It's not that I mind, although a girlfriend would be nice.

I made my way up the busy Harper Street pedestrian precinct, threading my way around the now late grim faced office workers hurtling along the pavement like guided missiles, hanging onto their designer cardboard Costa-Coffee cups as if their lives depended upon them. Without even glancing up I pushed open the doors of the modern glass, pink and green monstrosity of a building that now houses the Bedford library and stepped inside.

The furnace hit me as soon as I entered the building. Jay, our head librarian was a cold bloodied woman and liked the heating cranked up to at least 40 degrees Celsius. I liked to imagine that underneath her professional but severe blue-suited exterior there might be a cold-blooded alien reptile hiding, perhaps part of the advance party for an imminent invasion of the earth.

I felt the sweat begin to trickle down my back before I even had a chance to get my jacket off.

"Good morning James, you're ten minutes late again," Jay shouted across the heads of at least three customers who turned to glare at me.

"Sorry, yes won't happen again Miss Peppershall."

The disapproving customer's eyes lingered on me for a few seconds longer before they returned to their own dreary lives again. I hung my old jacket on a peg inside the little cupboard behind the librarian's desk and turned to face the steely eyed Jay.

"This can't keep happening James, you're a good worker but you're in your own little world and you need to snap out of it sometimes. Now, can you get down into the back storeroom and start unpacking and cataloguing those boxes of old books, let's see if there's anything we can use shall we?"

"Yes, Certainly Miss Peppershall." I grinned at the alien but she didn't smile back. *Her species probably doesn't have the facial muscles to allow it* I thought.

I meandered through the library, which now had half a dozen people browsing the shelves even at this early part of the day. As I turned right into the historical section I spotted the old man sitting at one of the tables studying a large rather ancient looking leather bound book. He seemed to be in the library at least once every day lately, and always appeared to stay for a few hours. The long black Crombie style coat and black felt Homburg hat he always wore - and never took off even in the sub-tropical heat of the library - presented him as an eccentric, peculiar old gentleman. Although that's perhaps a little unfair as I'd never even spoken to him, so he may well be as normal as me.

All said and done, despite my reptilian boss I did rather like my job. An assistant librarian may not be the most exciting job in the world for a young twenty five year old, and it certainly didn't do much to help me cultivate a dashing, adventurous image with which to attract the girls, but dull as it might be, I enjoyed it all the same. I love being around books, especially old ones, I always have. It's the feel of a book that excites me, the weight in my hands, the softness and quality of the leather, the design of the cover, the smell of the paper and the craftsmanship involved in the binding. You can't get any of that from a Kindle. Although to be fair I've never owned a Kindle so shouldn't be too judgemental. In fact, I don't even own a mobile phone, I'm not that good with technology.

As I reached the end of the history section I slowed down and glanced at the large selection of local history works, running my finger along the colourful spines as I dawdled past. Yes I did enjoy my work, but the one big problem with the job was the pay, or rather the lack of it. My earnings just about covered the cost of my lodgings, food and the occasional pint; but didn't stretch to a car, new clothes or going out on the town, which is probably one major reason why there wasn't a girlfriend.

Moving on I passed the racks of Z listed authors, such as Émile Zola, Rachel Zadoc and Timothy Zahn, and came to a blue door set in the end wall of the library. As I approached the door a sizzling sensation in my head began. I can only describe it as being similar to the buzzing you experience in your head when the anaesthetic knocks you out before an operation, only this is more intense and becomes significantly more painful the closer I get to the door. It's weird and completely unexplainable. That pain in my head is why I hated going to the storeroom. Once or twice when I had to go right into the storeroom I almost passed out. I mentioned it to Jay on a number of occasions but I think she thought I was either shirking or simply insane. She may well have been right on the latter.

The boxes I needed to sort were just inside the storeroom to the right of the door, so my plan was to pull the first one out fast and do the sorting on the floor in the back of the library, as far away from the storeroom as I could get. I pushed the door open and peered into the dark windowless room. With my left hand I fumbled along the wall for the light switch and clicked it on. I might as well have lit a candle for all the illumination the single dust covered light bulb gave out. As the bulb warmed up a stench of burning dust filled the small room.

Nausea accompanied the pain in my head which had suddenly become more intense, so I dropped to my knees and crawled into the room a few feet, feeling around on my right until my hands touched the dusty top of a large cardboard box. With the agony in my head increasing every second, I grappled with the heavy box and dragged it from the room.

Once outside I kicked the storeroom door closed and the pain began to diminish. By the time I was six feet away from the door the pain had vanished. It was the strangest thing ever and as I said I had no explanation for it. I had no intention of making a big issue out of it either as even I realised no one would believe me.

I lugged the heavy box further along the wall and about ten feet away from the storeroom door I slumped down on the floor next to the dusty carton. The arms and front of my previously white shirt were streaked in sweat and black dust, which, as I had no means of washing clothes in my bedsit, meant I was going to have to ask my landlady, Mrs King, if I could use her washing machine again, and she always charged heavily for the privilege. Luckily enough, my trousers were dark brown, so I reckoned they would last another couple of weeks without washing. I sure hoped there was something interesting in the box to make it all bloody worthwhile.

I settled down to examine the carton, which was about three feet by two and held around fifty books by my estimation. The cardboard was old and dusty and held together with a mile of string that had been expertly wound around the box. I pulled my little penknife out of my trouser pocket and started to cut through the tight strings on the top. A tinge of excitement ran down my spine and I shivered. Although I grumbled to Jay about taking on this cataloguing work, in reality I adored delving into the past almost as much as I adored books, and I'd been looking forward to getting my hands on these boxes for the past few days.

The story goes that they had been in deep storage ever since the old library had been hit by a V2 bomb at the end of the last war and a large number of the books suffered fire and water damage. The surviving books were boxed up and kept safe while the library building was repaired, but for one reason or another there were a few boxes that never made their way back onto the shelves again. The janitor discovered these a month ago and we've only now got around to opening them up after all these years.

My luck was in as the janitor had dragged all the boxes from the back of the storeroom and placed them near the front. I don't think I would have made it if I'd had to go that far into the storeroom. It seemed he didn't suffer from the same pains in his head as I did.

I pulled the string away from the box and examined the handwritten label that had been pasted onto the topside. Written in a neat hand in deep blue ink was the name and address of the library, the number of books inside, 52, the date, 31st December 1944 and a lady's name, Miss Bonnie Ohain. *Some other poor sod working late into the night on that New Year's Eve* I thought to myself.

I cut around the label with my knife so as not to damage it, pulled open the cardboard lid and was immediately covered in another layer of fresh black dust. After sneezing black gunge into my one and only tissue, the thought crossed my mind that I had to be the first person in over 70 years to peer into the box, ever since Miss Bonnie

Ohain, whoever she was, had sealed it up so carefully that lonely night.

It was almost a spiritual moment as I held back the cardboard flap with one hand whilst my other trembling hand reached into the box and lifted out the first tome which was neatly wrapped in a thick brown paper. I warmed to Miss Bonnie Ohain and her obvious love of books. After unfolding the little parcel I stared at the perfectly preserved hardback revealed in my hands; *The Story of the Malakand Field Force* by Winston Churchill. I had read that edition a number of years previous and recalled the story. In truth I've read most of Winston Churchill's works; he's always been a bit of a hero of mine. This one was an early edition by the looks of it and in almost mint condition. With care I opened the cover and saw it immediately. I don't think I quite comprehended what I was seeing at first, my mind was too slow to register, but all of a sudden the shock hit me and I felt my throat tightening and my heart pounding in my ears. Tucked inside the front cover was a folded piece of paper with a name written on the front in a bold black ink. The note was addressed to Mr James Cunnion. My name.

I stared at the note in stunned silence for what seemed like an age. My head felt light and my hands trembled as my eyes registered what was in front of me but my mind couldn't accept the reality of what my eyes were seeing. The note inside this book obviously hadn't seen the light of day for almost 70 years, and it was addressed to me.

I glanced up and scanned the room, but there was no one else in sight. With a deep breath I reached into the book and picked up the note. The texture of the yellowed paper told me it was a good quality stationery. Even to an untrained eye like mine the note was obviously old and had all the appearance of having been folded up inside the book for 70 years.

With trembling fingers I unfolded the paper and spotted more of the same neat block writing inside. It contained just one line and said simply: *'you are not who you think you are.'*

I stared at the piece of paper, reading and re-reading the line over and over, struggling to process the information in my mind. What on earth could it possibly mean?

A sense of unease settled over me and I had the strangest sensation of being spied on as I lifted my head and scanned the room again. The strange old man in the black coat and hat was pulling another book from the shelves over to my left, but he wasn't looking at me. Other than that the area seemed deserted. I still couldn't shake the sensation of being watched though.

I folded the paper back up and slid the note into my shirt pocket. With my heart in my mouth I spent the next ten minutes pulling out the other books from the box. I was no longer taking any interest in what they were, I only had one thing on my mind, searching for more notes inside. There weren't any.

I slumped back against the wall amidst the jumble of old books. What the hell was going on I thought. How in God's name could a note be addressed to me and placed inside a book 44 years before I was even born? Unless of course it had been addressed to another James Cunnion. Yes that was it, of course, how daft. I can't be the only James Cunnion who's ever lived around here. It's a coincidence, a big one I grant you, but just a coincidence all the same. Although I didn't believe that for one minute.

Trying to ignore the note that weighed heavy inside my shirt pocket, I grabbed my pencil and pad and spent the next few hours cataloguing each book by title, author, date published and edition, and included a short summary of the content of each book. It was mid-afternoon by the time I'd finished collating books and my back was breaking. I'd almost forgotten the note.

I packed the box back up and marked the lid with my bright red felt marker with the single word DONE. As good fortune would have it, Barry our janitor lumbered past as I finished taping the lid down.

"Barry, would you mind helping me get this box back in the storeroom?"

"Sure James, no worries, I'll get it," he said as he bent down, wrapped his huge hairy arms around the box and lifted it as if it weighed no more than a box of tissues. "You just get the door old mate."

I was only too pleased not to be going into that storeroom again.

"You're looking a right old mess James, you'll need to get tidied up before the dragon sees you in that state. She won't like you making the place look untidy," he said as he stepped back out of the storeroom, clicking the door shut behind him and grinning from ear to ear.

"You're right there," I said, grinning back at him. We acted like a couple of school boys caught raiding the tuck shop. "I'll sneak over to the washroom now. Thanks for your help."

"Anytime mate," Barry said as he sauntered away whistling something quite tuneless, but which might have been the theme tune from Jaws.

I made a dash for the washroom that was unfortunately on the other side of the library, but didn't get that far.

"James, what on earth..."

It was the reptilian invader.

"Look at the mess you're in. What will our visitors think?"

"Em...that I've been working?"

"Don't give me the backchat lad. It's three thirty now anyway, I suggest you remove yourself from the library, go home and get your clothes washed ready for tomorrow. How is the cataloguing coming along?"

Bloody lad? She was in her mid-thirties at most.

"I've done 52 books Miss Peppershall," I said, grinning as I handed my neatly pencilled notes over to her. Jay frowned as she glanced down at the crumpled papers in her hand, but didn't say anything.

Needing no further prompting to get off home, I took two steps backwards, turned and made a sharp exit for the front doors.

"And don't be late," she yelled after me.

"Don't worry, I won't Miss Peppershall," I yelled back over my shoulder.

I grabbed my tatty jacket from the cupboard behind the front desk and dashed out through the front doors before Jay changed her mind. Off home an hour and a half early, that was a result. Mind you, I had worked through my lunch break so I reasoned that it evened out. Not that I had any lunch to eat mind you, or any money to buy lunch with, so there hadn't been much point in stopping work just to listen to my stomach rumble.

The late afternoon felt cold and crisp and the bright winter sun hung low in the clear blue skies over Bedfordshire. Just the sort of day I loved.

I made my way back down Harper Street, gazing up at the brilliant white contrails contrasted against the blue sky. I'd never flown in an aeroplane and it was something I'd spent my whole life dreaming of. For as long as I can remember I've had a fascination with aeroplanes and anything to do with flying. I recall I used to drive my parents crazy as I spent hours locked away in my bedroom gluing together models of all the old military planes, Avrils, Bristols and Sopwith Camels. I'd also plague them to take me along to Abbotsinch aerodrome over near Paisley every weekend so I could watch the aircraft.

I glanced up on my way back past the Corn Exchange. I remembered all the great radio stars who used to perform there during the forties: Bing Crosby, Marlene Dietrich, Glenn Miller, Vera Lynn, Bob Hope, Humphrey Bogart, Gracie Fields, David Niven, the BBC Symphony Orchestra and the BBC Proms, after the Queen's Hall in London was bombed out. What an electrifying period of time that must have been.

I trudged on over the long road bridge crossing the River Ouse. Glancing down I watched as half a dozen young lads and girls paddled down river, gliding gracefully under the wide expanse of the bridge. As always, I stopped halfway over the bridge to admire the many wonderful old Victorian and Georgian buildings which ran along both sides of the river, gleaming in the sunshine. Walking on I tried not to glance at the modern carbuncle of the River Inn hotel situated on the riverside to the left of the bridge. *How do the modern town planners allow these blots on the landscape to be built?* I wondered.

A little further on past the bridge I arrived at the start of a row of old Georgian buildings. The first door in the row was mine, just before the Riobello Italian restaurant. As usual in the late afternoons the pungent smells of garlic and sauces being prepared reached my nostrils and made my mouth water.

Fumbling the single key out of my jacket pocket, I managed to get the door open, stepped into the tiny hallway and fell over a unicycle someone had left balanced against the wall. A bloody unicycle, why would anyone leave a unicycle in the hallway? Why would anyone want a bloody unicycle?

Slamming the door behind me, I stepped over the stupid unicycle and began the long climb up the five flights of bare wooden stairs to my bedsit in the attic, hoping and praying I wouldn't meet any of the other tenants on the way up. It's not that I'm completely anti-social, it's just that I get a bit tongue-tied and never seem to know what to say, so I've always avoided contact with other human beings as much as possible.

I had never seen anyone in the apartment on the ground floor, but Mrs King the landlady lived in the only flat on the first landing. I had no desire to face her so I tiptoed past and hurried up the next flight to the second floor as stealthily as my large frame allowed. So far so good. Relaxing a little I bounded up the third flight of stairs and ran straight into Miss Buxley. Sarah Buxley was a thirty something ex-model and stunning.

"Why James, it's lovely to see you. You're home early, is everything all right?"

I stood two steps down with my eyes just about level with her magnificent breasts. They seemed to be struggling to free themselves from a low cut and almost transparent t-shirt.

"Err...yes...late...no, sorry...early...yes," I said, rather eloquently I thought.

Sarah smiled and those huge sparkling blue eyes of hers made my knees wobble as she innocently smoothed her short black skirt down against her thighs. Her legs were the longest and shapeliest I had seen on any girl.

"I see, do you have anything exciting planned for this evening James?"

"Em...yes, no...err, no, I don't think so. Just washing my shirt."

Just washing my shirt? Jesus Christ, did I really say that? What was I thinking of? No bloody wonder I didn't have a girlfriend.

Sarah smiled. "Oh, that sounds nice James. Well you enjoy yourself. Is it cold out?"

"Em...no, well...actually I mean yes, I think," I soldiered on, relentlessly.

Sarah pressed her body against mine as she squeezed past me on the narrow stairs.

"Ah, OK. Well it's been lovely bumping into you James, enjoy your evening," she said, with a smile that looked suspiciously like one you'd have if you were studying an adorable but extremely stupid animal.

My face turned a horrible shade of crimson.

"No...I mean, yes, em of course...lovely."

Oh God, what a complete dork I thought to myself as I bounded up the last two flights of stairs, two at a time. As I ran I fished inside my inside jacket pocket and found the only other single Yale key I possessed, which I used to open the rather small sloping door on the top landing and dived into my attic bedsit, remembering to duck my head at the last minute.

"No, no, no, you complete bloody imbecile. Good grief, bloody washing my shirt? What is the matter with you?" I muttered out loud to myself. Sarah is a beautiful, adorable divorcee and I would love to take her out, hold her hand, and oh heaven, maybe even kiss those wonderful red lips of hers. But no, what chance do I ever stand of that when I can't even string a bloody sentence together in front of her?

Still shaking my head I threw my jacket onto the unmade bed and stared at myself in the full view mirror on the front of the old wardrobe door. On the positive side, tall, slim...well, if I'm being critical, bordering on emaciated, and still quite youthful looking. On the negative side, from the bottom up: old brown brogues which let in water, crumpled and shapeless dark brown woollen trousers at least a size too big for me, a white shirt with black dust stains all over the front, blue braces and an unruly mop of dark brown hair perched on the top of my head. Whatever makes me think Miss Buxley would even look twice at me?

I kicked my shoes off and went over to the small yellowing fridge that stood in the corner next to the decrepit four-ring Belling cooker. I'm not sure whether I hoped someone might have broken in while I'd been out, taken pity on me and put something tasty in my fridge, but no, to my constant surprise that hadn't happened. The one dried up slice of ham I'd been saving for a special occasion and the two Darylea triangles were still there. I took them out, put them on the small counter top and opened a single wall-mounted cupboard above where I discovered a lone pickled egg in a jar and two dried up slices of white bread which only had one or two bits of blue mould on so weren't too far gone. I picked out the mould as best I could, spread the Darylea slices over the bread, sliced up the pickled egg, lay that on top of the cheese spread and topped it all off with the slice of thin ham. A sandwich fit for a king.

After I'd clicked the kettle on for a cup of tea I carried my sandwich over to the big, well-used leather armchair that sat underneath the single skylight. I placed my sandwich down on top of a pile of books to the right of the chair and slumped down into the soft, cracked leather upholstery.

As I leaned forward to grab the sandwich, I remembered the note in my shirt pocket. For a brief moment I thought I might have dreamt it, but no, I felt the heavy paper in my pocket as I slid my fingers in, the note was still there. I eased it from my pocket and stared at the writing on the front again; 'Mr James Cunnion.' The ink was black and heavy, definitely from a fountain pen, not a Biro. I detected that from the way the ink flowed thicker at the corners as the nib formed the curves in each letter. Sherlock Holmes would have been proud of me. Carefully unfolding the yellowing paper I examined the words inside again; 'You are not who you think you are.'

What in heaven's name could that mean? I put the note down on the arm of the chair while I began to chew on the sandwich. *Of course I am who I think I am.* Aren't I? Good question.

I came to Bedford about 18 months ago after I finished University back in my home town of Glasgow. My parents were still there of course and I knew I should give them a call sometime soon, I couldn't recall the last time I spoke to them. I remembered my English Literature studies at the old University of Glasgow, and some of the good friends I made there. I knew I should try and look them up too, it had all been too long.

Too long? Too long? Something edged itself into my mind, teasing me, but I couldn't quite grasp it. *What was too long* I wondered? My mind drifted back to the university days before I came down south, remembering the antics we got up to, the old faces and all the events that always made me smile.

I managed to swallow the last of the dry sandwich and got up to make myself a cup of tea, still deep in thought. There was something niggling me about my university days and being here for the past 18 months, but what? The thought nibbled away at my mind, but I still couldn't latch onto it. When I tried to it slipped further away, maddeningly just out of reach.

The old white Ascot water heater gurgled and spat boiling hot water into the yellow stained sink while I grabbed the box of washing powder from under the small counter top and tipped the last of the powder into the light brown coloured water. I prayed my dust streaked shirt could be saved as I pushed the fraying dirty white cotton under the hot suds.

Wiping the soap suds on my trousers, I walked over to the wardrobe which stood next to the single bed in the other corner of the room and peered inside. My green and yellow coat hung beside a mustard-yellow woollen tank top, two pairs of jogging bottoms, two t-shirts and a pair of cheap white trainers which lay in the bottom of the wardrobe. But that was it, nothing else. I slid open a drawer and stared at the half dozen pairs of under-pants and socks.

Something niggled again, a hazy thought trying to take hold in my mind.

I turned and scanned the room. No photographs of my university pals, or my parents for that matter. In fact, nothing from my past life in Scotland. Did I really live like this? The thought started a swarm of butterflies churning in my stomach; something was wrong, that note had stirred something in me, a memory, but of what?

It wouldn't come, so I gave it up. My mother always said if you stopped thinking about what you were trying to remember, it would eventually come, creeping up on you when you were least expecting it. I hoped so.

I slipped my work trousers off and pulled on a pair of jogging bottoms and a t-shirt. I stared at the trousers as I hung them up and realised, as if for the first time, they were almost threadbare. Why did I live like this, I couldn't remember why I didn't have other trousers? It made no sense, no sense at all.

The TV that evening was crap. It was dark by five thirty and I was shivering and hungry so I climbed into bed at six thirty and read a copy of *Great Contemporaries* by Winston Churchill I'd borrowed from the library. I think I must have fallen asleep after about three pages.

Chapter Three - Bedford, Dec 13th 2015

I woke up with the sheets knotted around my body like a straight-jacket and Winston Churchill lying face down on the floor, closed, with the bookmark lying next to it. The nightmares had been vivid and the memories of fires, explosions, and the screaming of trapped people were all too fresh. I'd had nightmares before of course, but that night it had all seemed too real. Perhaps it was something to do with reading Churchill's book before I drifted off to sleep? But deep down I knew it wasn't that.

I struggled to see the time on my watch in the grey early light, it looked like eight o'clock. Uugh, I was going to be late again. I sat up on the edge of the bed and ran my fingers through the tangled mop of hair on my head. It was freezing. I hit the button on the old radio on top of the fridge as I passed by and Chris Evan's over energetic voice crackled into life. The ice cold water from the sink helped clear my head as I splashed it over my face and I had what could pass for a shave in the same cold water using a blunt Bic razor. I brushed my teeth but didn't bother trying to comb my hair, there was no point.

My now semi-white shirt hung from the makeshift line I'd rigged up between the curtain pole and the standard lamp with a piece of string. It was still damp so I slipped the yellow woollen tank top on over the top. It wasn't going to help much but I didn't fancy catching cold out there in the icy December wind. I even put my embarrassment to one side and pulled on my loud green and yellow coat that morning.

I forwent a cup of tea, thinking I might still make it to the library on time. I figured I could always have a tea in the little librarian's room, and I'd even be able to have milk with it there.

It was a dash through the busy streets of Bedford town centre that morning and I only managed a quick glance up at the Corn Exchange as I raced by. I bowled in through the doors of the library at one minute to nine.

"Ah, glad you could make it this morning," said Jay.

Trying to catch my breath, I smiled back at her with my most charming, but probably witless grin.

"Can you get on with cataloguing those old books again please James? I'd like to get them all finished off this week."

I'd forgotten all about the old boxes of books, and the note. A feeling of apprehension cast a shadow over me as the memories of yesterday flooded back. Would there be any more notes? It didn't seem likely but in that fleeting moment I had a feeling of certainty that there would be. Of course there would. My stomach lurched.

"Yes Miss Peppershall. I'll just make some tea first, would you like one?" I asked, with my sweetest sickly smile plastered across my face. Jay stared at me for a few seconds before turning on her heel and marching off. You know, now I come to think of it I don't think I ever saw her drinking tea before. Perhaps the reptiles from her planet don't?

I wasn't surprised to see the old man with the black Crombie coat and hat down at the historical fiction section again as I walked past trying not to spill my tea. He was always one of the first customers in the library in the morning and seemed to be around quite a lot lately. This time I managed to catch his eye and nod. He nodded back but didn't smile. He was a strange one.

The fizzing in my head started the moment I approached the stockroom door. I had planned to do exactly what I did the day before and grab the first box I came to inside the doorway and pull it out as quickly as I could. I had no intention of going right inside that stockroom, ever. I put my tea and notepad down on the floor alongside the back wall and went back to the stockroom. As I turned the handle and pushed the door inwards the pain in my head increased tenfold. I dropped to my knees and reached inside the doorway. The next dust covered box was just inside and I managed to slide it out of the room, slamming the door shut as soon as the box was out.

I dragged the box over to my tea and the fizzing in my head disappeared as quickly as it had come. I slumped down on the floor next to the box and sipped my hot, sweet tea. The box was pretty much indistinguishable to the one from yesterday, expertly tied up with string and with the same pasted on label on top. Identical neat blue handwriting adorned the label and as yesterday it detailed the name and address of the library, the number of books inside, 48 this time, the date, 1st January 1945 and that same name, Miss Bonnie Ohain. Whoever she was, she wasn't having a good start to the New Year of 1945.

I took out my pocket knife and flicked it open with one hand. The sharp blade sliced through the strings on top of the box with ease and I cut around the pasted label so I could open the flaps. Peering inside it was evident the box was stacked full of rows of books with their spines pointing upwards, but, as with the previous day there was one book lying flat on the top. *The River War* by Winston Churchill.

The butterflies immediately fired up in my stomach. Another book by Winston Churchill, lying on the top. It was too much of a coincidence and I had long ago stopped believing in coincidences. I reached in, picked up the book and stared at it. I even considered simply not opening it and ignoring the note I was certain would be inside, but I knew I was never going to be able to do that. With trembling fingers I eased back the front cover and sure enough, there inside the first page was another folded up piece of paper with my name clearly penned in black ink across the top. Holding the note between forefinger and thumb I placed the book down and compared the writing on the note to the handwritten label on the top of the box. It was neither the same ink nor the same handwriting. I pulled the note from yesterday out of my trouser pocket and studied both. The paper, ink and writing were identical to each other. It was obvious that the same person had written both notes, but it wasn't the same person who had boxed up the books and labelled the lid all those years ago.

I unfolded the new note and wasn't surprised to discover another single line in the same flourishing handwriting, but there was a little more this time. It read; 'You are not who you think you are James, do some research.' That was all it said. I read the line again and again and compared it with yesterday's note. This is impossible I thought. I examined the box again, it was simply not possible that it could have been tampered with. This box had not been opened since it was secured and sealed with that label nearly 70 years ago, I would stake my life on it.

But of course if the note was addressed to me that was impossible too, and I was certain the note was meant for me, it was no coincidence.

I remember there being an intense pain growing in my head, but this time not from whatever was going on in the storeroom. I leaned back against the wall and stared up at the ceiling. What the hell was going on, what did it mean, *I am not who I think I am*? Of course I am, I'm me, I've always been me. It's one of those things you just know isn't it?

But...and there was that fleeting thought again, just at the edge of my memory. I closed my eyes and tried to concentrate on it, grasp it. Something wasn't adding up, but what was it? I tried to calm my breathing down and relax and let the thought come.

There, it drifted into my consciousness again. Something about time, and this life I'm living in Bedford...but what was it? I opened my eyes and stared down at myself. It didn't seem to make sense that I had no real wardrobe of clothes, just these same clothes I keep washing and wearing, day after day. It's as if I'm leading a temporary life, but why hadn't I wondered about that before?

It was as I was taking another sip of tea I suddenly realised what didn't add up. The thought exploded into my mind like a tsunami, but it also brought with it a sense of relief. I had it, finally. That was it, my age doesn't match up with my memories. I closed my eyes again and focussed hard, I didn't want to let this one go again.

I knew I had attended university in Glasgow, my home city, back when I was around seventeen and a half. I remember it was straight after school. I had good marks for my school leaver's certificate and my mother and father, as poor as they were had somehow managed to scrimp and save enough money to put me into university. The University of Glasgow, no less. I was the talk of the neighbourhood I can tell you. My memories drifted to all the friends I had back then and all the tricks we got up to. I remembered old Jonathon Dooley, and Sammy McGregor, and the fun we had kicking around in the old close.

But back to the point in question, it still didn't add up. I know I did four years at university and came out with an exceptional pass in English literature. My parents, and the whole family were so proud of me that day, swaggering about in my black mortar board and gown, collecting my MA, and I was still only twenty one. The like had never been seen in Lyon Street before. I know I was the talk of the steamy for that whole summer, my mother never tired of telling everybody at every opportunity she got. They were both so proud of me. I understood what it meant to them, the first generation in our family to go to university and have an opportunity to make something more of themselves.

A few months after that I came down here to Bedford and started working at the library. That was a year ago now, when I was just coming up to my twenty-second birthday. But that's where it all goes wrong, that should make me exactly twenty two and eleven months old now, but I'm not am I? I'm almost twenty-five, there are two years missing somewhere. How can that be possible? My head spun, what the hell was happening to me? And why did I even come here from Glasgow, all the way down to Bedford for what? To work as an assistant in a small county library? Why did I do that, and perhaps more importantly, why haven't I asked myself before? What the hell have I been doing?

Too many questions and no bloody answers at all. My head hurt and it still wasn't because of that strange storeroom. I decided to do the only thing possible in circumstances like these; I needed to phone my mother, she would talk some sense into me.

I placed the book back in the box, stood up, folded both notes and slid them into my shirt pocket before weaving my way through the aisles towards the front desk. I had hoped Jay wouldn't be hovering around as I was wanting to use the phone urgently now, but there she was, sitting at the desk. "Damn!" I muttered under my breath.

Jay glanced up as I approached, she had been typing something at the computer. I thought I detected a look of concern on her face. Almost.

"James, are you all right?"

"Err, yes I think so, why?"

"Because you look absolutely ashen faced, like you've had a shock or something."

Hundreds of questions were jumbling around in my mind but in that instant I understood what I needed to do, I was going to confide in Jay, of all people. I wasn't at all certain it was the right thing to do as I had no idea how she was going to react, but in all honesty I had to tell someone. I was starting to think I'd gone mad.

"Yes Miss Peppershall, I think I have. Can I talk to you?"

A warm smile spread across Jay's face and her eyes lit up, something I can't recall ever having seen before.

"Yes of course James. It's quiet at the moment so come and sit yourself down here and tell me what's troubling you," she said, patting the empty chair next to her.

The hairs on the back of my neck stood up as I sat down next to her and tried to think about what I was going to say. I didn't want Jay calling the local loony bin to cart me away.

"You don't look well James, can I get you some water?"

"Em, no thanks, I'm fine," I lied, and then proceeded to fill her in on the events of the past two days. I think I managed to include all the details; I tried not to leave anything out. I even showed her the two notes that I hoped would help corroborate my story. When I finished we both sat staring at each other. I was beginning to wonder if I had made a grave mistake when finally Jay spoke.

"Oh my God James, I'll admit I'm struggling to accept what you've told me, but I believe you, and I don't think you're lying. You can't fake the way you look, that speaks volumes, so, you'd better get on and phone your mother, I think that'll be a good start." Jay got up from her seat.

"Would you prefer me to leave you in peace while you make your call? I don't mind."

Actually, I was hoping she would stay. I admit I felt a lot better since I told her everything and I sort of wanted her there in case there were any more shocks coming my way.

"Actually, would you mind staying, in case I need some support?"

"Of course James. It's no problem. Now, do you know your mother's phone number?"

"Yes I do. It's a landline number for their place in Glasgow. They should be in at this time of the morning."

I reached for the phone on the desk and pulled it towards me.

I rang my parent's number through my mind as I picked up the receiver and pressed the buttons; 041 945 1122. I held the receiver to my ear while the butterflies swarmed around my stomach. Jay perched on the desk next to me and smiled sympathetically. She was pretty when she smiled. *She should do it more often* I thought.

I heard a few clicks and whirls from somewhere far away and a repeating looped voice message came on the line, 'the number you've dialled has not been recognised, please try again.'

I put the receiver down, picked it up and tried again, and heard the same-recorded message.

"What's wrong James?"

"I don't know, I'm getting an unobtainable, listen," I said as I passed the receiver over to Jay.

"Are you sure you're dialling the number correctly? Here, you write it down and I'll dial it," she said as she slid a Post-it note and pen across. I wrote the number down and passed it back to her. Jay picked up the Post-it note and studied what I had written.

"Ah I can see the problem James, you missed out the one. There should be a one after the first zero. Glasgow is 0141."

I glanced at the note in her hand.

"No that's correct, the number is definitely right. I've always been good with numbers and I can remember the numbers of most of the people I know who have telephones." As soon as I'd finished the sentence I was aware it sounded odd. A frown creased Jay's forehead as she stared at me.

"No one remembers phone numbers James, they're stored in your mobile."

"I don't own a mobile," I said, and wondered why I didn't. I was still getting the slightly odd stare from Jay.

"But James, the number isn't right. Back in the 1990s BT ran out of telephone numbers, so to resolve the problem they changed all the phone numbers in the UK by adding a 01 onto the front of them. So for example Glasgow would have been 041 but after 1995 it became 0141. So the number you're dialling is definitely wrong. Here let me...," she said, as she redialled the number herself, but this time adding in the extra digit.

After a couple of clicks on the line I heard a ringing tone. Jay passed the phone back to me and I held it up to my ear. The ringing stopped and a female voice said, "Hello."

The accent was Glaswegian but I knew instantly it wasn't my mother.

"Hello, who is this?" came the voice again, a little agitated now.

"Em sorry, I think I must have a wrong number, I'm looking for Ellie...Mrs Ellie Cunnion."

The voice on the other end relaxed a little, "I'm sorry, there's no one here by that name."

"OK, I'm so sorry to disturb you. Can I just ask, are you in Lyon Street, Glasgow?"

"No I'm not, never heard of it."

I tried to thank the lady but she put the phone down before I could say any more. Jay smiled that knowing smile at me again.

"Look James, I know you think the number is right but maybe you've got a digit or two wrong. Please let me look it up on the on-line Yellow Pages?"

I had nothing to lose, and I had run out of ideas anyway so I saw no reason to stop her.

"OK, thanks for helping me, I appreciate it," I said, as I smiled back at her.

Jay slid down into her seat in front of the computer and she began clicking keys and sliding the black mouse around. I'd never really got into computers so I knew I wasn't going to be much help. Anyway, if the wide unblinking eyes and the compressed lips were anything to go by, Jay was obviously on a mission and I didn't want to disturb her.

"What is your parents address James?"

I had to think for a moment. "Em...16 Lyon Street, Glasgow."

"And the postcode?"

"The postcode? Err...I don't think they have one."

Jay stared at me. "Of course they have one, everyone has a postcode."

I racked my brains, but nothing came to mind. "No, sorry, I don't know, I've never heard of one."

"All right, never mind, I'm sure I can manage without." Jay stared at the screen for a few moments, looking increasingly frustrated.

"Did you say Lyon Street, Glasgow?"

"Yes, number 16. It's up a close in the first tenement up from Garscube Road, right next to the Garscube Bar."

Jay clicked and tapped for a few more moments.

"Nope, there's nothing listed. I even pulled up Google maps and there's no such road in Glasgow. I can see the Garscube Road you mention, but no sign of a Lyon Street."

I stared at the screen in front of her that was now filled with a large brightly coloured map. I could see Garscube Road in the centre of the screen but she was right, no Lyon Street.

"But it's definitely there, I lived there with my parents up until a year ago. This is crazy."

"Maybe I could switch to street view, you might recognise something?"

I wasn't entirely sure what she was talking about, but she seemed to know what she was doing so I said yes anyway. The screen instantly changed to a static and very clear picture of a road with modern looking buildings along both sides.

"Wow!" I said. "That's bloody amazing."

"Yes it is rather isn't it?" she said, grinning at the screen.

I stared at the picture on the screen as Jay somehow moved us along the road. I didn't recognise anything.

"I don't know where that is but it's not the Garscube Road I remember," I said.

Jay stared at me and frowned again. She turned back to the screen and her fingers resumed their dance at the keyboard.

"Rather than looking at maps I'm going to Google Lyon Road, Glasgow and see what comes up."

Different screens popped up on the computer and were closed again in a seemingly endless cascade of colours, pictures and text. I couldn't keep up with it so decided to try and make myself useful.

"Fancy a tea Miss Peppershall?"

"Yes please. And James, please stop calling me Miss Peppershall, my name is Jay," she said, without taking her eyes off the screen.

That made me smile. I had definitely warmed to Jay in the last ten minutes or so, perhaps she wasn't an alien reptile after all. I stood up and made my way over to the small staff kitchen area behind the front desk. I glanced around the library and spotted the old man with the black coat and hat staring at us. I grinned at him and nodded but he didn't smile back.

When I came back with two steaming mugs of tea Jay was still in her seat, but she was no longer looking at the screen. She was staring up at me and if I'm any judge of these things she was looking like she'd seen a ghost.

"Are you all right...err...Jay?" I said as I placed the two mugs carefully down on the blue and white striped coasters and slid back into my seat.

Jay didn't answer for a minute, she definitely seemed a little shell shocked. "I'm not sure James," she said, finally. "I'm really not sure."

I tried to keep it light. "So come on, what have you found out?" I asked, and followed that up with a pathetic chuckle.

"James, I don't even know where to begin with this. None of it makes any sense, but it's all there, in black and white so to speak."

"What is?" I asked, starting to feel my own anxiety levels rising again.

"I've discovered from a whole load of posts and on-line discussions that Lyon Street definitely doesn't exist James, it doesn't. But it used to."

"It used to? What do you mean, what happened to it?" My stomach was tying itself in knots.

"It's exactly as you explained James, Lyons Street did adjoin Garscube Road and there was a pub on that corner, a pub called the Garscube Bar just as you said. Lyons Street itself had half a dozen old Victorian built tenement buildings along both sides of the street. Can you remember anything else about it James?"

Instantly my mind was back in my childhood and I visualised growing up in that poverty stricken, grimy street that we called home. Living on Lyon Street certainly couldn't be described as an uplifting experience, but despite the hardships I had nothing but fond memories for those times.

"Yes, I remember it was a hard place, and the men, they were all as hard as nails. You know the sort, whisky for breakfast, fights with intruders from other districts, a quick game of pitch-and-toss and a few bob when you could pick it up. The story goes there was one time they hung an out of town policeman up on a lamppost by his braces and the wains danced round him like redskins. The police didn't usually go anywhere near that part of Garscube Road and Lyon Street, and definitely not alone. I remember the old folks saying that during the First World War, over 200 of the men from those half a dozen tenements in Lyon Street joined up and fought for their country. Fathers, sons, brothers and neighbours went, often all the men from a whole family. Most of them joined the Highland Light Infantry which had a barracks close by up on Maryhill Road. My father told me that many of the men were horribly injured and a lot never came back at all. He said that medals clinked in every close as the boys came marching home to unemployment and those grey, stark tenements. You know, Lyon Street became known as the highest decorated street in the country, one decorated soldier for every square foot of tenement."

Jay sat motionless, staring wide eyed at me as I spoke. I should have spotted something was wrong, but I didn't and pressed on regardless with my tale.

"I remember every armistice day a piper and a bugler used to march from the Maryhill barracks down to Lyon Street, which was always heavily decked out with bunting and flags. All the old soldiers were out in their Sunday best and covered in medals. The piper played a lament, there was a short service attended by the whole street, and then the bugler sounded the Last Post. Afterwards there was always a street party. It was harsh living there Jay, but it was a real friendly neighbourhood all the same."

"When was the last armistice day party you had there with your parents James?"

"It would have been the November before last, just after I finished University and before I came down here."

Jay's staring eyes didn't blink and it finally dawned on me she was in shock. I thought harder about the answer I had given her and realised of course there was something wrong.

"Sorry Jay, I haven't accounted for the missing two years have I? So now I'm not sure I know when I was last there until we sort this mystery out."

Jay continued to stare at me in silence. It seemed as if she was trying to formulate the words in her mind before she spoke.

"No James, it's not the two missing years I'm worried about. I'm not sure I believe any of this myself yet but you see...Lyon Street hasn't existed for 53 years James. It was bulldozed to the ground in October 1962 along with the Garscube Bar, and a new school, St Joseph's was built in its place. The last of the locally famous Lyon Street armistice parties was held at the beginning of the Second World War. That piper hasn't played his lament for over 75 years James."

I tried to digest the enormity of what Jay was saying.

"James, look at you, you dress like someone from the 1930s or 1940s, you have no idea about technology, it's like somehow you don't belong here at all, and if I'm honest I've always thought that. Now you're telling me that you were there when all these events were happening, but that was 75 years go James, in the 1930s and 40s."

For the first time I realised Jay was scared. I felt pretty shook up myself as it happens.

"But that's impossible Jay. I do remember it all, and what about my parents? They're still living there."

"No they're not James, no one has lived in Lyon Street for over 50 years. Wherever they are I don't know, but they're not there."

That hit me hard. All this was impossible, completely impossible. It couldn't be happening to me. My stomach was in knots, my heart pounded and pains were shooting across my forehead. I dropped my head into my hands and Jay put her arm around my shoulders. That was to be the one and only time Jay showed me any real affection, but I liked it all the same.

"Don't worry James, we'll track down your parents. I'm sure we'll get all this little mystery resolved one way or the other." Jay was saying all the right words but the frown on her face said she didn't believe it either. She was as confused and scared as I was.

"Do you want to go home James? I'll give this all a little more thought and I'll do some further research, and hopefully by tomorrow we'll have a plan?"

I wasn't sure if I wanted to go home alone to my unfriendly bedsit just yet. Since yesterday my apparent lack of a life there concerned me as much as anything else.

"No Jay, if it's all right with you I'd rather stay here and get back on sorting those old books. It might help me take my mind off things, and anyway, I may even find another mysterious note that'll explain everything for us?" I grinned, trying my best to appear relaxed and not look like the weirdo I was starting to feel I was.

"Well, OK James, if you're sure?" She smiled but didn't seem convinced either.

I stood up, walked around to the front of the desk but paused to glance back at her.

"Thank you Jay for helping me. I do appreciate it. There's no one else I can turn to."

Jay smiled a beautiful warm smile and nodded. She wasn't so bad after all. If I'd have known what the future held for me I might have kissed her goodbye there and then, but of course I didn't know. Who does?

As I walked back to the storeroom it crossed my mind that the strange old man with the black hat was nowhere to be seen.

Back in my sorting area I dropped down onto my knees and began to remove all the books from the cardboard box and stack them neatly into little piles. I grabbed my notepad and pen and began the laborious, but therapeutic task of examining and cataloguing each volume. I immersed myself in the task at hand and almost - but not quite - forgot all about the mysterious events surrounding me.

It's funny isn't it, perhaps it's an evolutionary coping mechanism or something, but when life comes along and bites you hard, and your world turns upside down, it never ceases to amaze me how quickly your mind settles into the new reality and you just get on with it? Something was indeed wrong, things didn't add up in my life, but on the positive side I had found a new friend in Jay and I was convinced we'd get to the bottom of the little mystery. Anyway, I reasoned there would be a totally logical explanation for everything.

How wrong could I be? Little did I know then of the even bigger bite life had waiting for me that afternoon. If I'd known, I probably wouldn't have stayed.

It took the best part of three hours to sort and catalogue four boxes of books. Fortunately Barry the janitor came past and pulled out the next three boxes for me. I peeked at my watch, it was approaching three thirty and all I had to do was push the four boxes back inside the storeroom and I could get off. Not that I had any real reason to want to get away, but I felt dusty, dirty and emotionally drained from the events of the morning. Jay had been by to check on me more than once and she was still smiling, so things were looking up there.

I slid the boxes over to the storeroom and lined them up before I pushed open the door. I intended spending as little time as possible in that doorway with the door open. I turned the handle, pushed the door inwards with my knee and began to slide the boxes in, one by one. The pain inside my head increased as I opened the door and by the time I'd managed to slide the last box into the room the pain had become almost unbearable. I gave the last box a final shove with my foot as I leaned into the room with the intention of grabbing the door handle.

That was when it happened.

Chapter Four - Bedford, Dec 13th 1944

Something moving at considerable speed slammed into the middle of my back and the wind was forced from my lungs. The momentum hurtled me forward through the open door and into the storeroom, there was no way of stopping myself. My feet connected with the last of the boxes I had just slid in and I tumbled forward, rolling over the stacked boxes and onto the empty floor in the middle of the storeroom. The unbearable pain increased until there was a pop inside my head, like the kind when your ears clear in a swimming pool, and then the agony stopped. The relief washed over me as I lay on the floor in a daze. I recall hearing someone, a man's voice, apologising over and over. My eyes began to focus again as I sat up and stared at the man in front of me who was now attempting to hold my hand, presumably with the intention of helping me to my feet. It was the old man with the black Crombie coat and the black Homburg hat.

"I'm so sorry, are you all right? I tripped over the carpet with my clumsy feet and knocked you down. I feel so bad, how are you feeling?" He was trying to smile, but his frown suggested an element of real concern too.

He sounded sincere enough, although I couldn't remember there being any carpet on the library floor and I didn't see how a little old man could have accidentally knocked me so hard through the doorway like that. Stranger things have happened I guess. I accepted his hand and made my first attempt at standing up. It didn't go so well, my head felt woozy and I slumped back down again.

"Ah don't worry, it's often like that. Just sit still for a minute and your head will return to normal."

I peered up at the old man, a little confused. I still hadn't yet fully entered the fog of unreality that would soon engulf me. What the hell did he mean by 'it's often like that?' Did he make a habit of knocking people over in libraries? I reached up again, he took my hand and this time I made it all the way up. I still felt a little light headed but managed to remain on my feet.

"How are you feeling now, would you like me to go and get you a drink of water?" he asked. His eyes again suggested a real concern.

I stared down at the little man. "No, I'm fine, honestly, thank you."

I think it was about then I realised I was no longer inside the storeroom, I was somehow outside in the main library. I had a sense of that fog of unreality thickening around me as I peered over the man's head at the deep mahogany panelled walls and the oak coloured wooden bookshelves. Nothing wrong with that in a library you'd think, it's just that the library I had been in all morning had white painted walls and stainless steel book racks, not oak and mahogany.

I stared open mouthed at the unfamiliar room as the little old man took two large steps backwards. He kept his eyes fixed on mine as he backed away, and he seemed somewhat wary. I had no intention of letting him go, he had some explaining to do and I was just about to make a grab for him when a female voice interrupted us.

"James, James, there you are, where have you been?"

I glanced over to my right and striding towards me was a girl. Not just any girl though. The bright red lipstick framed her perfect white smile and her striking red hair hung in ringlets that bounced like bedsprings as she walked. Her shoulders were back, her breasts strained against the fabric of her cotton dress and her tiny waist was accentuated by a fashionable wide belt that hung on her wider hips. Despite the over-painted lips, she was absolutely stunning in a natural and very innocent way. I couldn't take my eyes off her as she almost skipped towards me.

"James, where have you been hiding today? I haven't seen you since you came in."

Her smile sent friendly butterflies swarming through the pit of my stomach. Not knowing what to say I simply stared at the vision before me. Out of the corner of my eye I spotted the little old man had taken this opportunity to vanish, but at that moment I didn't much care, all of my attention was focussed on the girl. She seemed to know my name but who the hell was she? And where was I?

The girl stopped about a foot away from me, gazing upwards into my eyes. Even through the lenses of her tortoiseshell glasses I could see her eyes were a dazzling emerald colour which contrasted perfectly with her red hair. Her pupils seemed to sparkle with excitement behind her glasses.

She was still staring and smiling at me when I finally realised she was waiting for an answer.

"Em...I've been working, sorting boxes of books."

The smile froze on the girl's face and a frown appeared.

"Are you OK James, are you feeling all right?" she asked as she shifted her gaze and now seemed to be examining me from head to toe.

"What do you mean working and why would you be sorting books?"

"Err...wouldn't I?" I stammered.

"And your clothes James, I hadn't noticed before when you came in, but...em, I mean...sorry, I don't mean to be rude but I think I need to take you shopping for some new rags. These ones look a little worse for wear."

I glanced down at my clothes and then back at her.

"Oh...do they? Sorry."

She seemed a little embarrassed now.

"Oh I'm sorry James, I didn't mean to..."

"It's OK," I said, trying to help with the awkward situation. "I know, I do need a new outfit, if you could help I would love that." I grinned at her and she grinned back. A lovely warm feeling settled into the pit of my stomach. I'm not used to pretty girls actually wanting to talk to me, let alone help me with my wardrobe.

She raised her left hand and peered at the small leather strapped watch on her petite wrist. "Hmmm I'm just about to get off for the afternoon, would you like to...em, perhaps have a cup of tea with me?" As soon as the words were out she realised what she had just said. "Oh sorry, that's so forward of me, I didn't mean to..." It was her turn to stammer awkwardly now.

"I'd love to," I said.

It's an old cliché but her face actually lit up and I was sure her eyes sparkled even more. Perhaps it was just wishful thinking.

"Ooh great, shall we go to Rosie's tea room?"

I had no idea where that might be, or even where I was right now, so I thought it best to just go along with it.

"Fine by me."

The girl spun on her heel and began to walk away past the rows of books.

"Come on then," she called over her shoulder.

At that point I think I might still have been able to simply turn around and walk back through the head splitting divide to my library, my home, and I don't know why I didn't, although I suspect the girl might have had a lot to do with it.

So instead, I followed on obediently, enjoying the way her full hips swayed from side to side, rubbing against the tight cotton fabric of her floral patterned dress. We walked over to a large double pedestal wooden desk at the front of the library. There was another young lady sitting behind the desk and she was busy stamping the inside covers of a pile of books with a rubber stamp, occasionally dipping the end of the stamp into an ink pad on the table in front of her. I glanced over the desk and noticed straight away there was no computer, or any other tech stuff for that matter; no iPad's, no mobile phone, no chargers and no calculators. There was however a large old typewriter and the one single piece of technical equipment, a heavy looking black telephone.

"Sarah, I'm heading off now," said the girl standing in front of me. Sarah glanced up and smiled, looking first at the girl and then staring over at me.

"Oh hi James, I forgot you were in today. Yes of course, no problem Bonnie, I'll be here for another hour and a half. How are you James, do you want to hang around here with me?" she said, still staring up at me and pouting her red lips in a way that was designed to make my legs quiver.

Bonnie threw back her head and laughed out loud. "James is coming with me," she said, jabbing her thumb back at me. It seemed like the point wasn't up for debate.

Sarah grinned. "Ah well, God loves a trier. Some girls have all the luck."

Bonnie's face turned a wonderful shade of crimson.

"I'll grab your coat James and then we can get off," she said as she moved around to the other side of the desk and disappeared through an open doorway behind.

"My coat? Err, yes my coat," I whispered, wondering what on earth was going on. A worrying suspicion was also beginning to dawn on me that the Bonnie who had just tripped away to get my coat was the same Bonnie Ohain who had sealed up the boxes I had been sorting earlier this afternoon. I knew it was impossible as that was 70 years ago, but this Bonnie and that Bonnie were one and the same, I just knew it.

It felt like I'd stepped into some kind of science fiction or horror movie. Bonnie and Sarah most definitely weren't in the horror category, but there's always a pretty girl cast in all scary movies and I was thinking maybe we just hadn't got to the scary bit yet. Little did I know then just how right that would prove to be.

"Here James, here's your coat," said Bonnie as she emerged from the doorway holding up a long and rather heavy looking blue coat.

"Ah OK, thank you," I said, as I held out my hand and took the heavy woollen coat from her. "Are you sure this is mine?"

Bonnie laughed out loud again as she stared at me. "Oh James, of course it's yours, who else would have a coat like that around here?"

I held the coat up in front of me and recognised it immediately. The shoulder epaulettes with the two bands of gold braid and the heavy silver buttons with the King's crowns on were a big clue. It was a RAF greatcoat, just like the one Captain Jack Harkness wears in the Torchwood series. Nice.

Bonnie was staring at me expectantly so I decided I might just as well play out the movie and see where this went. Surprisingly, or perhaps not, the coat fitted me perfectly.

Sarah's lips parted into a beaming smile. "Have a great time you two," she said as she picked up her rubber stamp again, dipped it into the ink pad and resumed marking the books.

Bonnie smiled back. "I'm on duty over at Kempsford tomorrow and Friday, but I'll be back in again on Saturday on my day off so I'll see you then."

"OK, bye," shouted Sarah as Bonnie pulled on her own green and brown tweed coat, slung her battered brown leather handbag over her arm and pushed her way through the heavy double swing doors at the entrance to the library. I followed her out into the early fading light of an icy cold winter's afternoon and watched the hot breath escaping from our mouths as we made our way down the stone steps.

The RAF greatcoat was heavy and the woollen serge material was rough, but I was glad of the warmth it provided. I pulled up the large collar against the icy wind and shivered a little.

At the bottom of the steps I turned to stare up at the library building. Before I even had time to admire the magnificent Victorian architecture, I spotted the wall of sandbags piled up around the front of the building and the white Gaffer tape criss-crossed over the windows. The first thought that sprung to mind was 'the blitz.' Yep, the story line was going well, all the props were here. Bonnie had dated her box label as December 1944, so what else should I have expected? I didn't understand any of what was happening and if I cared to analyse it I might find I was in shock, but in another way it was quite exciting and I enjoyed the prospect of spending a little time with the beautiful Bonnie.

I wanted to ask her where we were, but just managed to stop myself as I realised how stupid that would sound. I thought it better to simply go along with everything for now and try not to put my foot in it.

Bonnie grasped my hand in hers and gave me an embarrassed stare.

"Do you mind?" she asked.

My heart gave a lurch as I glanced down at her delicate leather gloved hand in mine and thought how perfect it looked.

"Of course not," I said, and grinned at her as I gave her hand a little squeeze. Horror or not, I was starting to like this little movie.

Hand in hand we strode along the pavement, carefully avoiding the piles of snow which had been scraped away and piled up on the sides. I felt as if I were walking along in a dream as I began to take in some of the details of my new surroundings. It was different for sure, but I recognised the street we were in almost immediately. We were in Bedford town centre and walking along Harper Street towards St Paul's Square and the old Corn Exchange. A road I walked along twice a day, every day. The only thing wrong with this Harper Street was that it was no longer a pedestrian precinct. It was now a road, with cars running up and down puffing out clouds of white smoke into the icy atmosphere.

Despite the unreal, almost fantasy-like situation I'd found myself in, I was strangely comforted by the fact that at least I recognised most of the buildings around us and I knew where I was, even if I wasn't sure exactly 'when' I was.

The road wasn't busy. There were a few snow covered cars parked here and there by the kerbside and all of them were old enough to belong in a car museum. I recognised a few of the old classics as we walked down the street: a little black Ford Anglia, an even smaller two seater Austin 8, two Hillmans, a Morris 10 and a dark green Humber Super Snipe. *All of these cars belong to real people,* I thought as I touched the bonnet of the black Morris 10 as we walked by, the metal was icy cold, it was real.

I began to take notice of the other pedestrians around us too. Everyone seemed to be wrapped up like us against the falling snow and hurrying along minding their own business. It was the same, but again it was all so different. There were no bright green and yellow coats, no big clothing brands, no colourful sportswear, everyone looked so similar. The men all either had on military uniforms in blue and khaki, or long dark woollen trench coats, a formal hat, and trousers. No jeans to be seen here. The ladies, although more elegant, wore long coats, hats and short boots or court shoes. Again, no jeans or trainers, nothing remotely casual. The only colourful items of clothing I noticed were the scarves, otherwise it all seemed to be blacks, browns, blues and greys.

I almost jumped out of my skin at one point as an old motorcycle roared past with its engine coughing and banging and thick black smoke billowed out of the exhaust pipe, contaminating the fresh white snow which was starting to settle again on the road.

I thought I was coping well with my fall through the looking glass, but if I was being honest I'd have to admit I was freaking out just a little. I think a human mind that is moderately well balanced (as I like to believe mine is) can absorb a fair amount of strangeness before it goes tilt, but there is a limit, and I worried I was fast approaching it.

Bonnie pulled me along, turning left at the end of Harper Street and across in front of the Corn Exchange building. No one could have missed the giant colourful posters outside.

"Look!" I shouted at Bonnie as I pointed at one of the posters on the front of the building. "Well as I live and breathe, it's only the bloody Glen Miller band!"

Bonnie slapped my arm with her free hand.

"That's enough of your swearing James Cunnion! You're not out with the RAF boys now you know."

I looked at her and grinned. "Sorry Bonnie, but, wow! The Glen Miller Band."

Bonnie and I stared at the poster as we stood on the pavement directly in front of it. I think the realisation that I was definitely no longer in the second decade of the 21st Century and, bizarre as it might be, was now in wartime Britain in the 1940s finally hit me.

"Yes I know, he's great isn't he? I've been along to see the band twice this year already," said Bonnie.

I pulled her around and stared at her. "You...you've actually seen Glen Miller?" I was astounded. I've always had a real thing for the big band sound of the 1930s and 40s, especially the Glen Miller Band. The music was so clear and exciting back then. I've always thought I would have braved the war years just to be able to experience that music and the atmosphere for real, it must have been truly wonderful. And here I was, holding the hand of a girl who has apparently seen and danced to the music of Glen Miller himself.

Bonnie stared up at me through her misty glass lenses. I'm sure they were icing up.

"Haven't you ever been?"

"No," I admitted, honestly.

"Well then we simply have to go. We'll find out when his next concert is on and we'll go, he's always playing here."

"OK, is that a date then?" I said, grinning from ear to ear.

Bonnie looked embarrassed again. "Oh, I...I...didn't mean to..."

"It's OK," I said. "I would love to go with you, it would be a dream come true." And I meant it, but at the same time I was racking my brains to remember just when Glenn Miller died. I knew it was near to the end of the war sometime but I couldn't remember exactly when. I hoped we could go before he was lost to the world forever.

We held hands in front of the Corn Exchange, grinning at each other. I was thinking that maybe I had died and gone to heaven and I would have liked the moment to last forever, but Bonnie had other ideas.

"OK, come on, I'm getting cold, let's get to Rosie's and get some good hot tea inside us. You never know, she might even be able to manage a couple of hot chocolates. Anyway, it's getting dark and I think the weather might be coming in so you'll have to get your motorbike and get going soon. We should get a move on."

Did I hear her right? 'My motorbike?' I had the creepiest feeling we were now already moving into the next scene of that movie.

"Em...where did I leave my motorbike Bonnie?"

Bonnie stopped walking and turned to stare at me again.

"You are a strange one today James and no mistake. It'll be where you always park it won't it?"

That was going to be no help whatsoever, but I didn't want to press the matter any further just now. I'd work the conversation around to it again later over tea.

"Err...yes I guess so, of course it will. Come on, let's get that tea.'

We came to a small shop doorway set back into a wall. I wiped some fresh fallen snow from the small roundel glass leaded windows at the side of the door and peered inside. It was exactly how I imagined a quaint little old English tea shop should look like: little round tables covered with crisp white linen tablecloths, a long glass counter showing off a myriad of cakes, sandwiches and biscuits, and a waitress dressed in a black dress and starched white apron. Bonnie pushed open the door and I followed her into the warmth inside.

We were in luck, Rosie had hot chocolate on so Bonnie and I had a large cup, each topped with homemade marshmallows. I ordered spotted dick and custard and Bonnie went for a lemon meringue. It was all truly delicious.

"So, what are you going to be doing with your evening off, or wait, let me guess, you'll be sharing a few jars with your chums back at the base later I shouldn't wonder?" Bonnie said, with what seemed to be a sorrowful sort of smile, if there is such a thing.

I had no idea what she was talking about or how I was even going to attempt to answer that one, so I took a huge mouthful of spotted dick instead.

"Pig," Bonnie said, grinning at me.

I grinned back, or at least I tried to whilst still keeping the spongy mess inside my mouth. *No point in turning her off just yet* I thought. The tea room wasn't busy on that late Wednesday afternoon but a few customers did come in and more than one or two of the men slapped me on the back and smiled grim faced at me. I wasn't sure what that was all about and I didn't know any of them - why would I? - but Bonnie nodded to each of them as if it was an accepted gesture they all seemed to understand, and I was probably the only one who didn't, but couldn't ask.

"Do you fancy seeing Bing Crosby in Going My Way at the Odeon the next bit of leave you get? It's still showing there and I haven't seen it yet," Bonnie asked as I scraped my bowl to make sure I didn't miss any of the sweet custard.

"Err...yes I guess, yes, that would be lovely, can't wait," I said. She kept mentioning this leave thing. I was starting to think that in this movie I seemed to be starring in I was in the military or something. I suppose given there was a war on it would seem likely, and the RAF greatcoat was a bit of a giveaway. The thought crossed my mind that

I hoped no one expected me to fly a bloody aeroplane. I'd never even been up in one before.

"A penny for them?" said Bonnie, as she reached across the table and took both my hands in hers. I stared at her beautiful face framed by that gorgeous long red hair and wanted to die in her arms. I can't remember when I had last even chatted to a girl, let alone sit actually holding hands with such a pretty one. Then I noticed she had tears in her eyes. My heart gave another little lurch.

"What's wrong Bonnie, are you OK?"

Bonnie let go of my hands and produced a small white silk handkerchief from one of the sleeves of her dress as if by magic, and dabbed the tears away.

"Oh, sorry James. I'm just being silly. I'm the one who's sitting here safe and cosy, you're the ones who're risking everything every night. I have no right to cry, really I don't."

I still wasn't too sure what was happening but I had a sneaking suspicion, and I felt certain we were fast approaching that horror scene. I didn't know what to say so I just held her hands tight in mine again and smiled, hopefully reassuringly.

"OK James, we need to make a move. It's dark now and I think more snow is forecast for this evening so we'd better go. I don't want to but you've got such a long way to go on that bike and I hate the thought of you riding in the dark with the snow coming down. Even though we've had some of the blackout lifted now, it's still treacherous, especially on a motorbike."

I think I agreed with her so I nodded and stood up. The waitress brought our coats over and gave me the bill which I stared at for a moment, trying to make out what it said. It was the money that confused me. It said I owed 10s 6d. What the hell that meant I had no idea. I fished around in my pocket for money and brought out a five pound note and passed it to the waitress, who stared at it as if I'd just placed a condom in her hand.

"Err...what's this sir?" she asked.

Bonnie peered at the note and then she too stared at me rather curiously. She reached into her own pocket and took out a large mauve coloured note and a few coins and gave them to the waitress.

"There, keep the change," she said, smiling.

The waitress smiled back and walked off.

"What was that money?" Bonnie asked as we stepped back outside.

I didn't answer immediately, I didn't know how to.

"Ah, I suspect it was some of that escape money they give you, the foreign stuff wasn't it? Did you get it mixed up? Silly James," she said, grinning at me.

I could do nothing but agree with her and apologise for my absent mindedness. I promised Bonnie I'd buy her a slap up dinner next time, but she responded by smiling that sad smile once again.

We left the charming little tea shop and stepped out once more into the icy evening. The snow was driving a little harder against our frozen faces now as we walked together, hand in hand back up Harpur Street towards the library. Neither one of us tried to make conversation, I like to think we were both simply enjoying the physical closeness of each other. Talking didn't seem necessary. Besides, my mind kept focussing on the other little piece of detail I had spotted on the hand written bill the waitress had produced. The date; it had said Wednesday 13th December '44.

As we approached the now snow covered front steps of the library I thought we were going to stop, but Bonnie kept on walking, dragging me along around the corner. As soon as we rounded the corner wall of the library I spotted a large wide area of pavement next to the wall, and couldn't miss the big old black and chrome motorbike proudly sitting there, snow piled up on the black leather seat and handlebars.

"Well, here we are then," she said, coming to a halt in front of the bike. I had no idea as to what I was going to do next, but if I was going to have to ride this damn thing I only hoped and prayed I wouldn't have to do it in front of her. To the best of my knowledge I've never ridden a motorbike before, and this was a vintage model so I suspected it wasn't going to be easy, especially in this weather. I didn't even know if I had any keys for the bike, although I thought there was every chance they were in one of the many pockets of the greatcoat.

I turned to face her and took both of her gloved hands in mine. As I glanced down at her beautiful features I was overcome with the desire to kiss her and taste those wonderful looking lips. Not one to fight an impulse when it arrives, I leaned forward, put my arms around her and pressed my lips against hers. Her soft moist lips parted as they touched mine and I felt her sigh with pleasure. Her small tongue began probing inside my mouth and I squeezed her body closer to mine, wondering at the sensations she aroused within me, simply from kissing. It was amazing and I'm not being just a hopeless romantic when I say I fell deeply and passionately in love with her at that moment. I never thought that sort of stuff happened outside of the pages of a Mills and Boon, but there it was, in an instant I was smitten.

I've no idea how long we stood kissing and holding each other. It felt like hours but I suspect it was only a blissful five minutes at most. When we eventually parted I held on to Bonnie's hands and gazed down at her. Tears streamed down her smiling face.

"Thank you James," was all she said. She seemed a little nervous, or embarrassed, I couldn't tell which, and then she was gone, striding off around the corner without a single glance back. I stood quite motionless for some time, reeling at the memory of her and willing the blood pounding around my body to calm down. Eventually I shoved my freezing hands deep into my extra-large coat pockets and turned to stare at the motorbike.

"Now what?" I murmured to myself.

The sign on the side of the motorbike said Norton and it looked like a beast of a machine. I must admit, I didn't know anything about motorbikes or how they worked, but this one seemed like it might be an expensive one. I also had no real idea as to how to even ride the damn thing, which was always assuming I could get it started in the first place. And once started, where did I think I was actually going to go?

OK, so I'll admit, I'd been following the wonderful Bonnie around like a little lost pup for the past few hours and thoroughly enjoyed myself, but hadn't really given too much thought to my predicament. I still didn't know what had happened to me, and perhaps more importantly, what was I going to do about it?

It seemed to me, and I have sat through enough time travel movies to know, that I had somehow slipped back in time to 13th December 1944. I can only imagine it must have been something to do with the painful feeling in my head from that old storeroom in the library back in 2015. Maybe it was some kind of a time-portal or something and that little old man accidentally pushed me through it. Or was it really an accident? And who was he anyway? If it was a time portal, then the old man came through to this side with me and maybe he's still here, lost like me.

OK, this is all so ridiculously weird, but if I did come through a time portal, then surely all I have to do is go back into the library, step back through the portal and arrive in my library in 2015, and then I can go home. Easy.

Only, it's never quite so easy is it? With my mind made up I strode around to the front of the library only to find it now closed and locked up. My choices were diminishing by the minute. I could either break in, risk getting caught and going to jail in 1944, or find somewhere to sleep for the night and come back tomorrow. The only trouble with that option was where would I stay? Especially as I didn't have any 1940s currency on me. Or did I?

I sat down on the snow covered stone steps and started to search through the deep pockets of my newly acquired great coat. It sounds a little weird but I couldn't get the thought out of my mind that I was rifling through someone else's pockets. I'd never seen the coat before in my life, so it felt like it belonged to someone else, but Bonnie seemed to think it was mine, in fact there was no doubt in her mind it was my coat. Could she have mistaken me for someone else? If I'm honest, I didn't think so.

The first thing I came across was a set of keys. There were about five keys on a ring and they weren't marked in any way, but I was sure one of them would at least fit the motorbike. OK, so far so good. The next thing I came across was a wallet. Things were looking up. I opened the flap on the expensive feeling brown leather wallet and peered inside. There were a few banknotes folded up in one of the compartments so I carefully slid them out and unfolded them. There were three large white five-pound notes, six blue and pink notes which had one pound markings on them and two mauve coloured notes which had markings of ten shillings on them, identical to the one Bonnie gave the waitress. To add to that there were a few loose coins in the front compartment of the wallet, a few large pennies, three penny bits, a couple of silver sixpences and a large half a crown coin. I had no idea as to the value of any of it but thought it would all probably come in quite useful.

I spotted a piece of paper sticking out of the large compartment at the back of the wallet. I pulled it out and a small square photograph flew out along with the paper and dropped into my lap. I picked up the photograph and studied it. It was a black and white photograph of a couple in their late forties who appeared to be sitting on a wall on a beach front. It only took me a fraction of a second to realise it was my mother and father's faces smiling back at me. I peered closer and was able to make out an island on the horizon behind them. I recognised it instantly, the Isle of Arran. My childhood summer holidays were all spent on that very beach in the quiet seaside town of Ayr, in Ayrshire. Every year at Glasgow Fair when my father's print works closed down for the summer break, everyone from all the streets around us used to take the one hour train journey from Glasgow Central Station down to Ayr to spend a wonderful two weeks on that crowded beach. I remember we used to stay in a little bed and breakfast run by Mrs Murdoch about two streets back from the front. Wonderful woman she was, always laughing, but kind of sad too. My father said her husband had died in the first war and running the bed and breakfast was the only way she could make ends meet. I leaned back against the cold steps and smiled. Happy memories.

The photograph appeared to be a recent one, perhaps a year or two old. My mother had on her usual summer frock and my father, as always was wearing a shirt, tie and his old cap. His only concession to the summer was to remove his jacket and roll his sleeves up. That made me smile.

I unfolded the piece of paper and stared at the neat pencilled writing. It was a letter addressed to me, from my father.

Dear James,

I sincerely hope this letter finds you fit and well and in good spirits. Your mum and I are both well and enjoying rude health. The weather here is starting to turn, we both feel it has all the signs of being a harsh winter this year, but still, we won't be letting that trouble us. We are getting things ready for Christmas, and that cheers us both up a little. You know how mother loves Christmas so? This will be the second Christmas without you James and we are all missing you terribly. We are both praying this dreadful war will end soon and we will have you home safe and sound for next year.

Grandma and Pops send their love, as does old Mrs Cowan from upstairs in the close, and her young daughter too. Your mother thinks she carries a thing for you.

Thank you for your last letter. It's lovely to hear from you and we are both so relieved to hear you are safe and sound and doing so well. We so look forward to receiving your letters. We understand you can't tell us much of what is going on, and if I'm honest, when we read the newspapers we both fear the worst, but still we hope life is bearable for you and your chums, and you can at least enjoy some moments of peace and happiness.

Everyone here is so proud of you James. Who ever thought we would have an officer in the family? Your mother carries your picture (the one of you in your new uniform) everywhere with her and shows it to anyone who will look.

You must tell us more of this young lady you have met. Is it serious or too early to tell? Mother of course wants to know all the details.

If you need anything James, anything at all, just write and ask and we will do our best to send it.

That's it for now. We will write again before Christmas. Please stay as safe as you can son and come home to us soon.

Mother sends all her love.

Bye for now.

All my love - Dad

Wow! That hit me, I wasn't expecting anything like that. At the back of my mind there was a growing sense it all seemed familiar somehow, but I knew that was impossible. What did occur to me though was how much I realised I was missing my parents. It dawned on me I hadn't given them much thought over the past year or so, but now sitting here, with my father's words in my hands I was feeling quite raw and emotional. Why hadn't I contacted them before? What was happening to me? I didn't want to dwell on it too much, it definitely needed thinking about, but not right now.

I folded the letter up and slid it back into the wallet with the photograph. I then spotted one last item in the back of the wallet and pulled it out. It was a small red booklet made from card and had the words 'Driving License' printed on the front in small black printed letters. I opened the cover and read the first few lines. It said the issuing authority was 'Bedfordshire County Council' and it stated

'Road Traffic Act 1930-36 - Driving license for Mr James Cunnion of 16 Lyon Street, Glasgow.' Further down the page it said I was licensed to drive all groups of vehicles and the license was valid from 1st September 1944 to 31st August 1945. Fee of 5/- received.

Staring at the little red book in my cold hands I read that page over and over again. I knew what it was, but I couldn't seem to comprehend what it was saying. This was my driving license, it had my name and address on it, but it was for the year 1944/45 and dated 1st September 1944. How is any of that possible? All of it was starting to freak me out.

But if I thought that was worrying, what I found next was downright terrifying. Apart from a handkerchief and two large round boiled sweets, I found nothing further in the side pockets of the greatcoat, so I began rummaging through the inside pocket. There I discovered two items which sent a physical shock through my body, there is no other way to describe it.

Out of the inside pocket I pulled what was obviously an I.D. Card and a pair of identity discs, octagonal in shape, one green and one red. The identity discs were made of a sort of pressed fibre material and hung on what appeared to be leather bootlaces, one long and one short. These looked to me like the military dog-tags soldiers wore around their necks so they could be identified in case of death. I examined the tags a bit closer and saw they were stamped with: CUNNION, J.D. - 306001- R.C. - RAF. The ID card was blue in colour and appeared a bit crumpled and dog eared. It had obviously been hanging around in someone's pocket for a while. I stared at the emblem of the Royal Air Force on the cover of the ID card for some minutes before I plucked up the courage to peer inside. I knew what I was going to find. As I flipped open the ID card my eyes were instantly drawn to a black and white picture of me dressed in a blue RAF tunic, over stamped with an official looking RAF ink stamp stating: RAF STATION HARROGATE - 10TH SEPTEMBER 1942. Reading through the description of me the nasty butterflies were swarming in the pit of my stomach: Height: 6'2". Colour of Hair: Dark brown. Build: Medium. Colour of Eyes: Hazel. Date of Birth: 31st December 1920. Religion: Roman Catholic. Distinguishing Features: None. And then there it was, at the bottom of the ID card on the right hand side, my signature.

Yes, there was absolutely no doubt about it, it was my bloody signature. I was stunned as the realisation hit me; I knew I hadn't been rummaging through someone else's coat or prying into someone else's life, I don't know how this is even possible but this was my coat, my wallet, my money, my letter and my ID. No wonder Bonnie recognised me, this is me.

It was becoming all too weird and if I'm truthful, I couldn't deal with it. Trying to work it out was fruitless, something was very wrong and I didn't understand it. I was scared. I needed to find the old man with the black coat and hat as I felt sure he knew something and would be able to answer some questions, but for now it was dark and I was sitting on a set of stone steps in sub-zero temperatures with nowhere to stay for the night. That was my priority right now, and I had to remain practical. I needed somewhere warm to stay otherwise I was going to die of exposure and hypothermia out here. The old man would have to wait until the morning.

My mind wandered back to my conversation with Bonnie. What was it she'd said about what I was going to be doing this evening, sharing drinks with my chums back at the base? I tried to follow that line of thought while I stared at my ID card again. I must have missed it before but now I saw on the left hand side it stated I was temporarily based at R.A.F. Tempsford, Bedfordshire with 617 squadron. It also stated I had received a promotion to Flt Lt on 30th October 1944. I glanced down at the two lines of braid across the epaulettes on my greatcoat shoulders.

"You're kidding me, a bloody officer no less?" I murmured to myself. Troubled as I was, I think I managed a grin.

I stuffed the wallet, ID card and identity discs back inside my pocket, stood up and strode back around the corner with the set of keys in my hand, some semblance of a plan forming in my mind. Stupid maybe, but still a plan.

The motorbike appeared even darker and more imposing this time. I walked over to it and began examining the various levers and controls while I cleared the snow off the seat and handlebars. My mouth was dry and the recently digested spotted dick churned in my stomach. I don't recall ever having ridden a motorbike before, but there was something nagging at the back of my mind that I had, and in this strange alternative world I was now living in I was beginning to question everything I thought I understood about myself. I found a place for a key on the handlebars next to the speedometer, so I tried inserting the keys I had on the ring, one by one. The third key fitted OK and I turned it. Two red lights immediately came up on the display. So far so good. I liked that, I decided that would be my motto from then on; *so far so good.*

I had seen this done before with older motorbikes on lots of movies, so I scanned the rear of the bike and spotted the kick-start lever on the left hand side. I held loosely onto the bike, placed my right foot against the lever and gave it a half-hearted kick downwards. My foot barely depressed the lever more than a few inches when it shot back up again and nearly knocked me sprawling onto the pavement.

"Goddamn bloody stupid thing!" I shouted as I hobbled away rubbing my ankle. I was damn lucky it wasn't broken. I tried again, but this time I held firmly onto the handlebars and forced the lever down. The engine tried to turn over but it didn't start. I tried again another half a dozen times but still the engine wouldn't catch. My leg ached and I was winded.

"Bloody stupid bike."

"Are you OK mate? Do you need a hand?"

I whirled around and standing in front of me, his warm breath condensing in the frosty air, was a man in a long dark overcoat, thick woollen scarf, work boots and a flat woollen cap on his head. He appeared to be in his late thirties or early forties.

"Looks like you're having a bit of bother with yer bike?"

I stared down at the machine.

"Ah yes, a bit...yes. I can't seem to get it started."

"OK, well, anything to give one of you boys in blue a hand. I'm a bit of a dab hand at motorbikes and this one's a real scorcher. Let's have a look."

The man stepped forward and peered down at the side of the bike. He instantly leant forward, placed his hand on a small brass lever and turned it.

"There you go mate, I think that's the problem, the fuel lever was off. Easy old mistake to make," he said as he gripped the handlebars, put his foot on the kick-start lever and kicked down hard. The engine roared into life and the man stepped back with a broad grin on his face. The deep throaty popping and rumbling of the engine reverberated around the walls of the wide alleyway we were in.

"There you go mate. Lovely bike, wish it were mine, I'd give me right arm for a Norton like that. Jake, me name's Jake," he said as he took his glove off and thrust his hand towards me.

"Em...James, and thank you so much Jake, I appreciate your help," I said as I took his hand.

"Do I detect a Scottish accent there James?"

"Err yes, you do. I'm from Glasgow."

"Ah, a long way from home then eh mate? These are hard times eh, it's so rough for you young-uns?"

I suddenly saw an opportunity.

"Jake, it's late and it's cold. You've done me a favour, how about I do one for you in return. How about I give you a lift home, and tell you what, you can drive," I said, grinning, and hoping to hell he'd say yes. That might give me a chance to see how to ride the bloody bike before

I had to have a go by myself. It might make the difference between getting horribly mangled in the next few minutes or hopefully managing to remain alive.

Jake stared at me, almost aghast. He seemed a little speechless.

"You'd...you'd let me have a go? Just like that? On this Norton?"

I smiled at him. "Yes of course I would, I would be only too pleased to."

Jake stepped forward and started pumping my hand again while he slapped me on the shoulder.

"Why thank you so much mate, wait till my Doris hears about this." His grin spread across his face and he was rubbing his hands together in pure anticipation.

"So where are you going James?" he asked.

I had to think about it for a moment, then thought 'what the hell, in for a penny in for a pound.'

"Em, I'm going to my new posting, it's at a place called Tempsford, but I'm not too sure where that is. Perhaps you could help direct me when we've dropped you off home?"

Jake grinned at me. "We can do better than that. I live out all the way along the old Sandy Road up at Church End, right close to the ruddy Tempsford RAF base. After my house, it's a straight road for less than a mile and then you're home."

Relief washed over me. Maybe there was a God after all, I wondered.

Jake was almost drooling as he hitched his coat up and lifted his leg over to straddle the bike. I found a pair of huge leather gloves half sticking out of the old saddle bag on the back, and tucked inside one of the gloves was an old fashioned pair of black motorbike goggles. I offered these to Jake and he slipped them on while I turned up my collar and managed to swing my leg up and over to sit on the seat behind him. It was a big bike with a comfy thick padded seat and it didn't feel too intimate behind my new pal, which I was grateful for. Not that I think Jake would have noticed in any event, he was positively in heaven as he revved up the engine, engaged the clutch and slipped the lever down into first gear with his right boot.

I swear I heard him shriek with pleasure as we roared away from the library, back down Harper Street, around St Paul's square in front of the old Corn Exchange and up over the bridge, out of the town centre. I had my eyes closed most of the way but managed a quick glance at the white front door of my apartment as we flashed past. With a worried jolt I remembered I'd left my house keys in my old corduroy jacket pocket which was still on the floor of the library, back - or forward, depending on how you looked at it - in 2015. But it occurred to me that someone else would likely be living there for the next 70 years or so, therefore it probably didn't matter anyway.

We left the town buildings behind us and then Jake opened her up. The big Norton screamed along the dark country roads and I think I was screaming with it most of the way. Thankfully the snow went some way towards deadening any embarrassing noises I might have made. Eventually we slowed down to pass through a quaint little village. I just managed to spot a sign informing us we were leaving Blunham before Jake opened the Norton up again and we banged and roared along another dark country lane. Soon after that I spotted a row of what appeared to be three semi-detached cottages looming out of the darkness on our left. Jake pulled the bike to a halt in front of the end house.

I got off the bike first and rubbed my stiff legs. Jake bounded off and clasped his arms around my shoulders, beaming all over his face.

"Yeeeeahhh!" he yelled, in my ear. "Wait till Doris hears about this."

Jake stared at me for a moment and grinned again. "This is my place. Church End, Tempsford Village, lived here all my life I have, man and boy," he said, puffing out his chest.

"Stay right there James, I've got to get her out here to see this, she just won't believe me otherwise," he shouted before he leapt over the small wooden gate in one bound and dashed off up the garden path, disappearing into the gloom. I heard the banging on the door then a small slit of light appeared as the door creaked open. There was muffled talking in the distance, and then the slither of light disappeared and the voices came closer and grew more excited until Jake stood in front of me again with his arm around a plump and pleasant looking middle aged woman.

"James, meet Doris, my lovely wife."

"Pleased to meet you Doris," I said, shaking hands with her as she smiled up at me in the semi darkness, her eyes twinkling in the moonlight which reflected off the still falling snow.

"I'm so pleased to meet you too Flight Lieutenant James. Thank you for bringing my old man home safely, and early too, I wasn't expecting him for hours yet."

"The pleasure was all mine Doris, I would never have got my bike started or got to the base without the help of your husband, so I'm the one who's grateful."

Jake stepped forward, put his arm around my shoulder and stared straight into my eyes.

"James, none of us could ever do enough to repay you boys for what you're doing for all of us in this country, and that's a fact. If there's ever anything Doris or I can do for you James, I want you to ask. Anything. Don't hesitate, it would be a privilege for both of us."

Doris nodded her agreement. Jake handed me back my goggles before he stepped back and placed his arm around his wife's shoulders again. They both smiled warmly at me.

"Take the next turning on the right and your base is less than a mile straight up that lane, the entrance is on the left, you can't miss it," Jake called out, pointing up the road.

So, this was it then. They were both going to stand there and watch me make a fool of myself, if I was lucky, or break my bloody neck if I wasn't. I straddled the motorbike. Fortunately Jake had left it running so there was one less embarrassment to contend with. I had tried to study what Jake was doing while he was riding and I think I got the gist of it. Pull the clutch in with your left hand, engage the gear with your right foot and release the clutch slowly while you turn the throttle grip anti-clockwise towards you. Now what did he say about the gears? I remembered him mentioning it was one down and three up or something like that. I tried to forget about my audience as I pulled in the clutch lever, pushed the gear lever down with my right foot until I felt it clunk into gear, and throttled back as I let go of the clutch lever. To my utter amazement I was off and riding down the lane. Without thinking I smoothly changed gears into second and then third. It seemed all too easy. The only difficulty I had was seeing in the darkness. There were no street lights, everything for miles around was blacked out because of the war I presumed and the headlamp on the front of the bike was shaded, probably for war time regulations. But on the plus side my night vision was good and there were thick dark hedges along both sides of the road so I could sense where to place the bike. I just hoped I didn't meet anyone coming the other way.

Chapter Five - RAF Tempsford, Dec 13th 1944

Jake was right, even in the darkness I was able to make out the RAF base as I approached. I saw the break in the hedge along the left hand side and almost at the same time I spotted a couple of glowing red lights further up on my left. I slowed the bike down and prepared to turn into what appeared to be the entrance to the base. As I turned the bike in I could just make out in the darkness a large wooden hut on the right hand side and a long barrier across the roadway. The glowing red lights belonged to the two great-coated guards who were puffing away on their cigarettes.

Out of the darkness a torch flicked on and swept over my bike and me and shut off again. The white beam only flashed on for a couple of seconds but my night vision was ruined and all that remained was the flashing white light burned into my retinas.

"Sorry Mr Cunnion Sir I thought it was you, but just needed to make sure. You know how it is? Tom, pull up the gate will you and let the Flight Lieutenant in?"

Tom's shadow dipped to the left and I watched the barrier rising up.

"They'll all be in the mess by now Sir, I'm sure you'll like a pint with them before you turn in?" said the first guard. The flashing white lights in my eyes began to subside and I was close enough now to see the sergeant's stripes on the guard's arms. It was obvious he knew who I was so he already had me at a disadvantage. I played it safe.

"Thank you Sergeant, you have a good evening too," I said as I revved the growling and spitting engine of the Norton, pinged out the clutch like an expert and sped through the gate to face my next adventure.

The road surface wasn't good and it was icy so I kept the speed down and followed the roadway around to the right, heading for some low squat buildings that loomed out of the darkness. I had no idea where I was going but as the Norton rumbled up to the first group of buildings I spotted a sliver of light coming from a window in one of the huts in the centre, so I pulled the bike to a halt in front of the door, kicked the gear into neutral and turned the key, shutting off the engine.

The scene was like a Walt Disney winter wonderland with drifts of white snow bathed in a soft blue hue from the almost full moon above. It didn't seem much like an airfield though; in the eerie light the base had all the appearance of a disused farm, maybe even a pig farm judging by the odours wafting on the icy breeze. Most of the buildings sported thatched roofs and looked as if they hadn't been used in years, but maybe that was perhaps a trick of the light. I wasn't at all sure what this place was but it wasn't what I expected.

The sound of singing drifted across from the hut in front of me. The sign on the door said Officer's Mess.

I kicked down the stand with my left foot and lifted my stiff and frozen leg over the bike. The greatcoat had been a lifesaver but the cold had penetrated through my flimsy trousers and shoes and I could hardly feel my legs and feet at all. I wouldn't have been at all surprised to find out I now had frostbite to add to my woes. I staggered and stamped around to try and get some life back into my stiff legs and feet. I had no idea what or who I was going to face inside but I did have some dignity, I didn't want it to look like I'd just dismounted a bloody horse when I walked in.

I stashed my big leather gloves and goggles back in the saddle bag, sucked in a deep breath of icy air and marched up to the door of the hut. The singing inside had reached a crescendo. I couldn't make out the tune or any of the words, and I probably didn't want to, it had all the tone of a raucous night at the rugby club.

I'd be lying if I said my heart wasn't in my mouth when I pulled down the freezing cold handle and pushed open the door. The light, the noise and the smoke coming from inside the hut immediately assaulted me. I peered through the dense clouds of blue smoke inside and could make out at least a dozen men and women in blue uniforms, drinking, shouting and singing. Everyone was smoking and the atmosphere inside must have been roughly akin to the surface of Saturn.

To complete the scene, an old gramophone on a side table scratched out a song I thought I recognised as Lili Marlene, sung by the iconic Vera Lynn.

This was just like the movie where the victim pitches up one cold and menacing night at the old *Slaughtered Lamb* on the desolate moors. Everyone stopped talking and turned to stare at the newcomer standing in the doorway.

Vera Lynn continued to croon out *underneath the lantern, by the barrack gate* as I stared bug-eyed at the people in front of me, unsure of what to do next.

"Look what the cat's dragged in! It's Jock, get in here and get a brew down your neck, you've got some catching up to do," shouted the tall blond haired guy at the front, the one with the big boyish grin and a WAAF tucked under each arm.

"Come on Jock, you're just in time, it's your round," shouted another shorter uniformed man with bright red hair.

I opened my mouth but no words came out, and my feet were firmly rooted to the spot while everyone continued to stare at me. After a few increasingly embarrassing moments I managed to take a step forward into the choking atmosphere of the room. The only other man not in uniform, standing behind the bar over to my left, called out, "Shall I line them up Sir?"

I'm not sure quite what I was expecting, but I didn't think this was it. I nodded and smiled at the barman as I kicked the door closed behind me and took a few more uncertain steps into the room.

"You haven't been in that library again all day have you? I bet you've got a girl stashed away over there," said the loud blond haired man, grinning and untangling himself from the two grinning WAAFs. He stepped over, put an arm tightly around my shoulder and ushered me towards the bar.

"The usual sir?" asked the barman as he slid a thick glass tankard of dark brown liquid across the bar towards me.

"Thank you Reg," said the blond man as he picked up an identical glass the barman had placed next to mine.

"Thank you Reg," I said, thankful for the little piece of information gained. I now needed to find out the names of everyone else in the room before anyone suspected I was a fraud. I took a sip of the flat brown beer and licked the white foam from my top lip. There was a pleasant aroma and a distinct flavour of fresh hops, and it wasn't at all bad. The beer in this 1940s world sure tasted a lot better than any of the fizzy chemical stuff I remembered from 2015. The aftertaste also stirred some memories, of my father, strangely enough, and even perhaps of this place. Was it simply *Deja vu*, or was there more to it than that? A strange sense of having been here before crept up on me.

"So old mate, is there a lady involved in your constant visits to Bedford?"

I stared at the grinning blond man in front of me. He wore blue RAF battledress trousers and a light blue open necked shirt with the sleeves rolled up. He was about an inch taller than me and appeared to be a few years younger. It was obvious we were friends, or at least he thought we were. I was at a loss as to what to do or say next so I grinned back at him while I carefully set my beer down on the highly polished mahogany bar top, with a satisfying clunk.

"I'll take that as a yes then?" he said, slapping me hard on the back. I nearly spat my second mouthful of warm beer across the bar.

"Oh James, I'm glad you're back early," said a small blond girl in a RAF uniform with sergeant's stripes on each sleeve.

"Jackie's been waiting patiently for you mate," said my new pal, still grinning.

Name number two then. So far so good. It would be good to find out my blonde pal's name though.

"Oh Larry, stop it, I haven't!" said the blond WAAF, her face turning crimson.

Name number three.

At that moment the door swung open again and a short grey haired man in full RAF officer's uniform stepped authoritatively into the bar.

"Good evening everyone, hope you're having fun?" he said, and I spotted the faintest of smiles under his bushy grey moustache. A general murmured response of 'yes sir' echoed around the room.

The officer glanced over in our direction.

"James, Larry, special ops tomorrow night. Be in my office at 12.30 tomorrow for a briefing? General crew briefings at 16.00." That little smile crept across his lips again.

"Yes sir!" said Larry.

The officer stared directly at me now. It was obvious he was waiting for a response, a positive one. I had a sinking feeling in the pit of my stomach and a growing sense I was getting into something way over my head.

"Yes sir."

The officer smiled a little wider this time and nodded to both of us.

"Reg, a round of drinks for everyone on me, put them on my tab," he said.

A cheer went up around the room and comments of 'thank you sir' rebounded as the officer turned and left the room.

"Bloody old 'Mouse' Fielden, he's not a bad sort really is he?" said Larry.

"Err...no I suppose not," I answered.

"I take it we're on ops tomorrow then, any idea what's on?" slurred the short red haired man I'd spotted earlier as he staggered up to us. He was obviously Irish and obviously drunk, going on shit-faced. Short and stocky with a barrel chest, he looked like he should've taken up professional wrestling years ago. He slammed his heavy pint glass down on the bar, shoved a last piece of sandwich into his mouth and wiped his oversized hand over his trousers before leaning across Larry to shake my hand.

"Good to see you again sir," he said, grinning and flashing his green eyes.

His broad Irish accent was thicker than a banker's wallet and my finger bones almost melted into one another from the crush of his handshake.

"Alky O'Brien, the finest navigator this side of the Emerald Isle," roared Larry as he slapped the short man on the back.

"Good to see you Alky," I said, with relief as he let go and I tried to rub the feeling back into my fingers without anyone noticing.

"I've no idea what's going on Alky," said Larry, "I guess we'll find out tomorrow, but I suspect it'll be another secret squirrel one." Larry nodded at me and laughed. "Come on, let's get that beer in from old Mouse before he changes his bloody mind. Reg..."

Jackie glanced up at me and smiled. "Are you OK James?" she whispered.

I stared back at her kindly blue eyes. "Yes Jackie, I think so."

I swallowed a few more sips of the warm flat brew and began to relax. Leaning back against the bar I scanned the room. There were about eight guys in various pieces of RAF uniform, and four WAAFs who appeared significantly better turned out in their uniforms. The bar itself was pretty austere, like it had been built in a hurry and no one had bothered to decorate it, which was very probably true. An old upright piano sat along one wall next to a dartboard and a large noticeboard covered in sheets of paper. There was a black telephone in a booth in the corner.

The telephone reminded me again of my mother and father and my need to call them. I fished around in the greatcoat pocket and pulled out a handful of change.

"Just going to make a call," I said to no one in particular as I left the group and walked around the bar towards the phone. I remembered that hardly anyone in our street back home had a phone in their house, but my father was a part time fireman for the city so the fire service had installed a phone for emergencies. I had no idea whether this was going to work or if I would get the same unobtainable result as last time. I wasn't even sure what I would do or say if one of them did answer, or what that actually meant to me either way. If my parents existed now, in this time, then they couldn't exist in my life in 2015. But if that was the case, what the hell was going on. The mysterious messages in the books said I wasn't who I thought I was and I needed to investigate. Well, I was sure doing that, but it didn't seem to be getting any clearer.

I lifted the heavy black receiver from the telephone and put it to my ear. The line was dead. I put the receiver down and picked it up again. Still nothing. I stared at the phone and the little box it stood on for any clues. There was a coin slot and two black buttons, one marked 'A' and one marked 'B' and it occurred to me that maybe I needed to put some coins in the slot to make the phone work. I had no idea what to put in so I pulled a handful of coins out of my pocket and pushed a couple of sixpences and a few pennies in the slot. I heard a click, and a clear dialling tone hummed in my ear. Egged on by my success, I placed a finger in the dial and began the laborious process of dialling my parent's ten digit number, watching the dial slowly unwind before I could dial the next digit. As soon as I'd dialled the last number I heard a series of clicks and whirrs on the line as it tried to connect. I almost jumped when a large final click echoed in my ear and the line began ringing. Holding my breath I counted three, four, five rings and then there was another click and a voice.

"Glasgow 945 1122 Hello?"

It was my father.

"Hello dad, it's me, James," I almost shouted down the receiver, but the phone went dead again.

"What's the matter with this bloody thing?" I muttered under my breath, glaring at the receiver.

A slim delicate hand reached forward and pushed the button marked A. I glanced down into Jackie's smiling face. "Push button A," she said.

"Hello, hello, is that you James?" came the voice down the line. I mouthed 'thank you' to Jackie as she walked away, smiling back at me.

"Dad, yes it's me James," I said as a horde of butterflies swarmed around my stomach. "How are you?"

"James, it's so wonderful to hear from you my boy. Ellie! Ellie! Come quick, the lad's on the phone...yes, yes, it's James. How are you son?"

The excited shouting at the other end sent pains through my ear drum so I switched the receiver to the other ear. "I'm good dad, everything is fine. How's mum?"

"She's great James, we both are, especially now you've called. Oh it's so lovely to hear your voice son, you don't know what it means to both of us just to know you're safe. Here James, your mother wants to talk to you."

"James, James is that you?"

"Yes mum, it's me."

"Oh James..." Mother began to sob.

"How are you mum?"

I head snuffling and whispers at the other end and then father came back on. "Sorry son, mother is just composing herself. Where are you James, are you still in Bedford?"

"Yes dad, I'm in Bedford right now."

"Hold on, it's your mother again."

"James, sorry, I'm just a silly old woman. How are you my little baby, is everything all right?"

"Yes mum, everything is...fine. I'm just checking in with you and dad."

"Do you need anything son, do we need to do anything?"

I smiled at that. Good old mum, always looking after me. "No mum, I'm fine, I've got everything I need."

"And how about that young lady you've met James, how is that going?"

I wondered who it was she meant, perhaps Bonnie? I thought I'd better not commit myself to anything just yet.

"Oh, you know mum, everything going well. I'll let you know if anything happens."

A series of beeps sounded in my ear.

"Damn! That's the pips son, please take care, I love you and write soon?"

"Yes mum, I will and I'll phone again soon..." and then the line went dead.

Phew!

I placed the receiver back on the cradle and rested my forehead against the wall. OK, so that's that then? My parents are living here in 1944, not 2015. What did that mean for me? My head ached.

"Come on James, come and have a drink with us, you look like you need it." It was Jackie again, her soft warm hand finding mine and leading me back to the bar. I was grateful for the contact.

Larry, Alky and a few of the other airmen were at the bar, arms linked and swaying, singing the usual crew ditty:

"This bloody town's a bloody cuss,

No bloody trains and no bloody bus,

And nobody cares for bloody us,

Bloody Tempsford,"

Agreed, the song didn't contain much of a melody and it was hardly Lennon and McCartney, but at least it rhymed, sort of.

The next few hours were a bit of a blur. I remember downing a lot of beer and following that up with a few wee drams of whisky. Glenn Miller, Anne Shelton, Gracie Fields and good old George Formby pounded out from the gramophone as I sang and danced the night away with my odd new friends. A bevy of WAAFs hung around Larry for most of the night and he kept pushing Jackie at me. Mind you she didn't need much encouragement. I've never been particularly comfortable around members of the fairer sex, but Jackie's a lovely girl and easy to get along with. She insisted on holding my hand wherever possible and staring up into my ever drooping eyes.

By the end of the evening her arms were around me and it seemed impolite of me not to return the gesture. In Jackie's arms I didn't feel the way I had when I kissed Bonnie earlier, but nevertheless she was warm and fun to be with. A combination of a lack of female company for over a year, coupled with the alcohol suppressing any inhibitions I might've had soon started to have an effect. Eventually I found my arms inside her unbuttoned tunic and around her trim waist, holding her firm body close to mine and kissing her soft warm lips.

"Wow! James, you are a sly one. I love the way you kiss, it turns me on," she whispered, gasping as we eventually came up for air, "and I do detect you're a little excited too, shall we pop outside?"

Even through the drink I clearly remember the sultry smile on her beautiful, fresh young face. There was no way I could've resisted even if I'd wanted to, but I didn't see any reason to fight it anyway. I recall pulling on my greatcoat and walking out of the mess, hand in hand with Jackie to a cacophony of cat-calls and whistles coming from behind us.

The snow-storm had worsened and the icy cold air coupled with the wet snow on my face sobered me up a little as we stepped outside. As soon as the door shut behind us Jackie fell back in my arms again and we kissed passionately, her sweet warm tongue gliding around my mouth. I caressed her breasts beneath her tunic and she gave a little gasp when I managed to squeeze her nipples through the thick RAF regulation bra.

"Oh James, I want you so much," she whispered in my ear as we hugged. "Can we go somewhere the next time we both get leave, please?"

At that precise moment I couldn't think of anything much better to do so rather rashly I agreed. I think somewhere at the back of my befuddled half functioning brain I reasoned we'd both forget all this in the morning so I would be able to get out of it if I needed to anyway. Unfortunately, I hadn't even noticed that Jackie had been drinking nothing stronger than tea all evening and wasn't going to be in any rush to forget this night.

I seem to remember saying my last goodnights to Jackie with a lingering kiss and then staggering around aimlessly in the snow for a while before Larry came out of the mess and grabbed me by the collar.

"Come on old mate, you never were one for holding your drink were you? Still, you seemed to have rather brightened up young Jackie's evening, well done old man."

All I remember after that was Larry roaring with laughter like a demented Santa Claus as he dragged me through the snow and eventually hurled me onto a small camp-like bed, fully clothed.

At least that's where I found myself in the morning when the roar of growling and spitting engines woke me with a start.

Chapter Six - RAF Tempsford, Dec 14th 1944

My head banged and my mouth felt like the inside of a camel's arse. What was I thinking of? I hadn't had a drink in nearly a year and then I go and try to drink the bloody bar dry. When will I ever learn? I glanced at my watch, 11.30 am. The racket outside the little window next to the bed echoed around my aching brain. What the hell was going on outside? It sounded like the starting grid of a grand prix.

I wrapped my arms over my head and tried to get back to sleep, but someone was shaking my arm. I buried my face deeper into the pillow and tried to ignore the evil bastard, but whoever he or she was they sure were bloody persistent.

"Jock, Jock, come on, up you bloody get. We're seeing old Mousey in an hour, get your skates on."

It was Larry. I remembered then we had agreed to meet the CO at 12.30. Ugh, my head hurt.

I forced my eyes open and the light almost blinded me. As my pupils focussed, the grinning form of Larry materialised in front of me, less than six inches from my face.

"Ugh?" was all I could manage.

"Come on old man, you're not normally one to suffer like this. You need to get up."

"OK Larry, just give me 15 minutes will you," I said, closing my eyes again.

I heard a loud laugh.

"OK, see you in the mess, you'll need to get some eggs down you, it'll make you feel better," Larry called out as I heard his retreating heavy footsteps and a door bang shut.

Eggs? The thought half cooked yokes slopping around in grease made me want to heave. Holding my head with one hand I pulled the heavy grey woollen blankets back and swung my legs down onto the floor. I still had my shoes on. Almost the first thing I spotted when I was sitting upright was the picture of my parents in a little art-deco silver frame on the small metal cabinet next to the bed. I reached over and picked it up. They were a little younger in this picture and were standing outside our tenement building in Lyon Street with a small boy, me in fact.

I placed the picture frame back down and examined my new surroundings. The room appeared to be about eight feet wide at most and twenty feet long. I was at one end of the room and there were five other small beds placed between me and the door at the other end of the dormitory. A small metal side cabinet sat next to each bed and situated on the wall opposite each bunk was a much larger grey metal cabinet. There was a wooden foot locker at the end of each bed and that was pretty much it, no T.V., no mini-bar, not even a radio. I did notice that all of the other beds were neatly made and the whole room appeared tidy, apart from my bed.

But greater things were now pressing on my mind. The call of nature was fast becoming a priority and I had no idea where the nearest toilet was. Holding onto the bedside cabinet I pulled myself up onto my feet. I swayed a little on unsteady legs and felt rather light headed as my alcohol soaked blood tried to balance itself out, but that was the worst bit over with. There was a second door at my end of the room, so with hope in my heart and a hand on my bursting bladder I made for it.

Despite the thick rank odour that hit me as soon as I opened the door, the relief was palpable when I discovered the metal trough-like urinal, two toilet cubicles and two sinks with shaving mirrors in front of them. I made it to the urinal and fumbled with the buttons on my trousers for 30 worrying seconds before finally letting the steaming flow out. Heaven.

Relieved, I staggered over to the sink and filled the cracked porcelain with ice cold water, which was the only thing that seemed to come out of both taps. I stripped off my clothes and had a stand-up wash, which wasn't wonderful but did go some way towards waking me up. While I dried off with the small blue towel I found hanging next to the sink I spotted a line of six wash-bags sitting on a wooden shelf next to the mirrors. The one on the far end was a green tartan colour, so on the basis that was definitely a wash bag I would choose to buy I picked it up, unfolded the bag and examined the contents. Inside I discovered a round green coloured tin with Gibbs Dentifrice branding on the lid, a plain white toothbrush, a silver cut-throat razor and an ivory handled brush with thick white bristles, a comb and a small pair of scissors. I didn't fancy using the cut throat razor much as it seemed a tad dangerous, but staring at my reflection in the mirror it was obvious I wasn't going to get away with it. I needed a shave.

On the shelf I spotted a big old mug which seemed to have been used regularly for something. I recalled my old dad using a brush and a mug like that to lather up the soap he used to put on his face before shaving, so I gave it a go. I managed to get quite a lather up in the old mug with the brush and began plastering plenty of soap over my chin. Then came the exciting bit. I opened the razor up to expose the thin, sharp blade and with a trembling hand I dragged it downwards across my cheek. I was a bit hesitant with the blade at first, but it wasn't too bad and my confidence grew. That is until I saw the first streaks of red running down my neck. I gave up after the first half dozen cuts and used the towel to try and staunch the flow of blood. It had all the signs of a bloody massacre around the sink.

I tied the towel around my neck, scooped my clothes up from the floor and went back into the relative fresh air of the main room again, hunting for some clean clothes. I guessed the best place to start would be the locker opposite my bed, and I was proved right. As soon as I swung open the heavy door I spotted two eye-catching blue uniforms hanging up. The first one was a four pocket jacket with bright brass buttons and a belt, two lines of gold braid around the cuff of each sleeve, an embroidered RAF emblem with white wings just above the left breast pocket and two medal ribbons immediately below that, one white with thin diagonal blue stripes and the other red with a thin blue stripe on either side. The second jacket was a shorter blouse type affair with only two breast pockets and dull black buttons. That too had the gold braid on the sleeves, the RAF eagle emblem and the medal ribbons. Other than the two uniforms, the only other choice of clothes hanging up was a thick cream coloured woollen roll neck jumper and a spare pair of heavy blue trousers.

Wow! The uniforms were bloody superb, medals, badges and braid, just like the real thing. Actually I was forgetting, of course they were the real bloody thing. The thought crossed my mind as to whether the uniform would even fit me, but then, that was obvious, of course it would.

I found some underpants in the footlocker at the bottom of the bed, big old white Y-fronts, nothing too sexy, and some black socks and a vest which I didn't bother putting on. Several light blue shirts were hanging up in the wardrobe so I grabbed one of those and tried to put it on, before I realised the buttons only went half way down. Changing tactics I slipped the shirt over my head, buttoned up the top half and peered in the mirror which was stuck on the front of the locker. At first I couldn't see what was wrong with the shirt, but then I realised it didn't have a collar. I examined the drawer and found a stack of shirt collars in a little box in the corner. I pulled one out and spent the next ten minutes trying to button the damn thing on. Surely shirts with collars had been invented by now?

I went to do up the cuffs only to realise there were no buttons, they needed cufflinks. After a brief panic I discovered a pair of silver ones in my shirt collar box which had the RAF emblem imprinted on them. I thought the emblem was a nice touch, very British.

I couldn't make my mind up on which uniform to try first, but I finally decided on the longer four pocket one, purely on the basis the ornate brass buttons were shinier. My eagle eye spotted that not all the buttons were in fact the same. A close inspection highlighted two of them were different. One had RCAF engraved below the King's crown and eagle and the other had RAAF on it, the rest were regular RAF buttons with just the King's crown and eagle. How very odd I thought.

I found a pair of well-worn but highly polished black shoes in the bottom of the wardrobe so I slipped those on too and they fitted like a glove. Of course they did.

There was an officer's peaked cap sitting on top of the wardrobe which I considered putting on, but I thought it might be a bit overkill so eventually decided to leave it where it was.

I went over to the mirror on the back of the door, lifted off the dressing gown and admired myself for a minute or two. The uniform fitted like a glove and I have to admit I felt like a movie star.

The next task was to try and sort out the tangle of hair on my head. I've always kept my hair short on the sides and back, but the mop on the top has a tendency to curl up, so included in my usual morning routine was a fruitless attempt at straightening it. As I dragged my fingers through the knots I spotted the blood from my face trickling slowly down my neck and in imminent danger of staining the new collar.

I scanned the room and spotted a well-thumbed brown coloured magazine on a table which looked like it might help. The title said TEE-EMM and it appeared to be an RAF publication of some kind, full of articles and cartoons. It did look kind of interesting and I made a mental note to try and get time to peek at it later, but for now it had another far more valuable use. I tore a corner off the front page and went back to the mirror, then tore a smaller piece off for each of the slashes on my face and pressed the tiny pieces of paper onto each cut. The paper stuck easily to the oozing blood, it was a little trick I remember my father using. Staring at myself in the mirror again, my face and neck now covered in little bits of paper which were slowly turning red, I looked a lot less like a movie star now. Ah well.

'This is it,' I said to myself before opening the door and stepping out into the frosty winter sunshine.

The first thing I spotted was the wooden barn-like building that I had been drinking in the night before, away to the left, about 200 yards away. The Norton was still parked in front but now had snow piled up high on the seat. There were other smaller farm-like buildings on either side of the officer's mess but as yet I had no idea what they were for. I also noticed a much larger, derelict looking building with a duck pond in front of it, and there were even a few ducks slipping and sliding around on the frozen surface of the pond. What was this place?

People wrapped up in scarves, woollen hats and blue great coats were coming and going and everyone seemed to have a purpose, dashing around with clipboards or bits of paper in their hands. The cough, rumble and roar of aircraft engines in the distance caused the very air to vibrate around me and was more than a little disquieting. It sounded like an aerodrome, but didn't look much like one.

Turning around I realised the building I had just stepped out of was only one of a row of long black painted wooden huts which ran off into the distance to the right and left of me. There were doors in each one so I guessed they would all be individual dormitories, presumably identical to the one I'd come from. They looked exactly like the old pig pens my uncle Hamish had on his farm up in Stirling in the old days when my parents used to take me there for our summer holidays. The stench of those pigs in that July heat came back to me, it was exactly the same as the smell in the air here. Maybe these were old pig-pens then? I wouldn't have been at all surprised.

I glanced up at the door and noticed it had the lettering OB-47 stencilled on in white gloss paint. I figured I should try and remember that.

I peered at my watch. 12.00 midday. Half an hour to get ready, that wasn't bad. I reasoned that the mess Larry had mentioned might well also be the officer's mess I was in last night so I headed off in that direction. One or two people I passed saluted me so I did my best to salute back, unsure exactly how to do it. I hope I didn't embarrass myself too much.

My assumption regarding the mess was correct. I stepped into the stale, beer smelling bar which now had rows of tables lined up across the room and people in blue RAF uniforms lounged around with mugs of tea and plates of food in front of them. All of them wore caps. Most of them appeared to be smoking too.

Larry sat at a table with the usual group of laughing WAAFs surrounding him. I clocked he was wearing the short uniform jacket, open at the front with a white roll neck jumper on underneath. He was definitely loud and a bit of a charmer, not usually my type at all and I wondered how we had become the close friends we so obviously were. Larry spotted me straight away.

"Well, bless my soul, it's very nearly human! I see you had a battle with the razor this morning, and where's your tie old man? The boss won't like that, even though you've got your best blues on."

I must have seemed a little worried as Jackie came straight over, plonked a mug of tea in my hand, took off her tie and handed it over with a big smile.

"Here James, use this for now, I'll go and get a spare. You can give it back to me later," she said, peering up into my eyes and giving me a knowing wink that made my stomach drop. What had I said to her last night? I hoped it wasn't anything I might live to regret later.

"Thank you Jackie, thanks very much. I didn't even give a tie any thought."

Jackie frowned for a moment, then shrugged her shoulders.

"I'm just going to pop off and get my other tie before the dragon catches me without one," she said as she dashed out of the mess. "If you're gone by the time I get back, good luck with the CO"

"You having any breakfast Jock? I think they'd still be able to rustle you up something," said Larry.

My stomach churned. "No, thanks mate, I couldn't face it."

One of the WAAFs left the table so I slid into the vacant seat next to Larry.

"You are looking a bit green old feller," he said, grinning at me.

My stomach heaved again. "Yep, and I feel like I look. Listen, I'm going to take a little walk and get some fresh air before we see the CO. I'll meet you over there Larry,"

I finished my tea and stood up to go. I needed to get outside and quick.

"Sure, see you in 20 minutes old man."

I bolted for the door and felt relieved when I stepped back outside in the fresh icy air again. I had no idea where the CO's office was but I didn't think it would be too hard to spot. Knowing the military, there was bound to be a sign somewhere.

I was right. I found the central administration building within minutes and spotted a door inside with the name Group Captain Edward Fielden stencilled on it. It was still only quarter past twelve so I had fifteen minutes to kill.

My head ached as I wandered around the building, rubbing my freezing hands together and watching my breath condense in the icy atmosphere. I should've put my greatcoat on.

I spotted three large beech trees at the rear of the admin building so I headed that way. I'm not sure what caused me to look, and I'm not normally one for spying on others, but I glanced in one of the windows as I sauntered past and saw who I thought was the CO from last night sitting at his desk. He was talking to someone. Well, not just someone, it was the little old man in the black coat and hat from the library.

I almost stumbled over with the shock. I didn't think I had been spotted but I turned and flattened myself against the back wall of the building next to the window. My heart raced. I was certain of what I had seen but I needed another peek inside, just to be sure it wasn't my mind playing tricks. I needed to be careful, the CO was facing the window and he would easily spot me peering in at them if he happened to glance up at the window. I crouched down a little and edged my eye over to the bottom corner of the glass. If I was quick, a glance would be enough. I only wanted to confirm it was the old man from the library. I edged closer and peered in. I recognised the sharp features and the small head with the black Homberg hat instantly. Yep it was definitely him.

Still crouching, I stepped back away from the window when someone prodded me in the back.

"James! What are you creeping around back here for?"

Feeling a little ludicrous bent over, I turned and raised myself up to my full height as I leaned back against the wall next to the window. A smart red haired girl in full

WAAF uniform stood in front of me and she didn't appear too friendly.

My heart leapt when I realised it was Bonnie, but I was confused.

"Bonnie, what are you doing here, and why are you in uniform?" I whispered.

Bonnie continued to glare at me with a deep frown creasing her forehead and her luscious lips pursed tightly together. Her next move came as a bit of a shock.

She took a step forward and slapped me across the face with her right hand.

Even with my sluggish mind I managed to work out she was angry about something. The slap stung my left cheek and left the imprint of her hand burning my skin. My heart sunk as quickly as it had leapt only a brief moment before.

"What's wrong Bonnie?" I asked as I stepped forward, holding out my hand in an attempt at grasping hers. Her eyes flashed and she pulled her hand back.

"What's wrong James? Everything's wrong," she blurted out, tears welling up in her eyes. "I know what you've been through but how could you? With Jackie of all people, it's all over the base."

She sobbed, the tears running freely down both cheeks. My heart broke and a churning started in the pit of my stomach. My thoughts flicked back to the events of the previous night. Everyone must have spotted me kissing that WAAF Jackie in my drunken stupor. I knew it was just a stupid, drunken kiss and cuddle. It didn't mean anything, well, to me anyway, but that's obviously not how everyone else saw it, especially Bonnie. I had only met Bonnie yesterday - I think - but for some reason I felt completely devastated.

Obviously she did too, she seemed to be in shock. I wondered just what sort of a relationship we had? Somewhere deep inside I sensed that somehow we had been a part of each other's lives. I had to try and do something, say something.

"Bonnie, I was drunk, it didn't mean anything, nothing happened. I'm so sorry," I pleaded and tried once again to take her hand in mine, but she backed away, hot tears streaming down her ice cold face.

"How could you?" she almost shouted this time as she glared at me. We stood like that for a moment, face to face, neither quite knowing what to say next. I watched as her eyes eventually broke away from mine and seemed to take in our surroundings for the first time. A curious look spread across her face.

"And just why are you skulking around behind the CO's office, were you planning a secret rendezvous with her?"

"No of course not Bonnie," I pleaded again. "I'm just...well, I'm just...em...trying to see who's in there with the CO."

Bonnie glared at me. "Why?"

"Em...it's a long story but I think it's the man from the library."

Bonnie continued to stare at me for a few seconds, then turned on her heel and stormed away. She didn't look back.

"Well, that went well," I murmured to myself.

My watch said 12.30. After all that I was still going to be late. I dashed back around the building, up the step and stumbled in through the open front door. Larry stood inside the doorway in front of a small desk, behind which sat an officious looking adjutant with a prominent hooked nose. Next to Larry stood another tall and gangly sergeant in a tatty uniform with a white roll necked pullover on underneath, identical to Larry's.

"Thought you weren't coming old boy," Larry said, grinning at me.

The tall and awkward looking sergeant nodded and smiled, revealing a perfect set of brilliant white teeth underneath his bushy black moustache.

"What-ho old boy," he said in what must have been the best impersonation of Bertie Wooster I'd heard in a long time. I smiled nervously back at both of them but said nothing. My mouth was too dry for that.

"Go right in, the CO is waiting for you," said the adjutant. He didn't even glance up as he pointed at the door behind him.

Larry led the way, knocking on the closed door once and stepping in as the CO bellowed out, "Enter."

Group Captain Edward Fielden was still sitting behind his desk and there was no sign of the strange old man from the library.

"Ah, James, Larry, Bertie, come in, come in, pull up a chair," said the old man, in a surprisingly warm tone. He smiled broadly at the three of us as we each pushed a wooden chair up to the desk and sat down.

Bloody Bertie? He must be joking, it is bloody Bertie Wooster I thought, trying my best to suppress a snigger.

"How are we this morning? Looks like you all had a few jars in the mess last night?"

Larry, Bertie and I nodded in agreement, grinning sheepishly.

"And it seems like you had a fight with the razor this morning James?" he said, as Larry turned and grinned even wider at me.

"Yes sir, sorry sir," was the only response I could come up with. I needed to get the hang of that damn razor and quickly.

"Tea gentlemen?"

"Yes please," Bertie and I said, in unison.

"Colin, four teas please," the CO called out.

"Yes sir," came the reply from hook-nose on the other side of the door.

"Now, gentlemen, let's get down to business," the CO began. My stomach lurched again, it all sounded rather ominous.

"I've been chatting to your squadron CO, old Johnnie Fauquier over at HQ and 617 is on ops tonight. You'll be going with your Lancs from here and joining up with the rest of your squadron over the east coast. The usual mission briefings will be this afternoon but I have a favour to ask of you. I have to get four very special S.O.E. agents into Holland tonight and I don't have a spare aircraft available. It's a rush job and as usual highly secretive. I need you to take care of my agents and drop them in as close as you can to the drop zone, on the way to your target. This is an odd one and comes from the highest level, so I need the most experienced pilots on the job."

My stomach churned even more. Pilot?

"I've cleared it with Johnnie, and Larry we've agreed your crew will go and you'll lead the op. James, you'll be playing second dickey with Larry on this one and will be looking after my agents for me. Larry's mid-upper gunner, Harry, is still out of it with his back injury so you can double up as an air gunner too if you don't mind? Bertie, you'll take your crew in M-Mike and follow Larry in, drop your two agents and link up with the rest of your squadron on the mission."

I stared uncomprehending at the CO. Honestly, I had no bloody idea what he was talking about.

Larry turned and stared at me before he burst out laughing. "The great James Cunnion playing second dickey to me? Well, that's certainly one for the officer's mess."

I still had no idea what was going on.

"Now, now Larry, you should be honoured James has agreed to come along," the CO said, grinning at me.

I grinned back, inanely.

"James Cunnion, the man with the most gongs on the base and acting as my mid-upper gunner? That's going to go down a treat with the boys, wait until I tell them," said Larry, as he slapped me on the back.

The most gongs on the base? I wondered what that was all about. I needed to get a handle on this RAF slang and it also began to dawn on me that everyone in this life, or alternative world, whatever it was, seemed to know everything about me and yet I knew almost nothing about myself. Well, nothing apart from my childhood memories, my time at university, and my memories of the library and the little flat in Bedford in 2015 that was, but there was obviously a big bit missing in the middle somewhere. What the hell was going on with my mind?

The door banged open and hook-nose swept into the small office with a tray containing four steaming mugs of tea. He still couldn't manage a smile.

I took the tea offered to me and nearly scolded my fingers on the burning-hot white enamelled mug. I guess the RAF couldn't stretch to decent china mugs. We sipped our tea and the CO produced a packet of Garibaldi biscuits which we all dived into.

"So how is everything James, are you fairing up ok?" asked the CO, studying me closely. It was difficult knowing how to answer the question so I answered in the positive but I got the impression he didn't quite believe me.

Larry made some small talk about the impending runway repairs and the on-going testing of the latest SHORAN aircraft guidance system installed on our 617 squadron Lancasters based at Tempsford. As I didn't have a clue what he was talking about I kept out of the conversation as best I could and concentrated on the Garibaldis.

As Larry popped the last Garibaldi into his mouth and we drained the contents of our mugs, the CO glanced down at his watch.

"OK, thank you gentlemen, that's all for now. I'll have someone drive the agents over to you at dispersals later on. The rest of the details you'll get at your briefings this afternoon. And, once again, thank you, especially you James," he said as he stood up, leaned across the desk and took my hand in both of his, shaking it firmly while his deep blue eyes connected with mine. He was unable to hide the sadness in those eyes.

"Come on Jock, let's go and stretch our legs before the briefing," said Larry, who put his arm around my shoulder and led me towards the door. I sensed this was an emotional moment the CO and Larry were obviously sharing and I was completely in the dark.

Larry, Bertie and I left the CO's office and stepped out once again into the cold and frosty air. I shivered as I pulled up the collar of my jacket against the icy breeze

blowing across the exposed airfield, and not for the first

time that morning I wished I'd put on my greatcoat.

"Come on James, let's stretch our legs over to the old

kite and make sure the erks have got all the gremlins out

shall we? You coming Bertie?"

"No, I'll pop on over to mine. They're installing the

new Rose turrets today and I want to make jolly sure

everything's completed on time before the off," he said as

he jogged off across the snow covered airfield.

I had no idea what an erk was but I could probably

guess. I marched alongside Larry as we crunched over the

hard glistening grass away from the wooden huts and the

vast cavern-like aircraft hangar buildings towards the

perimeter of the airfield.

The activity going on around us reminded me of a

small colony of worker ants. Tractors raced along narrow

roadways pulling low trailers full of menacing looking

bombs, trucks were filled with men in oil covered overalls and literally hundreds of men and women, muffled in their hats, scarves, thick gloves and ever present blue uniforms, walked, ran or cycled from building to building. It seemed everyone had a purpose, everyone had a job to do, and there was none of the mucking around from last night. To a man they appeared grim faced and deadly serious. Operations were on.

A few people waved at us and smiled as we made our away across the snow covered grass to the aircraft sitting in their dispersal bays around the perimeter of the airfield. Larry made a bee-line towards the second of the huge four-engined Lancaster bombers, which seemed to be literally crawling with brown overalled personnel. By the time we approached the aircraft my face was red and my breath rasped in short white puffs.

"Looking a bit out of condition old man," said Larry, as he laughed and slapped me on the back again. If I hadn't been quite so out of puff I might have given him a suitable witty and sarcastic retort, assuming I could have thought of one that is.

We came to a halt about twenty feet away from the giant nose wheel of the Lancaster and both stood gaping upwards in the shadow of the monstrous aircraft. The ground crew (who I later discovered were the erks Larry had referred to) had swept the fresh snow from the massive wings and fuselage, and were now busily refuelling the wing tanks with high octane fuel from a large mobile bowser.

Glancing up I spotted armourers in the glass domed turrets on the top and rear of the aircraft loading the evil looking black cannons with hundreds of rounds of incendiary shells, each almost as large as their hands. Grease covered mechanics leaned inside the huge Merlin engines high up on the wings and a gang of brown overalled men with a crane loaded what appeared to be a massive bomb into the huge empty bay underneath the aircraft.

The dark painted bomber sat heavily on its huge smooth tyres and as I stared at it I couldn't clear from my mind the vision of a brooding and menacing dark hulk, waiting in silent anticipation of the horrors to come. An involuntary shiver ran down my spine.

A short and stocky man in brown overalls sauntered over to us.

"Good afternoon sirs," he said. He didn't salute.

"Good afternoon Percy, how's everything looking?" responded Larry.

I smiled and nodded at Percy, the grinning, grease-covered mechanic with the sergeant's stripes who so obviously loved his job.

"Tickety-boo sir. She's got a replacement starboard inner engine, the new Rose turret modifications on top and at the rear are complete, the new .50 inch cannons with the gun-laying radar you're trialling have been fitted, and we've patched up the flak holes from the other night sir. I've got everyone on it and she'll be good to go by 15.00 hours."

"How much fuel Percy?" asked Larry.

"Exactly 2,155 gallons of fuel on board sir," responded Percy as he attempted to remove the grease from his hands using an even greasier rag. "And a tallboy being loaded underneath."

Larry sucked in air through his teeth and glanced at me with a resigned shrug which clearly was supposed to mean something, but didn't.

"Could be bloody Berlin," was all he said. That didn't sound too good even with my lack of experience. "Maybe we're being sent over to drop off old Adolf's Christmas present eh?" Larry laughed as he spoke, but there was no humour in his eyes.

I gazed up again at the aircraft looming above us and for the first time spotted the brightly coloured decal painted on the side of the fuselage, just beneath the cockpit window. It was a well detailed cartoon image of Hitler's head clasped inside a pair of nutcrackers. I laughed out loud and pointed up.

"What's that Larry?"

Larry glanced up at the side of the aircraft and had a little chuckle too.

"You mean to tell me you haven't seen that before? That's our call-sign decal, Percy here painted it himself." He pointed along to the rear of the aircraft where there were three large red letters painted on the side of the aircraft. An 'A' and a 'J' before the RAF roundel and an 'N' immediately afterwards.

"We're N-for-Nuts," he said, rather proudly and without a hint of humour.

"N for Nuts? You've got to be bloody kidding!" I said. Percy the mechanic grinned maniacally and wiped more grease across his face with the back of his hand. I glanced up at the nutcracker decal and down again at my two grinning companions. *We're all going to hell in a bloody handcart* I thought.

"Come on then old man, how about a pint of wallop in the mess to settle our nerves before the briefings?" Larry said as he strolled off towards the dark painted huts in the distance.

I wasn't at all sure it was a good idea, especially after last night.

"Actually Larry I think I'll head back to my bunk, I need a bit more shut-eye." I did, and I needed some time to myself to think too.

"OK old man, your loss. See you at the briefing at 15.30 hours, or before if you change your mind? I can't wait to tell the boys we've got you on board, I'm sure they'll want to stand you a drink." Larry grinned at me once more and then jogged off in the direction of the large mess building, puffing clouds of icy white breath before him like a small locomotive.

With all the standing around the cold started to bite into my extremities, so I followed Larry's lead and jogged slowly back to the hut I had vacated only a few hours earlier, but which seemed like a lifetime ago now.

I found the door marked O-47, stepped into the now strangely familiar room, clicked the door shut behind me and leaned back on it, letting out a deep breath. Thankfully the room was empty.

I could still see my breath inside the building, which wasn't a good sign. A small black iron stove affair which might well have been a heater stood in the middle of the room, but on closer inspection it appeared to require coal to make it work and I couldn't see any immediately to hand, so I grabbed my greatcoat from the locker at the end of my bed and pulled it on. I threw myself down on the narrow bunk and stared up at the white paint peeling off the corrugated tin ceiling.

So, what the hell was going to happen now? It seemed obvious to me if I let the day run its course I would soon be attending briefings and joining Larry and his crew on a flight to God knows where, possibly even Berlin by the sounds of it. I had no concept of what that would be like, but despite Larry's outward show of nonchalance, even I had detected his underlying fear at the mention of Berlin. Whatever was likely to happen, it wasn't going to be a joy ride, that's for certain.

My mind wandered back to thoughts of Jay and the library back (or forwards - this is getting confusing) in 2015. I could of course simply grab my motorbike, ride back to Bedford and return through the wormhole, or whatever it was, and get back to my normal life. But see, there's the rub; how normal was that life when you analysed it? I had confirmed my parents lived in 1944 and my friends all seemed to be here too, even though I'm struggling to recognise any of them. Hell, even all of my personal paperwork and IDs are dated 1944. What actually did I have in 2015 when I came to think of it? It was a shell of a life, a limbo like existence. Perhaps this was my real life here, and something had gone wrong with my mind? Amnesia perhaps?

And what about Bonnie, what was going on there? Even the mere thought of her made my heart jolt. I lay on that tiny bunk imagining her smiling face, that beautiful bouncing red hair of hers and I felt a physical warmth begin in the pit of my stomach and flow outwards throughout my entire body. Was that love? Real love? I was a bit of a novice in that area but it certainly felt like it might be. But she was mad at me now, and would she even look at me again after this morning's events?

And then there's Larry and his crew, and the CO. What was I going to do there? Why were they all so excited to have me on board and was I really going to let them all down? Could I possibly do that?

Of course I couldn't. The thought of going with them in that monster of an aircraft terrified me, but what else could I do? And if I'm honest, there was just a little twinge of excitement at the thought too.

My thoughts wandered to Larry and Alky and the rest of the crew, whoever they might be, and the idea of that pint of beer with Larry suddenly appealed to me. I rolled off the little bed and went over to the wardrobe. Larry had been wearing his shorter tunic and a white roll neck pullover, which was most likely his flying uniform, so I decided to change. I swapped my best blues, as Larry called them, for the rather more worn but comfier blue trousers with the big front pockets, battledress jacket and white pullover. I spotted a pair of high, black leather sheepskin lined boots in the bottom of the locker and pulled those on instead of my dress shoes. I even put the cap on my head this time, making sure it was at the obligatory rakish angle of course. Staring at my reflection in the mirror I was more than a little impressed again. A real flying hero even if I said so myself. I wondered if I would be able to live up to it.

I grabbed the tie I had borrowed earlier from Jackie, stuffed it in my inside pocket and let myself out of the small dormitory. The afternoon sun hung low in the sky and the dull glow gave the snow covered backdrop an eerie orange hue, almost as if we existed within a fantasy world. Perhaps we did.

I pulled up my collar, tucked my hands deep into my trouser pockets and followed my puffs of frosty breath over to the officer's mess. I was grateful for the woollen pullover. I passed three WAAFs bundled up in greatcoats and scarves on my way, and they each presented me with a beaming smile and a little wave. Unfortunately none of them was Bonnie. Still, I was beginning to enjoy the relaxed atmosphere of this place.

Half a dozen officers were drinking mugs of tea and reading newspapers quietly in the mess when I walked in, but there was no sign of Larry and his crew. I noticed someone had locked up the pay phone I had used last night with a large chain and padlock. I wondered if that was anything to do with our imminent mission briefing and the powers that be not wanting anyone casually giving out confidential information over the wires. I suspect you can never be too sure as to who's listening?

"You looking for Larry?" shouted Reg from behind the bar. He had a red and white checked cloth in his hand and was lazily polishing a pint glass.

"Yes, I was actually Reg, any idea where he is?"

"Yes Sir, he's over at the sergeant's mess, he said to send you over there if you came in."

"Ah, ok, thanks Reg," I said as I backed out the door and clicked it shut behind me, trying my best not to disturb the rather tranquil atmosphere inside any more than I already had. I had no idea whether the officers inside would be on ops later that day, and if they were, what might be going through their minds. Maybe they needed some peace and quiet, to steady themselves before the approaching storm?

I also had no idea where the sergeant's mess was, but it didn't take me too long to find it. Only half a dozen buildings stood around the main CO's office and the sergeant's mess was the largest of them. What gave it away was the sign on the door which said 'Sergeant's Mess', although some wag had crossed out the word 'Sergeants' and replaced it with 'Bloody'.

The warm air hit me as soon as I opened the door. A burning stove sat in the middle of the room and uniformed men and women filled the soft leather sofas, dining tables and chairs which were scattered around it. *In the Mood* was playing somewhere in the background which added just the right ambiance to the scene.

I wandered in and immediately my eyes settled on Larry, Alky and the rest of his crew, sitting around a large table in the far corner of the room with mugs of tea and plates of toast in front of them.

"Jock, over here old man," shouted Larry as he waved his hands wildly in the air. Was he always on volume eleven? I wondered. I managed to thread my way around the mass of tables and chairs and sat down in a vacant seat next to Alky.

"I've been telling the lads you're on with us tonight old man," said Larry.

Larry, Alky and four other uniformed guys grinned across the table. I sensed they were waiting for some pearls of wisdom from me.

"Yep, looks like it, pleased to be with you chaps."
My words weren't exactly 'Churchill-esque' but they at
least elicited a round of 'pleased to have you on board'
comments from each of the crew. The man sitting next to
Alky was tall, slim and straight backed with thinning hair
on top. He had sergeant's stripes on his arm and a badge
with a single wing attached to an 'E' over his left breast
pocket.

"Richard, Richard Gravestone. I'm the Flight
Engineer," he said in a well-spoken, rather BBC English
accent as he leaned over to shake my hand. "Everyone calls
me Dicky."

I smiled and nodded at him. It seemed they all knew
who I was so I didn't think there was much point in
introducing myself. Next to him sat a mountain of a man
with piercing blue eyes and a mop of curly blonde hair
perched on top of his head. He was also displaying
sergeant's stripes and a single wing badge with 'WAG'

embroidered on it alongside another bizarre badge with a fist gripping three lightning bolts. His hands were calloused and the leathery skin on his face was a deep golden brown.

"How's it going mate? Ricky Kellow, I'm on wireless."

His accent was Australian, pure outback, and he sported a wide cheesy grin.

The shortest member of the crew stood up from the other side of the table and leaned over to shake my hand. Aside from his extremely short stature, he could only have been five foot and a couple of inches, the other immediately noticeable feature was the way his unnaturally taught, almost plastic looking skin stretched across his destroyed face. As I took his hand in mine I spotted the terrible burn scars on back of his hand. His other hand was sheathed in a tight black leather glove and I suspected it probably wasn't a real hand under there. He had a single line of blue braid around his jacket cuffs and epaulets, and a half wing badge like the others, but this time with a 'B' embroidered at the bottom. I also spotted he had two medal ribbons attached to his tunic. He appeared to be about twenty two years of age.

"Flying Officer Johnson, Eddie Johnson, I'm the bomb aimer and general dogsbody," he said in a pleasant sing-song West Country accent. A few chuckles rippled around the table.

Next to Eddie sat a tall, slim, dark haired sergeant with a bushy black moustache perched on his top lip. His long slender hand reached over and took mine. He was the cultural and physical opposite of the big Aussie, Ricky Kellow. His hands were soft and smooth, a musician's hands I guessed.

"Frankie Sutherland, pleased to meet you Sir, I've heard a lot about you of course and seen you around, but never had the pleasure." His smile was warm and his

Canadian accent had a soft lyrical note. "I'm the arse-end Charlie."

That surprised me. This man, with the soft elegant fingers, undoubtedly more suited to drawing a bow across fine strings than pouring hot death across the sky from his twin Browning machine guns, seemed so out of place, so out of balance with this setting, with this war. Yet here he was with all the rest of them, in uniform, far away from his home, his family, and probably his musical instruments.

"It's a pleasure to meet you too Frankie."

And it was. I doubted that any one of them were as old as me.

So, along with Alky the navigator and Larry up front driving, this was the crew of seven on 'N-for-Nuts', plus me now of course, tagging along for God knows what reason. I hoped I wasn't going to let any of them down.

"There you go Jock, the most experienced damn crew in Bomber Command, well apart from yours of course...oh...em, sorry...well...you know what I mean?," said Larry, crimson faced and obviously acutely embarrassed by what he'd just said. The rest of the crew suddenly tried to avoid eye contact, most stared down at their boots. I wasn't sure what Larry had meant, but I did have a growing suspicion. I tried to remember, did I have a crew and had something happened to them? There was the faintest of memories trying to edge into my mind, something...what was it? But try as I might I couldn't quite grasp it.

My desperate train of thought was disturbed by a lady in a light blue overall serving up plates of sausage, bacon and eggs. Well, one egg to be exact, and another mountain of toast.

As soon as the laden plates landed on the table, each man tucked into his greasy lunch. Was this a condemned man's last meal I wondered? My stomach started to complain before I even scooped the first fatty mouthful in, but overall the food turned out to be not too bad. I simply couldn't face the lukewarm grease covered fried egg though, and pushed that to the side of my plate.

"You're not going to leave that ruddy egg are you sir?" said Ricky in his unmistakable Australian drawl. "Outside they're like rocking-horse shit, no one gets them. The villagers would string you up if they knew you were wasting that egg." He stared at me expectantly until I pushed my plate towards him and he helped himself to the priceless fried egg.

"OK Lads," said Larry glancing down at his watch, "eat up, the briefing's in ten minutes."

"I thought we were going to down a beer or two," I said. I seriously had been looking forward to that.

"Nah, bloody crazy Wally won't play ball, he says it's CO's orders, no alcohol before ops. He's done it before but won't today, I reckon the old man's been on his back," said Larry, jerking his thumb over at the wild red haired man with the crooked eyes standing behind the bar and chatting to a sergeant WAAF. Crazy Wally indeed I thought.

Like us, everyone else in the sergeant's mess seemed to be getting up and making a move for the door. We all trooped out into the frosty December afternoon and I followed the rest of the crew to a large squat wooden building with smashed windows and a partially thatched roof. The rest of the roof looked like it had caved in years ago and the building appeared derelict.

'Gibraltar Farm, oh how I've come to hate this bloody place," said Frankie as we both stared at the dark, diseased looking building looming menacingly in front of us.

The big wooden barn doors stood ajar. In fact one hung almost off its hinges, so we all filed in one by one through the narrow gap. Once inside I stopped dead in my tracks and the Australian man-mountain behind me nearly knocked me flat on the floor.

"Sorry sir, didn't see you'd stopped," he said, staring at my gawping features.

The building inside was about the size of a tennis court, structurally sound, well lit, comfortably heated and newly painted. Neat rows of tables and chairs faced a raised wooden platform at the far end on which stood another table and two chairs. A large blue velvet curtain covered the back wall.

There was nothing even remotely derelict about this place on the inside. It was a mystery to me, but I began to understand this place wasn't at all as it appeared, or was supposed to appear.

Larry and his crew filed along behind a table on the left hand side of the room and sat down. I squeezed in at the end, next to Larry. Peering around the room I could see the chairs were quickly filling up with all sizes and shapes of men: big, small, skinny, bald, sergeants and officers, gentlemen and pit hands. There were only three things they had in common: they all wore blue uniforms, they were all volunteers and they were all young.

I spotted Bertie and his crew seated around him over to our right. Everyone chatted within their own small groups, although surprisingly the general noise level in the room still seemed quite subdued. Almost everyone kept glancing furtively up at the front of the room, there was a palpable sense of anticipation and nervousness in the air. What was behind that big blue curtain?

A door banged open at the other end of the room and the CO and another taller officer I didn't recognise marched up onto the platform. The CO faced the now silent room. I could hear Larry's breathing next to me.

The slightly statured CO's voice boomed out. "Gentlemen, thank you for your attendance. Despite the cold, you'll be pleased to hear we're on for tonight." A low groan rippled around the room in response. "There are three missions on tonight: some of you from 161 and 138 squadrons will be carrying out our usual agent drops with the Lysanders, we've got several locations on that, and the Halifax boys from 109 and our guests from 617 squadron with their Lancasters will be supporting the main Bomber Command mission tonight with their newly fitted Rose turrets and other trial equipment."

A general hubbub rippled around the room, but everyone remained focussed on the two men at the front and the mysterious curtain.

"Come on old man, let's see where we're going," whispered Larry.

As if in response to Larry - and just about everyone else in the room - the CO took a step backwards.

"And now Wing Commander Gus Rowe will take you through the details of tonight's raid," said the CO as he stepped to the side and sat down on one of the chairs on the platform.

The imposing, handlebar moustached Wing Commander stepped up to the curtain, lifted his hand and pulled hard on a string behind the curtain. The blue velvet material swung dramatically aside to reveal a map of Europe that filled the entire wall at the back of the stage. As soon as the map was exposed a second audible groan echoed around the room.

Peering at the map I could just make out the bright red lines of string pinned across the board.

The Wing Commander curled his moustache with his fingers. "So gentlemen, as you can see, our target tonight is Essen, the home of the Krupps armaments empire to be precise."

The hubbub in the room increased.

"Oh God, that's a tough one, bloody hell, back to the Ruhr. That bleeding place is ringed by at least 400 flack

guns and night fighters are still bloody operating too."
Larry sounded quite down for once, which was saying
something. I had a sinking feeling in the pit of my stomach
too, and I was blessed with not even knowing what to
expect. I wasn't entirely sure if that was a good thing or a
bad thing.

Scanning the room I spotted a lot of long faces
amongst most of the crews.

My attention came back to Wing Commander Gus
Rowe who now seemed to be explaining some of the
details. I presumed I needed to listen and take notes, but I
wasn't sure it would help much.

"Dispersals at 16.30. We go at 18.00. You'll be
routed north east out of here and link up with the main
force over Norfolk, leaving our coast at Yarmouth. Then
you'll be routed out over the North Sea, crossing the Dutch
coast at Harlingen and heading due east over Groningen.
M-Mike and N-Nuts have a special drop just east of

Groningen so will be leaving the pack for a while but will make every effort to catch up again before the target. Remember, keep pushing out window as soon as you're over the coast."

The wing commander cleared his throat and took a sip of water from the tumbler in front of him.

The occasional wisecrack rang out from the odd person in the room and I spotted a few grinning faces, but not many. The business of death was a serious one.

"You will continue on east until your turning point at Oldenburg, thirty miles west of Bremen. The main force will then head south-east on to Essen, approaching from the north to avoid the flak belt of towns along the Ruhr valley. 109 squadron will continue on to Bremen as a diversionary force. Hopefully the Luftwaffe controller will be fooled into thinking the main force is heading for either Bremen or Berlin and send the night fighters in that direction. To add to the confusion for the Luftwaffe, five Group will be conducting a simultaneous raid on the Dortmund-Ems Canal at Ladbergen."

A loud groan came from a number of tables on the other side of the room. I guessed they were the 109-squadron boys, going off to play catch-me-if-you-can with the deadly German nightjager. There weren't many more smiles coming from our table either.

"617 squadron, you'll be going in at angels 23,000 over the target area. With the exception of N-Nuts and M-Mike, your six Lancs will link up with the main 617 Pathfinder force tonight at 22.00, testing the new American modified SHORAN guidance system. You'll be dropping red target indicator incendiaries for the rest of the group. N-Nuts and M-Mike, you'll be playing catch up with the main force. You've got a couple of big old Tallboys loaded so make sure you're on target. We plan on finishing Krupps off tonight for good."

The wing commander took another sip of water. I glanced sideways and Larry had his head in his hands.

"Oh, and you eight crews in 617, do not, I repeat, do not lose your kites tonight. Those SHORAN sets the boffins put in are highly top secret and under no circumstances can they fall into Jerry's hands. If you're going down, make damn sure they burn!"

"Bloody nice," mumbled Alky.

"Your route out again will be due west and get over our own lines as fast as you can to avoid any more flak than is necessary. Cloud cover is expected very light tonight, about three-ten, and it's a full moon, so you boys will no doubt be enjoying the view while we're stuck here twiddling our thumbs hoping you don't do too much damage to our expensive aeroplanes. Gunners, remember to keep your eyes peeled for Jerry underneath the kite, we believe some of them may have modified upwards firing cannon. Navigators and bomb aimers, let's see you in the map room in ten minutes."

His briefing finished, the wing commander collected his paperwork from the table, nodded at the CO and marched grim faced from the platform.

The CO stood and scrutinised the men in the room.

"This one should put the final nail in the coffin of the Krupps German armaments production on the Ruhr. We're nearly there, but we still need to keep pushing. Good luck boys, let's see you all back here early tomorrow morning. Those of you on ops tonight from 161 and 138 squadrons, please stay behind now, the briefing for you guys is as usual top secret. Everyone else, go and collect your gear."

The sound of scraping chairs filled the room and the CO gave us his Sunday best smile as we all trooped out of the warm briefing room via the rear door this time.

The first thing I spotted as I stepped through the door were the neat rows of steel lockers running the length of the next room. No one said a word, everyone seemed to be lost in their own thoughts now, going through the motions required of them like automatons. Every man headed for a locker, as they would have done many tens of times before. For how many of these men would it be the last time? Would it be my first, and last time I wondered?

"Come on old man," said Larry, slapping me on the shoulder. Thank heaven for old Larry I thought. Brash, loud and bloody full of himself, but a good pal all the same. Larry sauntered along one of the rows of lockers, his arm draped casually around my shoulder.

"Jock, I know it's not been long since...well, you know...are you ready for this?"

I had no idea what he was asking me if I'm honest.

"Ready for what Larry?"

"Do you have everything tidied up and in order, do you need me to do anything?"

I was still none the wiser but if pushed I imagine I could guess what he was saying, so I just went along with it.

"I'm fine Larry, everything is cool."

Larry stopped and stared directly at me. "Cool? What's cool?" He seemed genuinely confused.

"I mean everything's tip top old chap," I said, in my best Surrey accent.

Larry grinned back at me and we continued walking down the aisle with identical steel lockers on both sides of us.

I had already worked out that we were there to collect our flying gear as I had spotted other lads opening their lockers and struggling into jackets, boots and hats, but I still wondered how on earth I was going to find my locker without making a fool of myself when Larry pulled us to a halt. In front of me stood a locker with a paper label glued to the front. On the paper label was typed the name FLT. LT. JAMES CUNNION.

Larry's locker was two away from mine. The lockers on either side of mine had no labels, just an outline of glue where a label had once been. I wasn't sure why, but it made me shiver.

Larry fished around in his battledress top pocket and came out with a key which he slipped into the lock and opened his locker door. It was as good a place to start looking as any so I slipped two fingers into my tunic top pocket too. Sure enough, human nature being what it is (we are so predictable sometimes), I discovered a single small key in my left breast pocket. I opened the locker door with a growing feeling of *Deja-vu* and peered inside.

The letter addressed to Mr and Mrs Cunnion propped up against a long sweet tin on the top shelf was the first thing I spotted. The ivory coloured envelope was sealed and I immediately knew what it was. This was the final letter to my parents should I not come back. I glanced across at Larry's locker and as he stuffed his wallet in I could make out a similar letter leaning up against the top shelf of his locker too. I wondered when I had written it and what I had said. Without any remaining doubt, At that moment I was certain that this was my locker and my letter. I had no idea what had happened to me, but it all fitted. This was my life.

Looking at the thick sheepskin lined brown leather Irvine flying jacket and leather helmet hanging up in front of me, I wasn't sure I was too excited about the revelation at all. Larry was already zipping himself into his jacket so I didn't have too much time to give it any thought. Thankfully.

I threw my cap onto the top of the locker, placed my own wallet onto the shelf next to my parent's letter and pulled on the heavy jacket over my RAF battledress tunic. I was sweating before I even had the zip halfway up.

"Don't forget you'll need the trousers too, and the over-suit old man, you're on mid-upper gunner duties tonight, no bloody heating up there," Larry said, looking serious for once.

I could already feel the sweat trickling down the middle of my back as I stared at the heavy sheepskin lined trousers and the large brown jump-suit still hanging up.

"Are you bloody sure I'll need it?"

"I know it's a load of clobber to be wearing but I'm not going up there with you if you're without it old man, and I'm certainly not going to go down in history as the one who caused the famous James Cunnion's old todger to fall off with frost-bite."

Famous or not, Larry appeared serious for the second time today so I did as I was told and struggled into the bulky trousers and over suit. By the time it was all on I could barely walk and sensed I was likely to faint from heat exhaustion if I didn't get outside in the cold pretty damn quick.

Larry sauntered out of the locker room in his flying jacket and sheepskin flying boots, and with his flying helmet and gloves in his hand. I swayed along next to him like the Stay-Puft Marshmallow Man, sweating like a pig and feeling like a jerk. Little did I know then my uncomfortably hot marshmallow-man suit was to be the only thing that separated me from life and a slow painful death within the next twelve hours.

We stepped out of the rear door of the Gibraltar Farm building into the welcome arms of the frosty December air. I breathed the ice laden air deep into my lungs and felt my body starting to cool down a little, the urge to vomit began to pass.

Larry crunched across the snow covered walkway towards a large aircraft hangar, following the footsteps of the aircrew who had gone before us. The big hanger doors sat open and inside I spotted an orderly line of aircrew bundled up in bulky flight leathers accepting packages of something or other from a line of WAAFs, equally bundled up in greatcoats, scarves and gloves.

When Larry and I arrived at the head of the queue a WAAF with a scarf covering most of her face shouted out, "James, James."

I stared into her sparking eyes but had no idea who she was. For a second my heart leaped at the thought it might be Bonnie, just as the girl said, "James, it's me Jackie."

My heart sank again. Not because it was Jackie, but because it wasn't Bonnie. I couldn't think of anything to say but knew she was waiting for me to say something.

"Err, I've got your tie in my pocket, but...em I can't get it out now with all this stuff on."

Hardly the sweet whispered words of love she was undoubtedly waiting for, but there you are, that's me all over, bloody useless. I think her eyes had lost just a little of that sparkle when she replied.

"Em...that's OK James, keep it close to your heart, it might bring you luck."

As soon as the words were out of her mouth she looked mortified.

"Oh James, I didn't mean that you needed luck, I mean nothing bad is going to happen is it, I mean..."

"Don't worry Jackie, it's fine. I do believe your tie will be a good luck charm." I was smiling my Sunday-best smile at her when Larry elbowed me in the ribs. I was holding up the queue, there were at least another thirty airmen lined up behind us, so I took the large canvas wrapped package Jackie held out to me and moved along the counter. Another WAAF presented me with a bright yellow Mae-West vest and a third WAAF at the end of the counter handed me a small brown cardboard box, a flask and another small, soft bag.

As we walked away from the hangar I spotted Larry pulling on his Mae-West life vest and stuffing the small soft bag inside his flight jacket, so I did likewise, trying to appear as familiar and full of confidence as he did, but failing miserably.

I was still trying to hold on to the large bag, which looked suspiciously like a parachute, and not drop the hot flask when a large open-backed truck careered around the corner of the hanger and slithered to a halt beside us. The petite WAAF driver with the non-regulation red woollen hat pulled down over her ears leaned through the open window and shouted out a muffled command.

"All aboard who's coming aboard!"

The aircrew gathered around us started to clamber onto the back of the truck. Ricky, the big Australian had joined us and he and Larry climbed up and pulled me up behind them. With the full flying suit on there was no way I was going to be able to climb up on my own. As soon as we had sat down on the wooden side benches, someone pulled up the tailgate and the truck lurched forward again. It was perhaps only my opinion, but the breakneck speed the WAAF drove at seemed most unsuitable for the road conditions, but no one else seemed to be bothered. I suppose that bearing in mind where we were going, having a minor traffic accident was hardly a great cause for concern?

We raced around the partially snow cleared aerodrome perimeter road and after about five minutes skidded to a halt underneath one of the dark brooding monsters sitting silently in its dispersal bay. The setting winter sun lengthened the shadows and gave the aircraft an almost sinister appearance. An involuntary shudder ran down my spine. Seven aircrew I hadn't seen before jumped off the rear of the truck. Two of them were trussed up in the same bulky outfits as me, but they definitely seemed to be coping better.

We roared off again and soon came to another Lancaster looming above us. Engineers and ground crew still crawled all over it like dark soldier ants. Bertie, the tall and gangly sergeant loaded down with big leather gloves, flying helmet, parachute pack, flask and cardboard box dropped off the back of the truck, followed by the other six members of his crew.

"Good luck Bertie!" shouted Larry.

Bertie turned and gazed back at us with a beaming smile across his heavily lined face.

"What-ho boys! See you back in the mess," he shouted. "The wallop's on me tonight."

I just had time to wave at him as the truck jolted forward again and we were off, racing towards N-for-Nuts waiting menacingly for us in the adjacent dispersal, 500 yards away.

I leapt off the back of the truck and would have gone arse-over-tit if Ricky hadn't caught me.

"Thanks mate, this bloody suit is an eff-ing nuisance."

"You'll be only too glad of it when you're up top," he said, jerking his thumb in the direction of the Perspex covered dome perched like a carbuncle on top of the Lancaster's fuselage. I peered up at the dome and spotted another dark soldier ant inside, no doubt checking the evil looking cannons over one last time, making sure they were well greased and ready to do their deathly duty.

Larry and Percy sauntered around the dark machine, stopping occasionally to peer up at the black, green and brown painted structure, Percy explaining something or other. The other crew members stood around smoking and chatting. I walked over and stood next to the only other member of the crew dressed the same as me, Frankie, the tall Canadian rear gunner. We looked like a couple of sumo wrestlers preparing to do battle.

"So what do you do back in Canada Frankie?" I asked.

For a split second he had a faraway look in his eyes, and then he smiled.

"I help my pa look after the family business up in Banff, in Alberta."

"Ah ok, and what business is that Frankie?"

"It's a gun store. Me and my two brothers help pa fix up the guns."

I wasn't expecting that.

"But I don't like guns much, I play the cello," he added, with that faraway look again.

I was expecting that.

"That's wonderful Frankie. And how are your family holding up with you over here?"

He seemed thoughtful for a moment and the smile left his face.

"Not so good sir. My brothers are over in France at the moment and I know my folks are struggling with the business and the worry of us. My ma never says it in her letters but I can tell."

There wasn't much I could say to that. I suspected my own parents felt the same way now I thought about it.

Larry finished his inspection of the aircraft and marched over to the rest of the crew.

"OK lads, I think we're good to go, shall we get on with it?" he said as he turned around and walked away, not towards the small open door in the side of the fuselage as I would have expected, but over towards the front of the aircraft. Alky and Dicky followed him and the three of them came to a halt underneath the Lancaster and turned to face the nose wheel. The rest of the crew walked towards the rear of the aircraft and stopped to face the real wheels. I thought perhaps they were all carrying out one final inspection of the wheels, but no, I couldn't have been more wrong. I stared wide eyed as the entire crew fumbled around in front of themselves and then the streams of hot urine appeared, steaming like geysers in the ice-laden air. They were all peeing over the tyres of the bloody aircraft.

"Come on James, get your bloody todger out and have a pee. You'll ruin our luck if you don't!" shouted Larry over his shoulder. Still trying to get my head around the bizarre scene in front of me, I walked towards the rear of the aircraft where there seemed to be more room around the twin sets of wheels and stood beside the others. I had no idea how the hell I was even going to burrow through all the clothes I had on to get my old-man out, let alone manage a pee, but it seemed as if it was my duty to at least try.

I placed my parachute, helmet, mask, gloves, flask and cardboard box down on the concrete next to all the others and began the long process of unzipping my way through several layers of clothing.

At last I managed to tug my penis from its well-hidden and snug home out into the icy air. It immediately recoiled and tried to sneak back in, but I hung on and finally managed to get a hot stream of pee onto the wheels just as the others finished. I thought it seemed a jolly strange way of de-icing the wheels, but who was I to question the long-established practices of the crew. I later learned this whole peeing thing was in fact a superstitious good-luck routine many aircrews went through prior to a mission. I had no idea what the connection was between urine and good-luck, but as I say, who am I to question the ways of men, especially in such dangerous and emotionally charged times as these.

I was still attempting to get everything back into place without getting my uniform wet, which I'm not entirely sure I succeeded in doing, when we all spotted a light blue car weaving its way around the snow drifts on the perimeter road, heading towards us.

"Hello, wonder what this is then?" said Frankie to no one in particular.

The car slid to a stop next to the Lancaster just as I picked up my kit. This time I jammed the leather helmet onto my head as everyone else had done. It was one less thing to carry.

The driver's door of the car opened rearwards and a young WAAF stepped out. I recognised Bonnie instantly. My heart leapt with excitement, but soon sunk in despair when the memory of this morning flashed into my head.

The rest of the crew were standing next to the door in the Lancaster's fuselage, chatting, so I took a few tentative steps towards the car. Bonnie opened the rear door and a young lady in a long drab brown coat and an orange headscarf emerged from the car at the same time as a tall slim man with a heavy black beard stepped out of the car on the other side. He wore a similarly coloured long dark coat and a brown cap pulled down tight on his head. He walked around the car to stand next to the young woman, took her arm in his and they both walked over to me, eyes staring. Was it fear I saw in those eyes? I wasn't sure.

The man held his hand out so I took it firmly in mine and we shook hands.

"It's a pleasure to meet you sir," I said, "my name's James, James Cunnion."

The man gave the faintest of smiles but there was no warmth in his eyes.

"It's a pleasure to meet you too Mr Cunnion, are you the pilot tonight?"

His accent was undetectable, his words were highly enunciated and I thought he sounded English, but he might also have been foreign. I wasn't sure. He gave nothing away, there was no warmth, nothing remotely friendly.

"Em, no, I'm not the pilot tonight. That's Larry, over there," I said as I turned to point vaguely in the direction of the crew who were now staring at us. The man gave the briefest of nods and stuffed his bare hands deep into his coat pockets.

The young lady glanced up at me and smiled. In contrast to the man there was a definite warmth in her smile. I held my hand out and she took it gently.

"Pleased to meet you miss," I said as I shook her trembling hand. The fact that neither of them had offered their name wasn't lost on me. She continued to stare into my eyes and I sensed she was not nearly as controlled as her companion. She seemed scared, possibly terrified, her eyes said it all and my heart went out to her. She couldn't have been more than 17 or 18 years of age.

"Are we boarding now?" the man asked, intruding in on my connection with the girl.

"Err, yes I think we are," I said.

I turned and spotted Larry dragging his sheepskin covered frame through the tiny doorway of the Lancaster. "Would you like to follow the crew in?" I said.

Neither the man nor the young lady spoke. He simply nodded at me, took the girl's arm in his again and walked her over to join the rest of the crew in the queue at the doorway. Her eyes stared unblinking with all the appearance of a rabbit caught in a car's headlights as she was led away.

Bonnie stood next to the car scrutinising me. I was almost afraid to look at her, but found the courage from somewhere.

"Hi Bonnie," I said, with what I hoped was my most conciliatory smile.

Bonnie studied me in silence. She appeared even more beautiful than ever and in that moment I knew I loved her with all my heart, but I still wasn't sure what her eyes were saying. Her face was expressionless, but to be fair at minus five degrees that was probably to be expected.

"Hello James," she said, eventually. Could that have been the flicker of a smile across her lips? I so wanted to believe it was. I was looking for a sign, any sign that I might have been forgiven.

We stood motionless, staring at each other, hardly daring to breathe for what seemed like a lifetime. Time had stood still: the crew clambering into the dark instrument of death behind me, the cold eyed young man, the trembling young lady, the people in Germany we were about to wreak destruction against, the German fighter pilot who was probably waiting for us right now in the skies over Europe, none of them existed in that moment, it was just Bonnie and me.

I took one step towards the woman I loved, heart racing. I felt certain that if the bloody Germans didn't get me the damn blood pressure would. Bonnie didn't move, she stood motionless, staring, her full red lips pressed tightly together.

I had to say something. I had no idea what might happen to me over the next few hours, I couldn't leave it like this.

"Bonnie, I...I...want to say, I'm so sorry about...well...about..."

Bonnie raised her hand into the air and silently cut me off. Still staring at me, she stepped forward as she peeled her brown leather gloves from her hands and tucked them into her tunic pocket. She reached behind her neck and then I glimpsed something glinting in her hand as she stood directly in front of me. I hoped it wasn't a knife.

I felt her warm breath on my face as she leaned in and brushed her soft lips against mine. I thought my heart was going to burst through my chest and I wanted to put my arms around her, to hold her tight and never let her get away from me again. But I couldn't, I was still holding the bloody parachute, flask, gloves and that stupid cardboard box. Bonnie's green eyes sparkled and a glimmer of a smile appeared on her lips, but to my despair she stepped back, held her hand out and pressed something into my hand. It was a small silver locket.

Finally she spoke.

"That's my great grandmother's locket. It's a family heirloom so you have to bring it back," she said. She leaned forward again, gave me one last lingering kiss and then she was gone. I watched as she sat back into the driver's seat of the car, swung her legs in and banged the door shut. The engine coughed into life and she was away without so much as a single glance back.

My heart sank to my boots. There was so much I wanted to say, so much I wanted to do, so much I wanted to plan. I wanted to live the rest of my life with her and I didn't get a chance to tell her. But then, perhaps she knew all that? What if I didn't come back? Maybe she was simply being realistic, young people were dying all around us after all. I hadn't thought too much about my own mortality until that moment and it hit me like a steam train. I didn't want to die, I wanted Bonnie.

A shrill whistle shook me out of my despair.

"Hey, Larry wants to know if you're coming with us or if you've got other plans now?" shouted Dicky the flight engineer who was leaning out of the small doorway in the side of the Lancaster. I glanced up at the cockpit window and spotted Larry giving me the V-sign. Childish as it was, all I could think of in response was to stick my tongue out at him. We both laughed and then Larry frowned as he gave me the thumbs up sign. I gave him the thumbs-up back. He was a caring guy deep down, underneath that macho, womanising exterior. I was beginning to realise why I liked him after all.

Without examining it I slipped the locket inside my right glove and pulled both gloves on. It was one less thing to carry and I figured I needed all the hands I had available to get my sumo-sized frame through that tiny doorway.

Getting into the aircraft with the bulky flying suit on proved to be as difficult as I had imagined. In the end Frankie had to grab hold of my flight suit and drag me through the hole. Like a rookie I ended up sprawled awkwardly across the bare metal floor of the aircraft, with fortunately only Frankie present to witness my embarrassment.

The cloying stench of grease and aviation fuel assaulted my senses as soon as I sat up. The smell hung heavy in the air and the acrid taste of oil instantly coated my mouth. The dark and claustrophobic atmosphere inside the Lancaster made me freak out for a moment and I almost panicked. I desperately needed to get out into the cold, fresh evening air again. With teeth clenched I sucked in a few deep breaths of the foul air through my mouth to try and regain some control again. I knew the smell and feeling of claustrophobia was something I needed to get over, and quickly. Little did I realise then just how much worse the atmosphere inside that Lancaster was going to become over the next few hours.

"Welcome to our world of Nuts," Frankie said, grinning and oblivious to my panic as he helped me to my feet. I grinned back. N-Nuts was such a wonderful name for a bomber, it seemed fitting somehow.

Frankie moved away to the back of the aircraft and I watched him hang his parachute up on a hook beside a pair of small black rubber doors which he proceeded to push aside. He climbed in awkwardly through the small hole and spent a few moments struggling to push himself into the tiny seat behind the large mounted guns of the rear gun turret. It seemed obvious to me that should an emergency occur he wasn't going to be getting out of there in any kind of a hurry.

I peered up at another Perspex covered gun turret directly above my head which I guessed would be the mid-upper gunner's position I was supposed to occupy, for at least part of the flight. Three steps led up to a small fold-down canvas seat in the base of the turret and there was a large metal hook on the steel beam at the side which I presumed was for hanging a parachute on. I wasn't relishing the thought of going up there at all.

Following Frankie's lead I hung my parachute on the hook, put my flask and the box up on the floor of the turret and thought I'd go and have a look-see up at the front of the aircraft. I managed to climb - or rather fall - clumsily over a large beam that ran across the fuselage just forward of the turret and spotted big Ricky perched in front of a bank of radios and dials. A tiny window was just about visible in the side of the fuselage to his left and above him another small Perspex covered dome was fitted into the top of the fuselage. I spotted a single step directly beneath the dome that I presumed allowed someone to stand up and peer out. Ricky didn't notice me. He had his leather flying helmet with the built in earphones and mask on and appeared to be talking intently to someone while he stared out of the window.

I climbed over the second large beam adjacent to Ricky and immediately spotted a thick, black floor-to-ceiling curtain hanging down on the left. I pulled the curtain aside and peered in. Alky sat at a small metal desk behind the curtain squinting at a dimly lit instrument panel in front of him. Maps, charts and notebooks were strewn across the desk and a dull red coloured lamp illuminated the whole scene in an eerie hellish glow. Alky turned and smiled up at me in the gloom before returning to the dials he had been analysing. Like Ricky, he was focussed on his work so I thought I'd best leave him alone.

As I dropped the curtain back down I spotted our two agent passengers sitting on the small area of floor opposite the curtain, leaning against the side of the fuselage. The young man and the young lady huddled close together beneath a large woollen blanket someone had been thoughtful enough to provide them with. They had their coat collars turned up and their hands tucked deep inside their coat pockets, but their breath still froze in front of them in the icy cold air of the Lancaster.

The young man's gaze was fixed on a spot somewhere in front of him but the young lady glanced up at me and managed a weak smile. I had no idea where they were going or what they planned to do behind enemy lines, and I probably didn't want to, but their shared stress was evident. The young lady looked ashen and appeared physically sick. She seemed so vulnerable and far too young to be on board this aircraft heading off to God only knows where. I wanted to sit down next to her and tell her everything was all going to be OK, but of course how could I know that. It most likely wasn't going to be, and they already knew it.

I managed to manoeuvre awkwardly around the pair and directly in front of them with his back to us I found

Dicky the flight engineer. He sat almost on the floor on a small fold away seat and was deep in conversation with Larry who sat up in the single seat on the raised portion of the left hand side of the cockpit. Underneath Dicky I could just make out Eddie, our disfigured bomb aimer, crouched down in a lower bay beneath the cockpit. Somehow this scene all seemed so familiar and there was that memory again, flitting at the edges of my mind, almost as if taunting me.

"Hey old boy, you decided to join us after all then?" said Larry, turning to face me. "We were taking bets on you running off with her, it was odds on you weren't coming with us." I couldn't see his grin behind the mask attached to his face but I knew it was there.

"Couldn't let you boys have all the fun could I?" I said.

"Glad to have you on board old boy," he said as his eyes caught mine. I believe he truly meant that too. He gave my leg a slap and then turned back to focus on the instruments in front of him. I decided to try and make myself useful and go back to see if I could fit myself into the upper gun turret. As I stepped carefully around the pair of agents the young lady glanced up at me again.

"The pilot said for us to sit here as he said this is the warmest part of the aircraft, the heat apparently blows out from under the wireless operator's table. Is it ok?" she asked.

I stared down at her shivering form beneath the thick dark blanket. I had no idea as it happened but didn't want to let her know that. I confirmed it was and decided the least I could do was to offer her my flask. I guessed it would have warm coffee or something in it which might help. It took me about ten minutes to clamber over the two beams, grab my flask from the turret and get back to where they sat. Moving around in that bloody suit was nigh on impossible, heaven help me if I needed to do anything in a hurry.

I bent down and offered the flask to the young lady.

"Here, this might warm you up,"

Hesitating, the girl stared at the flask and then back at me before she took it.

"Are you sure, won't you need it yourself?" she asked.

I thrust the flask into her gloved hands.

"No I'm fine, I can't pee in this suit anyway so there's no point drinking anything."

I finally saw a smile spread across her young face. She was beautiful.

"Thank you," she said as she accepted the flask.

I placed a hand on her shoulder and squeezed, it was a natural, almost fatherly gesture. She gazed up at me and we locked eyes. In that fleeting moment I sensed her fear, but also the deep gratitude for a moment's comfort from another human being who cared. She smiled again and that was the last time I would ever see that smile, perhaps it would be the last time anyone did, who knows.

I stumbled back along the cold bare metal obstacle course that was the inside of a Lancaster bomber and attempted to climb up into the mid gun turret. I grabbed my parachute on the way up but soon realised there was no way I could fit into the small canvas seat behind the guns with the bulky parachute strapped to me. There was simply no way it was going to fit inside the turret with me at all, so I had to leave it hanging on the hook beneath me. I had no burning desire to find out what it might be like to jump from an aeroplane, but if I did need to get out in a hurry I didn't think it would be a good idea to leave without a parachute, so I admit I felt more than a little uncomfortable having to leave it down there out of reach.

Perched in my rather uncomfortable seat behind the massive guns I began to try and familiarise myself with my new surroundings. I couldn't help but be impressed with the panoramic view. Sitting up in my perch on the top of the aircraft gave me a superb all-round view of the snow blanketed aerodrome with the white hills and fields beyond. The dark, almost derelict looking buildings with their strange thatched roofs were easily visible against the white background. Other menacing looking Lancaster bombers sat in their own dispersal bays on either side of us and engineers and ground crew still crawled all over their wings, engines and bomb bays making their final checks, as they were on ours.

The sky was a hazy opaque colour, which hung heavy with the promise of more snow. I wondered what it would be like thundering down the runway and up into those thick heavy clouds. I would find out soon enough.

Fortunately the reek of grease and petrol, although still present up in the turret was much less noticeable, probably due to the open section of panel in front of me. It seemed as if a pane of Perspex had been removed from the turret directly in front of the guns, probably to improve vision. It was bloody cold but I was grateful for the fresh air it provided.

There was a new odour though, something quite specific. If you've never been near a gun you perhaps wouldn't recognise it. Gun oil has a peculiarly sweet smell of its own and I recognised it immediately. I wondered when I had last been near a gun and had that fleeting memory again, but as before I couldn't quite grasp it.

A red-topped lever was positioned on either side of me. I pulled gently on the right hand one and with a loud rumbling sound of cogs and gears grinding against each other the turret swung violently around to the right. I pushed the lever forward again and pulled instinctively back on the left one. The turret lurched to the left and I found myself back facing the front of the aircraft again. *Well, at least that works* I thought. I pulled on the left hand lever again and swung the turret the whole way round through three hundred and sixty degrees. That made me a little nauseous so I made a mental note not to try and do too much of that.

The handles of the .50-inch guns sat directly in front of me, almost pressing against my chest. I slipped my hands inside and rested both index fingers against the curved triggers while I squinted through the cross-haired gun sight on top of the gun barrels. It all seemed strangely comfortable. I noticed the armourers had already fed the belts of bullets into the mechanism of the gun so I slipped my gloved hands off the triggers again before there was an accident. I hoped there would be no need to actually use these things. How naive was I?

Peering down at the metal panel in front of me I spotted two sockets to the left that were labelled OXYGEN and RADIO. The ends of the tube and the wire dangling from my leather flying helmet mask looked as if they might fit into the two holes, so I pushed them firmly into place and clipped the mask across my mouth. As soon as I pushed the brown wire into the socket I heard crackling and voices in my ear. The first voice I recognised was Larry talking to Frankie in his rear turret.

"You OK Frankie, are you receiving ok?"

"Yep, loud and clear skipper, all ship shape back here."

There was some distant muffled talking and then the crackling voice of Larry came through my earphones again. "James old boy, are you on yet?"

"Yes Larry, I'm here."

"Well bugger me old boy, it's nice of you to join in our little chat at last. We thought you might have been in the bog?" Larry's voice sounded a little mechanical and distorted but there was still no disguising his good-humoured ribbing.

"How is everything up there in the conservatory James?"

I peered around me. In reality how would I know?

"Em...yes all OK up here Larry."

"Spot-on James, the bods are nearly finished out there and the chair-borne division are telling us we're good to go on the dot of 18.00, that's 15 minutes from now. How are your passengers doing?"

My mind conjured up a picture of the somewhat detached young man and the scared looking young lady huddled down in the fuselage of the plane.

"They seem to be fairing up ok Larry."

"OK, bang-on old man. Alky will let us know when we're nearing the drop point, I'll take us right down to about a thousand feet and perhaps you could show them the door when Alky gives the OK?"

"Okey dokey Larry," I said.

There was a short pause before Larry responded.

"Okey dokey? I'll take that as a Rodger. Now you can put your feet up and enjoy the ride old boy."

Larry moved on to chat with the other members of the crew who each provided updates as to their own personal state of readiness. I half listened to the chatter coming through my ear phones as I peered out across the aerodrome, my thoughts inevitably switching back to Bonnie again. I pulled off my thick leather gloves and retrieved the silver locket she had handed me less than an hour ago. I'd almost forgotten about it. The delicate silver locket was tiny in my hand, quite plain in design, but even for a pea-brain like me I could tell the quality was excellent. I flicked open the tiny clip and inside found a single picture of Bonnie smiling back at me. She was beautiful and my heart ached for her again. I knew I was far too romantic for my own good sometimes, I imagined that my own photograph would sit rather comfortably in the empty space alongside hers. The more I thought about her the more my mind wandered, perhaps naturally, onto some of the exciting pastimes we could be enjoying together right now, rather than me sitting in this damn drafty turret.

Unfortunately my erotic fantasies didn't last long as the first of the massive Merlin engines coughed and spluttered into life, instantly jolting me from my day dreams. I peered out over the port wing just as the second engine coughed and roared and a plume of black exhaust drifted backwards across my canopy. By the time all four engines were running any hope of further quiet contemplation was long gone. Even with headphones on, the roar was tremendous. The vibrations from the four Rolls Royce engines reverberated throughout the Lancaster which creaked and twitched under the enormous power.

I hung the chain of the locket over a small hook to the right of my head so that I could still see Bonnie smiling at me and then pulled my gloves back on. I wondered if any of the other lads were as sad as me. I suspected they probably were.

"OK lads, this is it, we're off, it's beer and Berlin all the way and hopefully it won't be a bloody dicey-do." Larry's voiced crackled into my ears as the Lancaster's breaks were released and the aircraft lurched forward. I peered down at the group of ground crew who stood away to our left next to the now empty fuel bowser, waving enthusiastically up at us. I spotted Larry's arm pop out of the cockpit window below me and wave back at them. Not to be outdone I put my own arm up through the gap in the Perspex and waved too. *It was all very jolly* I thought.

On our left a Lancaster pulled forward out of its dispersal bay, tyres squealing as it turned onto the too narrow looking concrete taxiway. The snow was piled up in banks on either side where the roadway had been recently cleared and I stared fascinated as the propellers whirled, blowing the dry snow up into great blizzards on either side of the aircraft.

With the massive engines snarling, barking and spitting, Larry jerked N-Nuts forward and turned to follow the first aircraft on its precarious journey around the narrow taxiway towards the main runway. Any miscalculation now and we would be off the side of the taxi-way, stuck in the snow drifts, mission cancelled and the embarrassment of the squadron. As much as we didn't want to go, no one wanted that. An aborted mission didn't count towards a tour of operations anyway so there was no benefit in prolonging the agony, it still had to be done.

Inside the cold, dark and violently shaking turret the ice that had formed on the inside of the Perspex cover was melting and dripping onto my head. Despite the many layers and the thick sheepskin suit I was bundled up in, I shivered uncontrollably. I knew that each of the other crewmembers and our guests would be experiencing the same uncomfortable conditions inside the aircraft, but at least I was in in the relative fresh air with good visibility so didn't have too much to complain about, yet.

My earphones continued to crackle and even above the thundering of the engines I could hear Larry talking to the personnel in the control tower which was situated between the Gibraltar Farm building and the western end of the runway. I wondered if he might be chatting to Bonnie but I wasn't able to hear the other side of the conversation. The rest of the crew remained silent, listening like me and most likely lost deep in their own thoughts and worries as the snaking line of Lancasters continued their ungainly procession around the narrow, blue lit perimeter taxiway in a storm of whirling yellow tipped propellers and flying snow.

The Lancaster in front of us reached the end of the runway and turned just as I spotted a group of WAAFs standing knee deep in snow outside the watch office. They waved at the crew in the first aircraft and shouted unheard words of encouragement. A lump formed in my throat and my eyes filled up. I'm so glad I was on my own.

The controller's watch lamp flashed from red to green and the aircraft was off, roaring down the runway towards God only knew what. And then it was our turn. N-Nuts turned onto the runway with another squeal of tyres and waited, propellers whirling furiously as Larry held the massive bomber trembling against its brakes. The group of WAAFs freezing on the ground below us waved heroically again and I gave a wave back. I couldn't make out who they all were but I was touched by the gesture. I wondered if one of them might be Bonnie.

My eyes stared at the controller's red lamp on the roof of the watchtower. I knew Larry would be doing the same. The lamp flicked from red to green and I felt the Lancaster shudder with relief as the brakes released and the engines snarled and roared to full power. Inside the aircraft the entire fuselage shook, booming and echoing with the beating of the four Merlin engines at full power. The slightest miscalculation now, a swing off the narrow runway, a missed beat from one of the four massive engines, and the bomb and fuel laden aircraft would plough into the banked snow and frozen mud, the undercarriage would collapse and yet another crew would be blown to kingdom-come in the resulting red flash and rolling boom. My testicles tingled and lifted unconsciously at the thought of it.

I was pleased I'd remembered to strap myself into the seat at the last moment as I began to shake violently around inside the turret. My head banged hard off the Perspex canopy at least twice as I watched the perimeter fence at the end of the runway race towards us. I peered down along the fuselage and spotted the faint red glow of the cockpit light below me. I imagined Dicky the flight engineer holding the throttle levers full on whilst Larry wrestled with the severely vibrating control stick, trying his damnedest to keep us straight, and alive.

It seemed like an age thundering down that runway, the kicked up white snow pouring in through the gap in the Perspex and blinding me in my lofty turret. Squinting through my goggles into the whiteness, my eyes widened in horror as I spotted the fence and a small copse of trees looming up in front of us. I knew we weren't going to make it and braced my arms over my head as the wheels reluctantly left the runway and the massive hulk of the fully laden N-Nuts lifted oh so slowly into the air.

I'd swear we took the uppermost branches of the trees with us as we went over, but we'd made it. We were up and not burning to death in a red fireball. Well, not yet anyway. Relaxing a little, I gazed down and saw the white-blanketed aerodrome and surrounding fields fall away from us as we laboured upwards towards the thick grey clouds above.

The Lancaster in front of us had already disappeared into the cloud and turning the turret around I could still make out the shadowy outline of the aircraft following us in the darkness below. It made me feel a little better knowing we weren't alone up in that black sky.

The shaking and vibrating continued and my head pounded with the constant thundering and roar of the engines. To add to the discomfort, despite the layers of uniform and the bulky flying suit I was already starting to feel the icy cold seeping into my bones. My teeth began to chatter uncontrollably and I wasn't at all sure how long I could actually last sitting motionless in that exposed turret.

Just when I thought life couldn't get much worse, we reached the underside of the cloud, disappeared into the greyness and the banging and shuddering became even more violent.

I wasn't sure what the noise was but I very nearly emptied my bowels inside the flying suit when it happened.

At first I thought we were being fired at, but soon realised it was chunks of were ice smashing into the Perspex of my turret. As I peered into the gloom I spotted sheets of ice forming over the surface of the wings and along the top of the fuselage in front of me. Lumps broke off and flew back in the slipstream but more ice instantly reformed in its place. The Lancaster began to shudder violently and I sensed we were losing height as my headphones crackled into life.

"OK guys, we're in trouble, get ready to bale," came Larry's stressed voice over the intercom. *Bloody bale out? We've just got up here* I thought. I didn't even have my parachute on and had no idea how I was going to get to that and out of the small door before the aircraft hit the ground, we must have only been at an altitude of a thousand feet or so. I heard the pitch of the engines change and I felt sure we were about to stall in mid-air when the radio crackled again.

"Are we going out Skip?" came Frankie's surprisingly calm voice from the rear turret of the struggling aeroplane.

"Hold on, we're too low," came Larry's reply as the nose of the Lancaster dipped and we began to descend. "Fuck, fuck, fuck!" his terrified voice filled both my ears. "Fucking ice...fucking weather...we shouldn't be up in this, even the fucking pigeons are staying on the ground in this cold," he screamed at no one in particular.

The heavy bomber dropped and I almost lost the contents of my stomach. Engines screaming, I felt the nose rise up ever so slightly again, Larry was fighting this one all the way. Another slab of ice detached itself from the starboard wing and smashed into the fuselage directly in front of me just as I head-butted the side of the turret. My stomach tipped and rolled along with the aircraft and my world blanked out again as we entered the thick cloud for the second time. The shaking and the noise was incredible and I couldn't see any way in which this aircraft could stand the strain it was being put through. The ice forming on the outside of the Lancaster was dragging us down, and the engines were seconds away from stalling, that much was obvious. I closed my eyes and waited for the inevitable.

Fortunately the inevitable didn't come, thanks almost entirely to Larry's skills. After a ten minute roller-coaster ride we popped out on top of the cloud layer and everything settled down a bit. Thousands of stars shone brilliantly against the rich black velvet of the night sky and the full moon bathed the top of the clouds in a supernatural glow.

I scanned the strange world above the clouds but couldn't make out any sign of the aircraft that had been in front of us. We were now the lead aircraft.

"James, Frankie, see anything?" came Larry's voice over the intercom.

"Negative Skipper," responded Frankie in his relaxed Canadian drawl.

"I can't see anyone else up here either," I said as I stared across the top of the mountainous cloud-formed landscape towards the horizon. "Where's the aircraft gone that was in front of us?"

"Wait a minute Skip, one of ours has just popped up behind us. I think it's M-Mike," said Frankie.

"Good old Bertie," said Larry, "I think Y-Yankee in front has gone for a burton though chaps. Poor bastards. Alky, what's my heading?"

"Course zero four zero magnetic Skip. We should spot the main formation in about fifteen minutes."

"Roger, thanks Alky, keep your eyes peeled guys."

I couldn't stop thinking about the aircraft that had gone down right in front of us in that ice cloud, there was no way the crew could have baled out in time. I didn't know them but I couldn't shake the thought from my head.

Seven young lives snuffed out just like that, and we hadn't even started the bloody mission yet.

I was still thinking about the crew when I spotted a swarm of circling black dots in the distance that looked for all the world like flies buzzing around an evening light.

"Dicky here, formation ahead Skip," came Dicky's voice over the intercom.

"Yes, spotted them, we'll join up behind. What altitude Alky?"

"We're aiming for 15,000 feet Skip, we're at the bottom of the stack so we can dip out to drop our passengers."

"OK, Roger Alky."

As we flew steadily on in the eerie moonlight towards the swarm of aircraft ahead, I turned the turret through 360 degrees and scanned the formation of bombers lined up alongside and behind us. They seemed far too close for comfort as far as I was concerned. I sure hoped these young twenty-something year olds knew what they were doing.

It occurred to me that the constant shaking and vibrating of the Lancaster was only matched by the shaking and chattering of my own body. Despite the protective sheepskin clothing the icy cold had seeped deep into my bones and I knew I was losing the feeling in my hands, legs and feet. It shouldn't have been any surprise as it was around minus thirty or forty degrees Celsius up there, and not only did my part of the aircraft have absolutely no heating in it, there was also an open window in front of me. I started to become aware that my head felt light and dizzy and I realised almost too late that I had to do something or I was going to pass out.

My lungs were straining to take in enough oxygen so I glanced down at the oxygen hose and plug to make sure they were still connected. They were, but the previously flexible hose now felt stiff and hard in my fingers. I struggled to think, something was wrong, very wrong. It took a supreme effort just to work out how to unclip the hose from the panel. I sucked in as deep a breath as I could and held it while I pulled the hose off. I peered in the end and immediately saw the problem. A long cylinder of ice was jammed inside the hose, preventing the air from coming through. I banged the end of the hose against the metal panel and the lump of ice fell out. As soon as I plugged the hose back in again and took a few deep breaths the light-headedness and confusion disappeared as quickly as it had come. *Bloody hell, that was nearly a disaster* I thought, and who would have known? I'd have just passed quietly away up here without oxygen. I guessed the ice had formed from the moisture of my own breath in the mask and hose. I made a mental note to keep a check on it for the rest of the flight.

None of that helped with the cold situation though. I was in real danger of dying from hypothermia in the next half an hour or so if I didn't sort something out. I searched the area around me again and this time spotted another plughole in a side panel down by my right knee. The label next to it said 'HEAT'. Glancing down I also spotted a wire with a plug on the end dangling down from the right leg of my outer flying suit. How much did I feel like a complete idiot? I plugged the wire in and within minutes some beautiful if meagre warmth began to flow around my body. The suit was electrically heated. Larry mentioned as much in the locker room after the briefing, why hadn't I bloody listened?

I'd only been in the air for half an hour and already I had almost killed myself from two stupid mistakes only a greenhorn would make. The realisation dawned on me at that moment, this wasn't some boy's own adventure. I'd no memory of what I had perhaps once been, and without that memory, in this dangerous environment I was totally out of my depth and at real risk. It was a sobering thought.

Alky's Irish brogue crackled over the intercom. "Alky here Skip, we're in the stack now, circling until 19.00 then heading off on zero five zero magnetic."

"OK, Roger Alky got that."

The sight before me was awe-inspiring. There must have been more than 500 aircraft circling in a tower formation in the skies above Norfolk that night. Larry had taken us in at the bottom of the stack as planned and at exactly 19.00 the aircraft began to peel off and head out over what I presumed was the English Channel. Bertie in M-Mike flew alongside us and we were the only two aircraft at the bottom of the stack, everyone else was flying at various pre-planned altitudes above us. I also spotted a few smaller single engine aircraft buzzing around the edges of the formation. They looked to be Hurricanes or perhaps Spitfires.

The whole scene made the hairs stand on the back of my neck, it was a truly awesome sight. I tried to forget the fact that in reality we were all just instruments of darkness, nocturnal predators on a mission to bring terror to the night skies over Germany.

As we flew across the white crested waves of the English Channel far below us, I sat mesmerised in my Perspex dome, staring at the surreal moonlit cloud formations all around us. With my suit now providing a semblance of comforting warmth, I began to relax into what I can only describe as an almost meditative state of mind. It was all so serene, so unreal. Even the constant roar of the engines and the vibrating of the aircraft settled into my new normality. I could easily have stayed up there forever, enjoying a rare moment of tranquillity in a troubled world.

That tranquillity was soon shattered and I almost shit myself when the cannons boomed and the Lancaster shuddered. My stomach fell through my arse and remained there while I scanned the sky in blind panic. Was someone attacking us?

"Frankie here. Guns A-OK Skip," came Frankie's metallic voice.

"OK Frankie, thanks, keep your eyes peeled, not long to the Dutch coast. We may get fighter trouble," said Larry. "You asleep James?"

"No chance of that with all this bloody racket is there?" I replied, in a feeble attempt at sounding jovial and relaxed. I felt as far away from jovial at that point as anyone could be.

"Perhaps you'll give those guns a little check then old man?"

I glanced down at the two handles and attached triggers in front of me. Ah well, this is it I thought. I slid my gloved hands into the handles and eased my fingers onto the triggers. I looked out along the length of the black metal gun barrels and made sure they were aimed downwards into the vast emptiness of the clouds before I pulled back with both fingers.

A moment of panic ensued as the turret filled with red hot ejected shell casings, smoke and the stench of cordite, not to mention the assault on my ear drums from the twin recoiling cannons. I released both triggers after two to three seconds and the pounding and vibrating ceased. I hoped I wouldn't have to fire these again, I didn't trust myself not to blow our own aircraft out of the sky. Luckily I had no inkling of what was going to happen in the next few hours.

"Em...guns are OK Skip."

"Excellent," responded Larry.

"The Dutch coast is coming up Skip, Harlingen in about four minutes," came Alky's voice over the radio.

Chapter Seven - Holland Dec 14th 1944

"OK boys, now keep your eyes peeled, the cloud cover's light and we're over enemy occupied territory," came Larry's crackling voice.

As soon as he'd finished speaking I felt the aircraft begin to weave and roll from side to side. Somehow I understood instinctively it was a protective measure taken by Larry. The weaving also helped me to get a much better view under the aircraft as we swung from side to side, which I guess was the whole point of it.

"Ricky, if you've got a bit of quiet on the radio can you start chucking the window out to confuse the blighters?" asked Larry.

"Righto Blue, onto it now," responded Ricky.

After a minute or so I spotted the moonlight glinting off the little strips of foil cascading down beneath us. It was hard to imagine that something so basic could have such an impact on the enemy's radar systems.

It was then I experienced my first taste of real war, post the onset of my amnesia of course. I realised it was highly likely that I'd actually been through all of this many times in the past, and if that was the case I wasn't entirely sure I even wanted my memory back. The thought did occur to me that maybe I was subconsciously blocking something from that recent past.

The first searchlights appeared in front of us as sharp columns of light against the velvet black sky and began their steady weaving to and fro. It seemed as if the enemy had picked up something on their radar and were now searching for us. As N-Nuts rolled to starboard I spotted a dirty black puff of smoke appear just off to the left and below us. Then a steady line of similar black puffs appeared on either side of N-Nuts. As I stared at the innocent looking puffs of smoke the aircraft suddenly began to buck and weave and the ominous sound of tiny stones rattling along the fuselage made my buttocks clench.

"Tail gunner here Skip, mobile ship ack-ack below us," shouted Frankie, from the tail.

"Yep spotted it, he's not got our range though, we'll be over it soon."

I hoped Larry was right on that. The black puffs of smoke didn't appear too terrifying but I suspected a direct hit might be a whole different matter, especially with a full bomb load on board.

"Navigator here Skip, we'll be over Groningen in three zero minutes and then our drop zone will be another four minutes after that on our same course, due east. So hold the current course but begin the descent down to five hundred feet ready for the drop. After the drop we'll continue on the same course but you'll need to get us back up to 23,000 feet as quickly as you can."

"OK, Roger Alky, got that. James, can you get our passengers ready by the door for the drop? Alky will give you the nod when they need to go. The static lines have been set up ready. Oh, and don't forget your oxygen old man, you'll still need it until we're below 10,000 feet."

My stomach lurched. I hadn't forgotten the oxygen, I nearly died from a lack of that earlier, but I hadn't thought about moving around the aircraft without it either until Larry warned me. That was very nearly another potential disaster. I scanned the turret and discovered a small oxygen bottle clipped to the side wall just below me and to the right. It had the same fitting as the plug on the panel in front of me, which was a bit of a clue, even for me. I pulled the bottle out of the clip, unplugged my oxygen tube from the panel and then connected it to the bottle, remembering at the last minute to open the wheel on the top of the bottle to let the oxygen flow. I hung the bottle around my neck using the attached strap and then unplugged my wireless and heater cords.

Moving my cold and numb legs wasn't as easy as I'd anticipated and it took me a minute or two to swing my legs around in the cramped space and ease my body off the tiny seat before I almost fell down the three steps to the floor of the fuselage.

I climbed over the two spars spanning the fuselage and made my way along to Alky's navigator's position just behind the cockpit. It was unnerving being inside that cold, dark, vibrating metal tube with just a faint glow of red light to see by. I had got used to my all-round views of the night sky up in the turret and it felt claustrophobic down inside the aircraft by comparison. Ricky waved at me from his wireless operator's position as I staggered past.

I spotted the two agents huddled under the thick blanket where I'd last left them. They both appeared shaken and obviously suffering from the cold. I suspected the heated air blowing out from under Alky's position wasn't as warm as they'd have liked.

I dropped down onto my knees in front of them. They were both wearing masks attached to a large oxygen cylinder which had been strapped to the fuselage beside them, most likely for the purpose of carrying the agents. I hadn't spotted that before and was pleased to see someone had shown them how to put on their oxygen masks. I'd nearly managed to kill myself so I was thankful I hadn't been left fully in charge of our passengers. I'd probably have had their deaths on my hands too.

"Are you two ok?" I asked. They both nodded, unconvincingly.

"Need to go soon," I shouted, theatrically pointing to my wristwatch. They both nodded understanding.

"Do you have your parachutes on?" I shouted. I wasn't sure how to mime that one but it seemed I didn't have to. The young man pulled the blanket down to expose their parachutes strapped to each of their chests. I also noted that they had donned full length RAF flying overalls over their coats. I gave them the thumbs up as I stepped over them to peer into the cockpit. Dicky stared at his dials whilst making notes on a pad and Larry peered intently out at the blackness in front of the cockpit windows. I tapped him on his shoulder and he very nearly jumped out of his skin.

Larry pulled the mask off his face and turned towards me with his usual grin.

"4,500 feet. We're OK without the oxygen," he said.

I turned the valve on my oxygen bottle to shut off the flow, pulled my own mask off, and grinned back at him.

"How are our passengers doing?" he asked.

"I think they're OK, just a tad cold. Shall I get them ready now?"

"Yes, we'll be over the drop zone in five minutes so get them lined-up at the door. I'll get Alky to let Ricky know when they're to go and he'll give you the nod. Once they're out get that ruddy door closed up and we'll get some altitude again."

I smiled and nodded at Larry. He smiled back, gave me the thumbs up and returned to the job in hand. I clambered back to the two agents and indicated to them they could take their masks off.

"OK, let's go," I shouted over the roaring of the engines, pointing towards the door in the rear end of the aircraft. The young man stood up and hanging onto the sides of the aircraft began to make his way down the fuselage towards the rear. The young girl faltered, her skin had turned an ashen grey colour and she seemed terrified.

"Are you OK?" I asked, gently taking her trembling arm. She glanced up, her lifeless eyes staring. She was past pretending, the fear had set in. I put my arm around her shoulders and gave her a hug. Her beautiful eyes seemed to clear for a moment and connected with mine, tears welling up and rolling freely down her delicate cheeks. A desperate sadness sunk over me and every instinct screamed at me to tuck her up under the blanket and take her home again. But I knew that wasn't going to happen.

As if reaching the same conclusion, the girl took a deep breath, bit her lip and nodded at me. Before I could change my mind I grabbed her gloved hand in mine and led the way to the rear door of the aircraft where the young man already waited with his parachute line attached to a rail bolted to the roof of the fuselage, immediately above the door. Almost mechanically the young lady attached her parachute line behind her colleague's and stood hanging on grimly in that shaking, freezing cold aircraft. They had obviously run through this procedure many times before, but safely on the ground I thought, when it was all still a great adventure. Her eyes were tightly closed and I could only imagine what terrifying thoughts churned behind those delicate eyelids.

At first I couldn't get the bloody door open. The handle appeared to be frozen in place, so I resorted to a minute or two of kicking, which at least helped to warm me up a little. With my heated suit now unplugged the cold had begun to seep into my body again. The door finally gave and it took all my strength to pull the door open against the slipstream outside and tie it back. The noise of the engines was now drowned out by the roaring of the wind in the doorway, which was doing its best to suck me out into the freezing night sky.

It was only then I realised my next mistake. My own parachute was hanging up on the hook at the bottom of the mid turret and not attached to me, where it probably should have been. If I were to be sucked out I wouldn't have stood a bloody chance. I gripped one of the struts to the left of the doorway and flattened my back against the fuselage, the roaring wind thundering in my ears.

I stared at the two agents. They only had their regular suits and coats on under those flying overalls and were unsurprisingly shuddering with the cold. The young girl's eyes remained closed. The man stared out into the darkness.

Ricky glanced over at me from his wireless operator's position and held up one finger. I took that to mean one minute to drop, so I turned to the young man and held up one finger in front of his face. There was absolutely no point in trying to shout. The man nodded and holding onto the side of the door he lowered himself into the open doorway and sat down on the edge with his legs dangling out in the slipstream. His facial expression hadn't changed, he simply stared into the abyss.

I risked a glance out of the open doorway. Snowflakes rushed past, white against the inky blackness of the sky, and the open fields below were blanketed in a dull white snow. No lights interrupted the darkness down there, but the snow was partly bathed in moonlight, so visibility was quite good. I wasn't too sure if that was a good thing or bad. Probably bad.

Ricky glanced over at me again, raised his right arm and let it drop. The sign was unmistakable, even to a novice like me. I leaned down and tapped the young man hard on the shoulder. Before I even had time to draw my next breath he was gone and the young lady was taking his place in the doorway. Her eyes were wide open, staring, unblinking. She made no eye contact with me as she sat down and placed her arms across her chest. Within a blink she too was gone and I was left staring at the now empty doorway with the two empty lines dangling in front of me.

The feel of the rushing air trying to pull me out to my doom snapped me out of my transfixed stare and I needed no further prompting to get the door closed in a hurry. Once I had it latched shut I gave Ricky the thumbs up sign. He returned the gesture and swung back round to his wireless set. Almost immediately I heard the engine tone change and the aircraft began its ascent again. That was my cue to return to my seat and face the next, and far more perilous part of the mission.

I settled back into my uncomfortable little seat as the Lancaster began its long struggle back up to the planned altitude of 23,000 feet. Spinning my turret around I spotted M-Mike behind and to our starboard side. It seemed as if we were the only two aeroplanes out over Europe on that beautiful winter evening, but I knew that was far from the truth.

Larry's continual weaving of the Lancaster gave me a good view of the ground far beneath us. The cloud cover was light and the moonlight reflecting off the snow presented an almost surreal fantasy landscape down there. Only an occasional light could be seen, I presumed black-outs were still in force.

"Navigator here Skip, Oldenburg two minutes ahead. This is our turning point, we'll need to switch to heading two four two magnetic, I repeat two four two."

"OK Alky, got it."

The bomber made its turn over the small-darkened Dutch town far below. I wondered what the people down there were doing. I had no idea whether they were in enemy or allied held territory or even if the poor bastards were right in the middle of a war zone. Then I wondered if they could hear us and what they would be thinking if they had? Friend or foe I guessed. That's always going to be the only question that matters isn't it?

"OK, keep your eyes peeled lads, it's been fairly quiet so far but not sure that'll last once they know where we are." Larry's words vibrated in my ears.

My eyes began to tire from the constant searching of the skies as we weaved and droned across Holland. Twice I spotted a reddish orange flash in the distance ahead of us.

"Some poor bastard's just gone down," said Dicky as the second flash faded gradually from my retina.

"Flak or fighters do you think?" came Frankie's calm voice from the rear.

"Can't see any flak," crackled Eddie from below.

"Can't see any fighters either," said Frankie.

"Keep watching lads," added Larry, unnecessarily. Even I could sense the tension building in that dark, freezing Lancaster.

As I unplugged another lump of ice from the end of my oxygen pipe I spotted a reddish glow on the horizon. I pushed the intercom button on my mask and spoke.

"Something on the horizon Skipper, a red glow."

The radio remained silent for a moment before it crackled into life again.

"Ah, thanks old man, I've spotted it now. Looks like the fun's started, that's Essen."

As I gazed out at the burning red glow which inched ever closer, I was able to make out the still tiny but distinct columns of white light desperately searching out the harbingers of death in the sky above. It was all too easy to imagine other guys like us, sitting terrified in their bombers over that red glow. I knew I wouldn't have to imagine it for much longer, it would soon be our turn to face that inferno. It was a terrifying and quite surreal thought.

I spotted two more sudden reddish orange flashes in the sky directly above the glow. I knew now they were aircraft like ours, exploding in mid-air with a full bomb load still on board. Instant death to the crew of seven young men on board. I hoped the poor bastards didn't feel too much, I prayed I wouldn't if it happened to us when our turn came. My stomach churned and swallowing had all of a sudden ceased to become an option.

"Navigator here Skip, target ahead," crackled Alky.

"I see it Alky."

"What's it look like Skip," came Frankie's metallic voice from the rear gun turret.

"You remember the last time Frankie?"

"Yes Skip."

"Well it's ten times worse."

I thought I heard a groan in response from the rear of the aircraft.

My eyes remained glued to the brightly burning city that grew steadily in size before us, exactly what I had been warned not to do. I hadn't been searching the dark skies around us and my night vision was now temporarily ruined. I thought I glimpsed a dark shadow out of the corner of my eye when my radio crackled.

"Engineer here Skip, I think a Jerry fighter just passed over the top of us, port to starboard."

"OK, thanks Dicky. Gunners, see anything?"

"Nothing Skip," shouted Frankie.

I frantically rotated my turret in the direction I thought the shadow had gone when all hell broke loose again. I heard the banging of Frankie's cannons reverberating through the Lancaster's fuselage.

"Jesus! ME-109, turning and coming back at us Skip."

Bang, Bang, Bang, Bang thudded Frankie's cannons again.

I rotated the turret back and forwards but still couldn't see anything in the darkness.

"Where is he?" shouted Larry.

"He's gone," crackled a breathless Frankie. "I think I ventilated his kite a little for him, must have been a new boy."

"Well done old man, good work," said Larry. No joking around this time, it was all business now.

I began to feel more than a little inadequate. I hadn't even seen the fighter, much less shoot at it. I knew I was making too many mistakes; I needed to sort myself out and focus.

"Navigator here Skip."

"Yes Alky?"

"Five minutes to go."

"OK, thanks for reminding me."

As we approached Essen the scene in front of us began to unfold. An inferno raged across a good portion of the city which lit the night sky for miles around. The devastation below must have been appalling and I couldn't even bring myself to think of anyone trying to survive down there. The scene in the air above was no less terrifying.

Giant searchlights ringed the city, swaying to and fro, which gave the sky directly above the appearance of a brightly lit arena. Inside the arena a wall of deadly flak was being thrown up from below and dark shapes could be seen flitting around in the melee. Strangely beautiful coloured lines of tracer streaked across the sky and the occasional bright orange flash of an aeroplane taking a direct hit just added to add to this unique vision of hell.

Hundreds of dark bombers like ours circled outside the arena, trying to remain in the relative safety of the darkness for as long as possible before they were called in for their turn in the limelight. I watched as bomber after bomber peeled away from the circle outside and disappeared into the arena of death for their own roll of the dice. I didn't believe anything could exist inside that inferno in the sky.

I felt the sweat trickling down my face and running into my mask. For the first time since we'd taken off I had no sense of the cold. There was only fear, nothing else but fear.

"Engineer here Skip, keep weaving, there's a lot of stuff coming up, it's falling off a bit low but I think they're getting the range."

"Yes I've spotted it, thanks Dicky. Will you put the revs up a bit?"

"OK, revs up Skipper."

"Plenty of fighters over the target Skip, not looking good," said Eddie from his prone Perspex bubble at the front of the Lancaster.

No one responded to that, we had all seen them.

"Search lights and flares going up on our left," I said, wanting to contribute something to the unfolding drama.

"Thanks old man, yes spotted those. Fighter flares I think."

I had no idea what they were but it didn't sound good.

"Wireless here Skip. We're joining the back of that mob over there to port at 21,000 feet. We'll be following Y-Yoyo in. About three minutes."

"OK, Rodger Ricky."

Larry joined the circling Lancasters and we waited for the inevitable. Flak burst all around us but thankfully all that hit us was the rattling of the shards of white hot metal bouncing off the fuselage. For now.

Y-Yoyo banked to port and began his run into the jaws of hell.

"OK Skip, that's us."

"Rodger Ricky. OK lads, we're going in. Let's do our bit to put the mighty Krupps out of action once and for all."

Bright flashes of deadly red tracer followed by a roaring dark shadow flashed over the turret, inches above my head as we went in. The Jerry fighters were in the arena with us, facing their own deadly flak in their desperate attempt to shoot down the British bombers. It was utter suicide and I saw absolutely no way on earth how we would ever come through it alive.

The Lancaster rocked and pitched and began to shake violently as it entered the wall of flak. Twice we were coned by a searchlight and were all momentarily blinded by the burning light as the beam of death thankfully swept past us. My eyesight was ruined. All I could see from the turret were flashes of tracer, flak shells blasting all around us, blinding lights and the terrifying swooping of dark shapes which had the appearance of gigantic pterodactyls searching for something to feed on.

Over my headset I heard Ricky the wireless operator jamming the German night-fighter wavelength. It caused a faint screeching in my ears and occasionally screaming German voices could be heard breaking through. It certainly added to the terror, as if that was needed.

The sky was thick with black smoke and the air smelt of cordite. At one point I recall glancing up and spotting a dark, sinister looking Lancaster bomber directly above us with its bomb doors opening. It was only then that I noticed other slow moving dark shapes to the side and below us. *Jesus Christ, they're going to drop their bombs on us* I thought as a dark cylinder shape hurtled out of the sky and crashed through the starboard wing of Y-Yoyo in front of us, taking the entire wing right off. The aircraft immediately erupted into flames and spiralled downwards into the black smoke below. I didn't spot any parachutes. The bastards never stood a chance, and it was one of our own bombs that got them. I couldn't get the thought out of my head.

It was the banging of Frankie's cannons filling my ears again that pulled me out of my shock. I gripped the gun handles a little tighter and eased my fingers back on the triggers, staring down the long barrels at the sights. I had no idea how I was going to make sure I didn't hit another one of our aircraft out there, but I knew I had to help somehow.

I didn't have to wait long. A dark shape screamed down on us from the starboard side, spitting fire as it came. I swung my heavy turret around, set my cross hairs on the approaching fighter and pulled both triggers hard. The cannons kicked and spat in my hands and the turret filled with acrid smoke and hot shell casings. I stared transfixed as my cannon shells ripped into the front and underbelly of the aircraft as it roared over us. I immediately glanced over my left shoulder and saw the plane erupt into a ball of fire just below us.

"Yeeehaw! You got the bastard!" shouted Frankie from the rear.

"Well done old man, confirmed kill," said Larry.

I wasn't sure whether I was happy about that or not, but I felt elated all the same. At last I'd done something to help. I didn't have too much time to ponder on it though.

The explosion ripped through us amidships. I felt the buck of the aircraft and watched holes being torn through the top of the fuselage in front of me before I even heard the explosion. The Lancaster rolled violently to port and I thought we were going down. I could only imagine what was going on in the cockpit as Larry fought to regain control of the aircraft, assuming he was still alive that is. As quickly as it had happened, N-Nuts levelled out again and carried on its previous course, albeit possibly a hundred feet lower.

"Is everyone all right?" came Larry's unreasonably calm voice over the radio.

"Rear gunner here, A-OK."

"Bomb aimer here. All OK. Jesus. I think it was somewhere behind me."

"Navigator here. All OK I think. Phew, that was fucking close!"

I clicked on my radio button. "Mid-upper gunner here. All OK. There are holes everywhere across the top of the fuselage."

"OK, thanks James."

There was silence over the radio for a moment before Larry spoke again.

"Ricky, you OK?"

Another long silence.

"Alky, can you go and see what's up with Ricky?"

"Yes skip."

We crashed and banged onwards while we all waited for news of Ricky.

"Bomb-aimer here Skip, one minute to target."

"Hello bomb-aimer, we're OK when you are. Over to you."

I peered downwards through the smoke and hoped to God that we weren't going to drop our bombs onto anyone else below us like we had seen with Y-Yoyo. The thought hit me that it must happen all the time. I glanced upwards at the dark shadows above.

"OK skip, a bit further yet though. I can see the red indicator flares...steady...right a bit...spotted the green flares now...right a bit more...OK...steady... steady. Visibility is good, only three tenths cloud, I can just make out what's left of the Krupp's factory, Christ what a mess. OK...steady...right a little...steady...steady...steady...OK bombs gone."

The aircraft surged upwards as the 12,000 lb Tallboy bomb was released from the bay underneath. I could almost imagine the Lancaster groan with relief as we easily gained a few hundred feet in altitude.

"Bay clear Eddie?"

"Yes skip. Bomb doors closing."

"OK lads, let's get out of this hell and get ourselves home."

I doubt there was anyone on board who didn't agree with Larry on that.

"Navigator here skip, Ricky's shot up a bit. I think that flak caught him. I've bandaged him as best I can and he's on the bunk."

"OK, thanks Alky, keep an eye on him and we'll get him home as fast as we can. Can you give me a course home?"

"Course two eight zero magnetic skip, repeat two eight zero."

"OK Rodger Alky."

I continued scanning the sky as the starboard wing dipped and we turned west for home. The feeling of relief that started to settle over me was short lived when brilliant white light bathed the turret and I was blinded again.

"We're coned," shouted Dicky from his position next to Larry.

Larry threw the Lancaster into a steep dive in his struggle to evade the deadly searchlight beam. The sound of Frankie's cannons banging away again made my stomach drop even further.

"Fuck! Bandit on us, port screw! Port screw!" crackled Frankie's voice over the radio. He sounded, distant, his grim battle somehow separated from me in my own little world. Seconds later his world collided with mine when lines of tracer smashed through the Perspex canopy right in front of me. In the mayhem of splintering metal and Perspex I somehow managed to aim and fire my own cannons at the aircraft roaring past, inches from my turret. I didn't have the remotest idea whether or not I had even come close to hitting him, and I would never find out.

The searchlight followed Larry's desperate attempt to dive us out of trouble and I remained blinded by the burning white light. The increasing sound of flak pinging through the fuselage told me that the gunners below had us in their sights. The aircraft shuddered and shook with the stress of the terrifying dive and I had to clamp my teeth together to stop my head vibrating. It felt to me as if the whole aircraft was going to fall apart. Wind roared in through the shattered canopy as I surveyed the damage. It seemed like hundreds of pieces of shattered metal and Perspex were sticking out of my flight suit.

Fortunately I couldn't feel any pain so I didn't think I was hurt, but I couldn't be one hundred percent sure. Unfortunately my oxygen pipe had been sliced clean through and the ends of my gun barrels were smashed and mangled, so it looked like I was out of action. Smoke was also beginning to waft into my mask from the freely flapping oxygen pipe. Things weren't looking too good.

Two things happened simultaneously. The aircraft suddenly bucked and reared upwards and the lights went out. All I could do was hold on grimly in the sudden darkness as the aircraft rocked and rolled on its late night roller coaster ride. The bright neon light was still burning my retinas and to all intents and purposes I was quite blind. I hoped and prayed that Larry was able to see more than I could. At least no one seemed to be shooting at us anymore, but as it turned out that was the least of our worries.

I peered through the shattered Perspex into the darkness and spotted immediately the roaring ball of flame that used to be our port side number one engine. Almost as if I were a detached observer I watched fascinated as the flames crept along the wing, which was probably still half full of high-octane fuel. I glanced right to check the starboard wing and noticed that only the outer propeller was still spinning. The propeller of the inner engine rotated gently in the slipstream, but was otherwise useless.

As I turned back to the port wing a jet of gas sprayed out through the engine and the fire dimmed and finally went out. The propellers on that engine then stopped spinning. I presume Larry had somehow extinguished the fire. The two remaining engines were screaming under the strain and a whole host of new banging and clattering noises were now coming from the stressed airframe.

Despite that, it did seem to me as if N-Nuts had levelled out and stabilised a bit. Perhaps that was just wishful thinking.

"Jesus! Is everyone OK?" came Larry's surprisingly calm voice over the radio. At least that was still working.

"Engineer here Skip. I'm fine."

"Navigator here Skip. A bit battered and bruised but OK. I'm just going to check on Ricky."

"Rodger that Alky. Can you give me a new course for home first?"

"Yes Skip, head out on course two seven five, I repeat, two seven five. I'll be back in a minute and check that again."

"OK Alky. Is everyone else OK? Please report."

I pressed the talk button on my mask.

"Mid-upper here. I'm OK Skipper but the turret took a hit, the guns look done and my oxygen is gone. I'll have to switch to the portable canister."

"OK, Rodger old man. Anyone else?"

The radio remained silent.

"Eddie, Frankie, come in."

Silence.

"Engineer here Skip. Jesus Christ I've just looked down and the bomb-aimer's position has gone. I mean there's nothing there...nothing. It's all shot away. Eddie's gone! There's just a great big bloody hole."

"OK Dicky, did you see if his chute was still there?"

"No Skip. There's nothing down there. It's all gone."

"OK Dicky. James, can you go back and check on Frankie? I can smell burning coming from somewhere back there too, can you have a peek for me?"

"OK Skip, my guns are shot so there's not much point in sitting up here anyway."

I unplugged my radio and pulled off my now useless mask and fitted the one attached to the mobile oxygen canister. It was just in time as I'd already started to feel a little light headed and confused.

As I clambered down from my lofty perch and dropped into the main fuselage below I was confronted by a wall of thick black smoke. Peering through the blackness towards the rear of the aircraft I spotted bright orange flames flickering around the rear turret.

"Frankie!" I shouted, as I stumbled along the fuselage. Flames were licking past the one remaining rubberised door which led into the turret. I could see Frankie's body slumped forward over his guns, his flying suit alight in numerous places. I had no idea whether he was already dead or not but I needed to try something.

I spotted what appeared to be a red painted fire extinguisher strapped to the fuselage next to the rear turret entrance. It was marked 'Meythel Bromide'. I didn't know what that was or how dangerous it might be but I didn't really have much time to think about it. I hauled the extinguisher off its mount and jammed my gloved fist down hard on the top lever while I aimed it into the rear turret and held on tight. An opaque jet was forced from the fire extinguisher and filled the rear turret with a misty cloud of gas and steam.

I made sure the fire was out before I dropped the extinguisher onto the floor and battled my way into the rear turret. It was absolute carnage inside. The entire turret canopy had been blown away and the guns were a tangled mess of twisted and melted metal. It had all the signs of having been hit by a stream of incendiary shells.

Frankie was slumped either unconscious or dead in his seat, but fortunately still strapped in otherwise he would have long ago been sucked out into the night. His flight suit was torn and bloody but I had no way of assessing the extent of his injuries. The only thing I could do was to somehow get him back into the aircraft.

I leaned into the smashed turret and grabbed Frankie's harness in my hand before I released his seat belt. I didn't want to lose him now. I somehow managed to manhandle him backwards over the seat and dropped him down onto the floor of the fuselage alongside me. I patted the flames from his burning suit out as fast as I could.

I was no medic but common sense told me his first need would be oxygen, assuming he was still alive that is. I pulled back his mask and took half of the skin off his face with it, exposing his perfect set of pearly white teeth. I nearly vomited there and then. I pulled my own oxygen mask off and pulled the strap over his head, easing the mask over his burnt and disfigured face. He groaned in pain as I placed the mask over his mouth. OK, so he was still alive but I wasn't all that sure he would thank me for saving him, even if I could.

Getting up onto my knees I searched his body for any other damage. There was loads. His flying suit was covered in holes, tears and burns and blood was oozing out here and there and staining the brown overalls. I knew there was no point in trying to remove his suit to attempt patching anything up, it was totally beyond me and I knew I'd probably only make matters worse. All I could do was grab his parachute from the hook and tuck it under his head to try and make him as comfortable as I could.

I kept thinking about those slender, delicate fingers of his, now burnt and mangled inside his bloody and burned gloves.

I was worried about my own lack of oxygen but I'd sensed the aircraft dropping for some time and I hoped we might soon be down to a level where I could breathe.

I left Frankie lying there and crawled along the vibrating and banging fuselage. Holes had been torn into the thin skin of the Lancaster in various places and I had to battle against the freezing cold air howling through the aircraft as I made my way forward.

Australian Ricky was still strapped to the bunk next to the toilet (for emergency use only) and I checked on him before I struggled over the two main spars towards the cockpit. Alky was in his curtained off position, desperately studying maps and his H2S navigation system. I didn't disturb him.

The scene in the cockpit didn't install me with any more confidence. The Perspex canopy had large holes smashed through it and debris was everywhere. Larry and Dicky were both hauling back on the flight controls, trying desperately to keep N-Nuts from going into a dive and I spotted a large jagged piece of bloody metal sticking out of the side of Larry's thigh. Smoke was pouring up from somewhere below and filling the cockpit, so I could only imagine we had other problems too.

Larry turned his head and pulled his mask to one side.

"James, how are things at the back?"

"Not good, I put a fire out in the rear and managed to pull Freddie out. He's badly burned and unconscious but I think he's still alive.

Larry simply nodded.

"We had to feather two engines old man and we're at 10,000 feet and dropping. I doubt we can make it home and I'm not sure we've got any landing gear anyway, so I think we're going to have to bale this side of the channel."

I didn't like the sound of that. I definitely wasn't warming to the idea of trusting my life to a fragile piece of silk.

"I'm so sorry old man, I know you've been here before, but at least this time Alky tells us we're over allied occupied territory."

That stopped me in my tracks, but somewhere deep inside I knew he was right. The memory was fleeting but I had been here before, I knew it.

"James, could you go and make sure Frankie and Ricky are clipped into their chutes, and get yours on too. Alky is telling us it's a maximum of ten minutes to the coast. We'll probably be down to a couple of thousand feet or so by then, we have to get out before we reach the water."

As if in agreement a loud bang came from somewhere beneath us and N-Nuts gave a violent shudder. I nodded at Larry but he had already returned to his battle with the controls.

I stumbled back along the narrow fuselage and spotted Ricky's parachute hanging up on a hook next to his wireless desk. I grabbed it and kneeled down next to his oversized form on the tiny sick bunk. I scanned Ricky's torn and blood spattered flight suit before I noticed his eyes were open and he was staring at me. I pulled his oxygen mask away from his face.

"You OK Ricky?"

"Never been better mate."

OK, so there wasn't a lot I could say to that.

"Ricky, Larry says we're going down, we're going to have to bale."

If there was any fear in Ricky's bright blue eyes I didn't spot it. He simply nodded and rolled onto his back so I could attach the parachute to his chest harness. I couldn't remember doing it before but it seemed simple enough. There was a clip on each corner of the parachute pack which matched up with four rings on the harness. Simple. I laid it on his chest and clipped the first ring in when I felt Ricky's massive hand on mine.

"It's upside down," was all he said.

I gave him a weak smile, unclipped the pack and turned it around. Ricky gave me a thumbs up and as I started to clip in the rings I spotted an arrow on the top of the pack pointing upwards. Kids' stuff I know, but I missed it. When I'd finished, Ricky rolled his large frame off the bunk and onto the floor. I half dragged him over and sat him next to the door the agents had vanished out of only a few hours ago.

"I'm going to sort Frankie, are you going to be OK?" I asked.

Ricky managed a thumbs up and another grin.

I found Frankie's parachute hanging up on the hook behind his turret. It was scorched from the flames but it still appeared to be in working condition and I had it clipped onto his chest in a few seconds, this time the right way up. Frankie was still unconscious so I slid my arms under his and dragged his body closer to the doorway. I was just easing his head down onto the floor of the aircraft again when Alky and Dicky appeared next to me.

"Jeez, I feckin hate jumping don't you?" Alky shouted. "The Skip asked us to come back here and help you get the lads out. We'll have to be quick; Larry can't hold her up for much longer. He'll be going out the front in five minutes and once this kite starts to spin down we'll never get out."

310

With that, Alky stood up and grasped the lever for the door. I just had time to turn around, grab my own parachute from the hook it had been hanging on ever since we came on board and clip it onto my harness before the door was flung open. The noise of the rushing wind once again filled my ears. Talking was pointless so we went back to miming again.

Alky grabbed hold of Ricky's harness and eased him into the open doorway. Ricky helped where he could but he was weak and in obvious pain. Alky steadied Ricky in the open doorway while he placed the parachute release handle in his palm and closed his fingers around it. He nodded at Ricky and Ricky nodded back.

Alky glanced up at me and pointed first to Ricky and then to himself. The message was clear, he was going to follow Ricky out. Someone would need to be with him assuming they made it to the ground alive. Alky grasped Ricky's harness with both hands and heaved him out into the blizzard. No sooner had he disappeared, Alky dropped out after him.

That left me and Dicky with the unconscious Frankie. We each grabbed hold of his harness and slid him along the floor to the doorway. There was no time to turn him around or try to sit him up, we were going to have to push him out head first. I was still trying to work out how we might get his chute to open on the way down and tried to come up with some way of rigging up another static line like the agents had used when Dicky reached down and pulled Frankie's release cord. The parachute now lay exposed in the pack on Frankie's chest. I glanced up at Dicky and he shrugged. It was obvious he had no idea whether the plan was going to work or not, but we had run out of time, it was the best we could do for him. Dicky pointed to Frankie and then himself. I nodded and smiled at him.

We both heaved Frankie into the open doorway and as we let him go his body was sucked out into the slipstream with a strange popping sound. Without a moment's hesitation Dicky dived out headfirst behind him.

I've never been one for all that God stuff, even as a child I thought the whole thing was all nonsense - as well as a complete waste of a perfectly good Sunday morning - but at that moment I prayed if there was someone or something out there watching over us, they bloody needed to pay special attention to those two.

I dropped down in the open doorway and with my heart in my mouth I swung my legs out into the speeding air. The suction pulling on my body was incredible. I glanced down at my parachute pack, checked that the arrow was on top for the fourth or fifth time and grabbed the release cord handle in my right hand. All I needed to do now was let go with my left hand and I would be out.

As I began to release my gloved fingers from the fuselage I remembered Bonnie's locket, I'd left the bloody thing hanging up in the turret. Irrational as it was, she'd made me promise to bring it back to her and I had no intention of letting her down a second time, so I let go of the parachute release handle and grabbed hold of the doorway with both hands.

Rolling back into the aircraft wasn't as easy as going out but I made it and struggled back through the now smoke filled fuselage. Fortunately the mid-upper gun turret was only a few feet away and I managed to feel my way up the three steps into what had been my place of work for the past six or seven hours. With some relief I spotted the locket still hanging on the metal spar where I'd left it. I pulled off my glove, dropped the locket in and pulled it back on. I didn't have any time to find a safe pocket and anyway, I liked the feel of the locket against the palm of my hand. It was somehow reassuring, as if Bonnie was with me.

Time had run out, I needed to go. I turned and dropped down the few steps onto the floor of the fuselage when it all went wrong again. The nose of N-Nuts dropped without warning and the bomber went into a steep dive. My feet left the ground and I was thrown forward, almost along the full length of the fuselage in one go. My head struck something solid along the way and I came to a sudden halt when I crashed into the back of the flight engineer's seat inside the cockpit.

I almost passed out with the sudden blinding pain behind my eyes and I tasted vomit rising up my throat. My right arm seemed to be pinned underneath me and I couldn't move either of my legs. Peering upwards, or was it down? I couldn't tell anymore, I could see that Larry had already baled out through the front hatch which was left wide open, and the screaming of the engines told me we were in a steep dive. I had no idea how long I had left, but I knew I was about to meet a pretty violent end if I didn't do something fast.

The first heave of vomit, when it came, intensified the pain in my head and I almost passed out. The second one I think cleared my head a little. I reached up with my left hand and grasped the back of what had been Larry's seat. Pulling hard I managed to lift my torso enough to free my other arm and then I had two arms to pull myself out. I recall screaming obscenities I didn't even think I knew as I yanked, pulled and slithered my way across the back of the pilot's seat until all of a sudden I felt my legs come free.

At that angle there was no way I could climb back up to the fuselage doorway, and I still hadn't the foggiest idea as to what I was actually going to do. As I dragged myself up onto my feet and looked out of the smashed cockpit window I realised there weren't many choices left.

The moonlight reflected off the crest of each wave top as they flowed majestically by, about a thousand feet below. If it wasn't for the fact that I faced an imminent violent death, the scene below would have been quite awe inspiring. I realised there was no time to jump now, the plane was going in and I was going with it. The only chance I had was to try and ease off the angle of the dive and hopefully ditch rather than smash myself into a million pieces, which was precisely what was going to happen at this rate.

As I clambered over the controls to get into the pilot's seat I soon realised I wasn't going to fit in with my parachute on. It was useless now anyway, so with a little relief I ditched the bulky pack and slithered down into the soft leather seat that Larry had recently vacated. I'd never wanted to jump out with that bloody chute anyway.

I thought it might be a good idea to clip the seat harness on as I assumed the rest of the ride down might be a little rough. I placed both gloved hands on the control stick in front of me, which felt strangely comfortable, and pulled back as hard as I could, as I'd seen Larry and Dicky doing. The stick felt rock solid in my hands but inch-by-inch I managed to heave it back towards me.

With eyes transfixed on the waves below rushing up to meet me, I focussed all my remaining strength into pulling back that stick. I don't think the shrieking engines; the howling wind, the shuddering air-frame or the billowing smoke even came into my consciousness in those last few remaining moments. My whole world centred on that control stick and my only choice was to hang on as if my life depended on it, which of course it most probably did.

I sensed the rate of descent slowing as the horizon inched into view in front of me, and there was a moment of elation as I dared allow myself the thought that I might actually survive this, but that was short lived when I spotted the orange flames licking up through the floor beneath my seat.

N-Nuts shuddered, banged and vibrated even more violently in those last few grim moments of its life, and all I could do was hang on. My recollection of the actual moment we made contact with that moonlit sea is limited to the violent jarring and battering my body received as the cockpit all but disintegrated around me, and the terrible screeching sounds of tortured, tearing metal and the hissing and steaming of the fires beneath me as they extinguished themselves in the icy water.

The moments following the ditching seemed like a dream, or perhaps a nightmare to be more exact. After all the noise of the past few hours the sudden silence was eerie and I think the immediate sense of relief I felt at still being alive almost paralysed me. If it hadn't been for the ice cold water rushing into the cockpit stirring me into action I might have sat there forever.

It took me a few seconds to find the release for the harness before I dragged myself up onto the seat and reached up to clamber out of the open escape hatch Larry had gone out of. Once out on top of the fuselage it became obvious that N-Nuts was sinking rapidly. The cockpit was almost full of water and dark waves began to lap over the burnt and shattered wings.

I pulled the cord on my yellow Mae West jacket and with a small bang it filled instantly with air. I knew I was going in for a swim, but I didn't know how long I could last in that icy water.

A much louder bang startled me and I watched in astonishment as a bright yellow life-raft exploded out of a box on the side of the fuselage and began to inflate. Before I even became conscious of it my legs were running along the top of the torn and holed fuselage towards the one thing that might even yet save my life. I had to get to it before the life-raft drifted off the wing and floated away out of reach. I knew I'd never be able to swim to it, and even if I did I wasn't at all sure I would be able to pull my body up and into the raft, especially weighed down with a sodden sheepskin flying suit.

Without any hesitation I ran past my shattered gun turret and in three strides was off the top of the fuselage and dropping the six or so feet down into the now floating life-raft. Fortunately my aim was good and I landed with a slight roll inside the raft. As it turns out I was just in time as N-Nuts sank beneath the waves.

I stared as the sea rushed into my smashed turret until that too sank out of sight. N-Nuts eased downwards into the depths, briefly taking on the form of a huge shadowy winged sea creature before it finally disappeared from sight.

I felt sure any of the real crew of N-Nuts might have shed a tear and said a few words at that moment, but I for one was bloody glad to see the back of it. All I hoped was that the sea would prove deep enough in this area to satisfy the requirements of the CO. I certainly didn't want to be the one responsible for letting our top secret radar set fall into the hands of the Germans. Anyway, it was probably bad enough losing the aircraft. I seriously wondered if the good old RAF docked your pay for that? If this really was my second downed aircraft I reckoned I might be bankrupt by the end of the war.

Chapter Eight - The English Channel Dec 15th 1944

The life-raft was designed and manufactured for a crew of seven, so that was a positive. I discovered an emergency box in the raft that contained water, hard-tack biscuits and chocolate rations for seven. There were also a couple of packs of malted milk tablets and a fishing kit, which would have been handy if I'd had any bloody idea how to fish. At least I wasn't going to starve for a while.

The real negative of the new situation I found myself in was that I was floating aimlessly somewhere in the English Channel, at night, and in sub-zero temperatures in the worst winter Europe had experienced for years. If I hadn't been wearing my full sheepskin flying kit I doubt I would've lasted more than an hour or so. My one consolation was at least I'd managed to keep myself dry, it might have been a different story if I hadn't.

The raft seemed stable enough in the water but the up and down movement over the small waves began to make me queasy. I wasn't a good sailor at the best of times and I hoped the waves weren't going to get any bigger. Moving safely around the raft also took a bit of getting used to. I found it best to keep low and perform a rolling, crawling motion if I needed to move, but there wasn't much point anyway. I wasn't going anywhere.

At first I scanned the horizon in all directions every few seconds. The moonlight still glinted off the wave crests and visibility was generally good, but there was nothing to see other than sea and sky. Cloud cover was light, which made for a startling display of bright twinkling stars against the velvety black sky that on any other night might have been enchanting.

The thought crossed my mind that I should try to work out my position from the stars. I recognised the Plough and Orion's Belt quick enough, but that still told me nothing about where I was. I had a vague recollection of the North Star being in a straight line from the end star of the

Plough. In my mind I traced along an imaginary line and spotted a quite unimpressive faint star sitting alone in the sky. That might've been it, but I wasn't at all sure what I thought I was going to do with the knowledge even if I was right.

There was no means of propelling the raft other than leaning over the side and paddling with the small hand paddles I'd found in the emergency box, which I had absolutely no intention of doing. There seemed no point in getting wet when I didn't even know what direction I should be going in, and I doubted I'd get very far anyway.

The realisation dawned on me that the only hope I had of surviving was to sit tight, try not to freeze to death and pray that someone spotted me quickly. My life again appeared to be in the lap of the gods; something I was getting used to.

Time dragged by over the next few hours of darkness. I gave up scanning the horizon and lay curled up in the bottom of the raft for the most part, trying to conserve any warmth left in me and sleeping fitfully. The suit saved me, of that there was no doubt, but I was still freezing and didn't know how long I could survive like that before any potential rescuers came along. I wondered how many other downed airman survived a wrecked aircraft only to die alone and freezing in that cold and unforgiving sea.

On at least three occasions I listened to the droning of aircraft engines and spotted a dark winged shape high above me. I guessed they were bombers returning to England from their nocturnal missions over Europe. The last of those aircraft was burning brightly and left a spectacular fiery arc trailing across the sky from horizon to horizon. I suspect the crew left on board battling to save their lives wouldn't have appreciated the wondrous sight they created. At least the direction the aircraft were travelling in gave me a rough indication of east and west, not that it helped my situation much. I assumed I was drifting in one direction or another but I had no real sensation of it.

At one point during the night I needed a pee. I held onto it for as long as possible, trying to pretend the feeling wasn't really there, as you so often do in the middle of the night, but I accepted I would eventually have to do something about it. For ages I planned how to have a pee without losing too much heat or risking falling overboard. In the end I removed my gloves, took the opportunity to slip Bonnie's locket into an inside pocket of my tunic, and proceeded to try and coax my old-man out through five layers of clothing. In sub-zero temperatures that in itself proved no mean feat as everything had shrivelled up. Eventually I managed it though and attempted to pee over the side from a kneeling position. I had no intention of standing up. I suspect most of the urine remained either in the boat or on me, but I was almost past caring by that point.

A spectacular sunrise provided me with two positives to grasp hold of: It confirmed my east and west points and the sun heralded a slight increase in daytime temperature. I had at least survived the night. On the down side, I didn't think I would survive another one.

During the next few hours I continuously scanned the horizon for boats. Visibility remained quite poor, a dull grey cloud now hung low over the sea and the occasional snow flurry came in just to try and make my situation a little more desperate. I spotted one or two shadowy ships in the distance and I set off one of the flares in desperation, but they were so far away and the visibility so poor I knew it was a waste of time. I decided not to waste any more of the remaining flares until something came a little closer.

The skies were unusually quiet and by mid-morning I hadn't heard or seen a single aircraft up there. I'd heard the RAF often sent up crews in the morning to do a sweeping search of the channel, looking for any downed crews from the night before, but I suspected the temperatures and conditions might have been too poor for safe flying that day. Just my bloody luck.

Assuming my watch was still accurate, I think it might have been around midday when the droning of a large number of heavy aircraft could be heard high above the cloud cover. From the sound it would seem they were British or American aircraft heading towards Europe. Someone was going to get it I thought. That didn't make me any happier.

I'd lost all sense of time bobbing around on that freezing raft, but I didn't think it was too long after that when I heard another similar sound of aircraft flying from east to west, towards England. For all I knew it might well have been the same aircraft coming back, or perhaps a flight of German bombers making an appearance. If it was the same aircraft they hadn't been gone long, certainly not long enough to get to Germany and back. I was still pondering the question when all hell broke loose.

Streams of dark shapes appeared through the cloud and dropped in long neat rows into the sea around me. Dull, wet, thumping explosions erupted across the surface of the sea. I held my hands over my head and rolled up in a ball on the floor of my flimsy life-raft and my testicles tightened as the sea boiled and churned all around me.

My luck held though, fortunately none of the bombs came close enough to blow me to bits or even capsize me, although I did manage to get soaked in spray before the rain of terror passed on over. I watched the bombs continuing to fall in the distance as the bombers disposed of their dangerous cargo, 'safely' into the Channel. The irony wasn't lost on me.

No sooner had the bombers vanished into the mist my ears filled with yet another terrifying noise. The unmistakable sound of a screaming engine, an aircraft in trouble, and it seemed to be heading for me.

I'd been on my own is this vast empty sea for the past twelve hours or so and now it seemed every ruddy thing in the sky wanted to be on top of me. I was still scanning the underside of the clouds when my new visitor arrived. It was a small single engined aeroplane and appeared to be in serious trouble. I no longer heard the sound of an engine and the single propeller didn't seem to be spinning so I guessed the engine had packed up. The pilot desperately fought with the machine that now appeared to be tumbling out of control. As it came closer I spotted two people inside the small Perspex covered cockpit. I felt helpless watching the poor bastards struggle with what might well be their last moments of life.

For one all too brief moment I thought the pilot had managed to bring the aircraft under a semblance of control. The nose lifted up momentarily and my heart stopped as I watched the struggle, but tragically in those last few seconds the port wing dipped and clipped the top of the waves. That was the end for them. The plane cartwheeled twice and with an agonising shriek the thin metal structure tore and broke up under the tremendous strain. The wing and the tail came off in one instant and as I stared at the catastrophe unfolding in front of my eyes I spotted a dark suited figure being ejected from the wreckage. Debris flew in every direction but I kept my eyes on the body as it hit the water about a hundred yards from me.

Without hesitation I gripped on tight to the rope running around the sides of the raft and began paddling with my free hand towards the still churning spot where the plane was going down. It was slow progress, even with the small paddle I'd found. Inch by frustrating inch I moved towards the figure still bobbing up and down in the water. Thankfully the yellow life jacket he had on was keeping him afloat and made him easy to spot, otherwise I might have lost him.

The rest of the aircraft wreckage had almost all disappeared below the waves and I saw no sign of the other airman I'd spotted in the cockpit. I could only assume he was either still trapped somewhere inside the sinking wreck or was already dead. I hoped for his sake he was already dead.

The bobbing airman's eyes were closed and his head rolled around lifelessly by the time I finally reached him. He was either unconscious or dead, I'd no way of telling. A bloody gash ran along the side of his forehead but the rest of his body was under water so I couldn't tell whether or not there might have been any further serious injuries.

As I pulled alongside him I grabbed the Mae West with my free hand. Having no other alternative, I let go of the rope with my other hand and started to heave the airman up into the life-raft. I had no desire to get pulled in with the guy but on my own there wasn't any other way.

I heaved and hauled on the lifeless body. The most difficult bit proved to be getting him over the inflated side of the raft. The sodden weight of the fully clothed man was unbelievable and I dropped him back in twice, but still managed to hang on. As the minutes ticked by I could feel my own strength ebbing and the icy cold water beginning to seep into my gloves. I knew I had to get him into the raft within the next few moments or I would have to let him go, there would be only one last chance. I cried out as I gave a final desperate heave and relief washed over me as something gave and the body slipped across the smooth wet vinyl and slithered into the bottom of the raft in a heap.

I desperately tried to remember some of the basic first aid I'd learned as I placed my ear close to the man's blue coloured lips. I couldn't feel or hear any signs of breathing. Not good.

I pulled the airman over onto his back and his unseeing eyes rolled in his head. Not good at all. I pulled open the bright yellow Mae West and began compressing his chest with the palms of my hands. I wasn't at all sure whether I might save him or make things worse, but I figured they couldn't get much worse anyway so what the hell. The bouncing raft didn't make things any easier, but I did the best I could.

The airman's brown leather flight jacket and tan coloured trousers were sodden. The insignia looked American and I was no expert but he appeared to be an officer.

After about thirty pushes on his chest the airman's eyes bulged and a rush of water gushed out of his open mouth. He began to cough. It was weak at first, but he soon began to sound like a hundred a day man as he hacked, wheezed and vomited the destructive salt water from his lungs. I rolled him onto his side to make the process easier and after about five minutes his eyes focussed a little and he stared at me.

"Are you OK mate?" I asked.

OK, so it was obvious he wasn't, but it was the only thing I could think of, and I am British after all, masters of understatement.

The airman continued his fixed stare and the frown across his face suggested he was still struggling to work out what had happened to him.

I scanned his body and spotted a large rip down the left arm of his jacket. Blood flowed freely from the wound, too freely in fact.

"Sorry pal, you're bleeding heavy, we need to have a look at that," I said as I pulled off his Mae West, unzipped his jacket and yanked it from his injured arm. He groaned in pain as I pulled the arm free and he vomited again. I tried not to notice the fresh blood mixing with the vomit and whatever else was already swirling around in the bottom of the raft. All in all it was getting just a little messy in our tiny boat and I decided I didn't feel too good myself.

Underneath the leather jacket he had on an officer's tunic and a thick brown woollen pullover. Bright red blood still pumped from the wound so I figured I didn't have enough time to undress him, and frankly I was worried he'd freeze to death before I could fix his wound anyway. His teeth chattered incessantly and his body began to shake. I wasn't sure if it was from shock or cold, but I sensed neither would be too good for him.

I ripped open the already torn arm of the tunic, jumper and the shirt beneath, exposing the gaping tear in his flesh. It almost made me want to puke. The white of his bone was clearly visible and I knew I needed to stop the bleeding first or he wasn't going to last many more minutes. I needed a tourniquet. Thinking fast the only thing that sprang to mind was Jackie's tie, which I remembered

I'd shoved into the top pocket of my tunic. *Thanks Jackie you're a lifesaver* I thought.

Shaking with the cold, exertion and probably fright, I finally managed to fumble my way beneath my flight suit, flight jacket and into my tunic to pull the tie free. As soon as I'd tightened the knot around the airman's upper arm the flow of lost blood eased off. Either he'd run out of blood or the tourniquet was working. His skin was an ash grey colour but he appeared to still be breathing so I hoped it was the latter.

Leaving him for a moment I grabbed the first aid kit from the emergency box and pulled out some gauze and bandages. I managed to pull the gaping sides of the open wound together as best I could, cover the hole with gauze and then bandage the whole arm up tightly. It was slow work with frozen fingers and I knew I had to get my own gloves back on as soon as possible or I was going to suffer from frostbite myself, or worse.

I eased off the tourniquet a little to allow some blood to flow into his lower arm and then pulled his leather jacket around him. I tucked the heavy woollen blanket I'd found in the emergency box over him and flopped back against the side of the raft. There wasn't any more I could do and I was too exhausted anyway.

Over the next few hours of drifting aimlessly I tried not to look at what was swirling around in the bottom of the boat and ate a few pieces of the cheap waxy chocolate. I even attempted to mix up the malted milk tablets in some of the water. The cold white mixture was lumpy, sweet and disgusting but I managed to get my airman friend to swallow a little of it. He drifted in and out of consciousness and tried to speak to me on a few occasions, but mostly it consisted of unintelligible groaning.

The American had lost quite a lot of blood, was still soaking wet and I suspected hypothermia might be setting in. If we weren't rescued soon I guessed he wasn't going to live for long, which was obvious even to me. I wasn't sure how much longer I was going to last either.

After searching through the silk bag that contained my escape kit the WAAFs had given me before we left Tempsford, I found a compass, a knife and a silk map of north Western Europe. The compass proved useful, at least I knew we were drifting northeast which meant we would hit the mainland European coastline at some point. What I didn't know was whether it would be allied liberated coast or the remaining part of the Dutch coast that remained in German hands. Either way, things were so bad it probably didn't matter very much which part of the coast we landed on, we had to get off that freezing raft and into some warmth or we'd both be toast, if that isn't a contradiction of terms?

As it turns out we didn't have long to wait. My watch stopped working after it became soaked hauling my airman friend in, but the sun was still up when I first sighted land so I guessed it was sometime in the mid-afternoon. The tide felt strong and the details of the coastline became more defined as every minute passed. I was able to make out a couple of tall church spires in the distance, which at least meant civilisation wasn't too far away. That had to be a good sign as my friend needed medical help as soon as possible and I needed warmth. Now that I had an objective I assisted the current with some paddling of my own and I breathed a sigh of relief as we finally approached the coast and the sea bottom came into view.

I spotted a wide sandy beach and headed for that. It appeared deserted but I reasoned it might be a fairly safe place to land and I hoped I'd still be able to find some assistance quickly. After ten minutes of dragging the pathetically small paddle through the tide I landed the raft on the firm wet sand at the edge of the beach.

After about three tries I managed to roll myself over the side and into the shallow lapping water. Layers of thin ice covered the soft wet sand at the water's edge, and I remember it cracking under my body weight as I dragged myself up out of the water. The beach still appeared deserted.

With the little remaining strength I had left I hauled the raft up onto the dry sand behind me and lay down beside it. I had no intention of trying to lift my airman friend out, and I doubted I could even if I'd tried. I was well past that.

I remember lying there staring up at a solitary seagull drifting and screeching on the breeze above me and finally closing my eyes. It wasn't a good time to sleep, I accepted that, but I was beyond exhaustion.

The dreamlike rhythm of the lapping waves was telling me to sleep and I seriously wondered if I'd ever have enough strength to get up again. In fact, I was so comfortable lying there, getting up again was probably the last thing on my mind. I could've stayed there forever, and might have if it hadn't been for the distant sounds of shouting drifting towards me across the sand covered dunes.

The approaching voices seemed to be coming from another world to mine, distorted somehow. I thought I made out the rumble of a vehicle somewhere close by and a couple of shrill blasts on a whistle startled me, but the last thing I recall before I drifted off again were voices right next to me, and they weren't speaking English. I remember hoping they were friendly.

Chapter Nine - Holland Dec 16th 1944

The fact that I woke up on a small bunk staring at a barred window suggested they weren't too friendly. The taste of salt on my lips and the sweat beading on my face indicated I was hot, very hot in fact. I couldn't recall being warm since arriving in 1944 so it was a bit of a novel experience and I might even have been happy about it if it wasn't for the fact the heat was becoming downright unbearable.

Gripping onto the side of the bunk I pulled myself upright and the world spun. I had to get my flight suit off before I threw up, or worse, passed out again with the heat. My outer suit had disappeared, as had my sheepskin flying trousers, but I still had my sheepskin flight jacket on. I slipped it off and dropped the heavy leather jacket onto the floor.

As my faculties and what memory I possessed returned, my hand shot involuntarily to the left breast pocket of my tunic. I breathed a sigh of relief as my fingers closed over the hard lump of the silver locket stashed away inside. However, the relief proved to be short lived. The intense heat still threatened to boil my blood away to vapour, so I pulled off my tunic and threw that on top of the flight jacket. Sweat plastered my blue shirt to my skin.

The six foot by six foot room consisted of four bare whitewashed brick walls with a barred window set high up in one wall and a black painted steel door in the wall opposite. The door had no handle on the inside. It didn't need Einstein to work out the room was a cell.

Shaking, I pushed myself up from the bunk onto two trembling legs and took three steps towards the door. With both palms and the side of my cheek flattened against the cold black painted steel I managed to stay upright and banged hard.

"Hello! Hello! Is anyone there?"

I waited for a response.

Nothing.

"Hello! Hello! I need this door open now, it's stifling in here." I banged the door again for good measure but doubted it was going to make any difference.

I turned and leaned against the door as I yanked off my sheepskin flying boots, followed by my heavy wool uniform trousers. I didn't stop there either. I unbuttoned my silk long-Johns and stepped out, leaving just my sodden Y-fronts and socks sticking to my bare skin.

With my breath coming in rasps and my head spinning I decided it might be a good idea to get closer to the floor before I fell down. I lay flat on the bare concrete floor and gained some relief from the relative coolness of the floor, but not much. What the hell was going on?

Sweat pooled underneath my body and my ability to hold a coherent thought seemed to be slipping away.

I have no recollection of how long I lay on that cell floor. I couldn't even tell you whether I thought I was in the real world or asleep, but I do recall in my dream, if indeed that's what it was, distant footsteps echoed against a hard stone floor, coming closer. I remember dreaming of the door creaking open and beautiful cool air flowing around my body. The relief was instant, like downing your first cold pint on a hot summer's day.

The kick in my ribs when it came was far too painful to be a dream. Instinctively curling up into a ball I tried to protect myself but my kidneys took the next kick and I thought I was going to pass out again.

"So, Englander, you are awake yes?"

I didn't respond and took another hard kick in the ribs for my trouble. It seemed the better option might be to do as I was told for a while.

"Yes."

"Good, good. So what brings you here Englander?"

Was I missing something or was that just the most stupid question I'd heard in a long while? Thankfully I managed to refrain from saying so.

I peered up at my attacker, a short wiry man with thin wisps of brown hair slicked back over his balding crown, a twisted nose that must have been broken on more than one occasion, and perhaps his least endearing feature, a distorted puffy hole on the left side of his head where his ear seemed to have been forcibly removed at some point in the past. I hope I'm getting the point across, handsome he was not.

His long black leather coat hung open at the front displaying an immaculately pressed blue pinstriped double-breasted suit beneath. I spotted a reflection of my half naked prone form in the gleaming black leather of his shoes. I hoped he hadn't scuffed them against my sweating skin, I would hate to be in his company if he got annoyed.

"Where am I?" I didn't really expect an answer but I had to start somewhere.

The shriek that passed for laughter was no more endearing than his features. I supposed someone somewhere loved him, his mother maybe? But in all honesty I sincerely doubted it.

"You are in the Third Reich Englander and you are most welcome." He shrieked again at his attempt at humour. If his laughter was intended to unsettle me, it was working extremely well.

"So you are an Englander terrorfleiger no?"

I was going to take umbrage with him over his use of the term Englander and explain the subtle differences between the various parts of the British Isles, and Scotland in particular, but I decided the nuances would probably be lost on him. I wasn't too sure what a terrorfleiger was either, but I could've hazarded a guess. In the end I opted to remain on the offensive.

"Why have I been locked in this cell with the heating turned full on? I have rights as a prisoner of war." Well at least I thought I did. I definitely remember it being mentioned in any number of war films I'd watched over the past year. I recall it being something to do with the Geneva Convention. I hoped he'd heard of it too.

The little man's screeching laughter suggested he didn't take that threat too seriously.

It was about then I spotted the uniformed policeman standing in the open doorway, his heavy eyes staring directly at me. As my eyes met his he immediately found something more interesting to stare at on the end of his boot.

"So Englander, you are aware of the recent order from Mr Goebbels regarding terrorfleigers?"

That was easy, I wasn't. I shook my head.

"As a result of the death and destruction you have wrought on the good people of Europe he has decreed that we no longer protect terrorfleigers from the civilian mobs who may wish to rip them limb from limb, and we the authorities are at liberty to use any force we judge fit should you attempt to escape or cause us any harm. In other words, I can do anything I wish with you."

The leather coated troll glared down at me, spittle and foam gathering in both corners of his sneering grin.

For the briefest moment I thought about questioning 'who' exactly the good people of Europe were, and possibly raising the obviously thorny issue of the Geneva Convention again, but I thought better of it. In all the war movies I'd ever seen the prisoners of war only said one thing, so I thought I'd give that a go.

"Flight Lieutenant James Cunnion, number...em...em"

On a positive note, the kick to my stomach saved me from having to remember the service number I'd spotted on my passbook - which I would probably have got wrong anyway - but it didn't do much for my overall health and wellbeing. A wave of pain passed through my body and I prayed no internal damage had been done.

"I've read all that from your dog tags. Do you think we care? Now what I really want to know is why you were in a life-raft with an American flyer?"

The question jolted me, I'd forgotten all about the American airman. I didn't even know if he had survived, but I saw no reason not to tell the truth. Granted I had no idea who the American was or what mission he might have been on, and I hadn't even had the chance to speak with him so I was completely in the dark on that score which meant I was on relatively safe ground. The American would need to answer those questions himself, assuming he was still alive of course.

Still, even though I was happy to answer I wasn't going to let an opportunity to gain a little something for myself slip by.

"I'll be happy to tell you how we came to be together but only if you turn off the bloody heating and let me get dressed again."

I waited for the inevitable kick to the stomach, but this time it didn't come. I risked a glance up at the vile little man and caught him wiping the sweat from his forehead with a white handkerchief. I liked the fact he was suffering too. He turned to the policeman in the doorway.

"Sergeant, go and turn off the heating to this room."

The police Sergeant nodded as he turned on his heel and disappeared from the doorway, the sound of his heavy boots against the stone floor receded into the distance. The German took one step back so I took that as my cue to get up and pull my wringing wet clothes back on.

Trying to pull my wet cotton shirt on was like some mad game from *It's A Knockout*, but the cool fresh air being sucked in from the hallway felt so refreshing I almost didn't mind.

"So, you were telling me your story?"

Holding my ribs that still throbbed from the last kick I eased myself down onto the small bunk and paused for a moment to decide on where exactly I should start, without giving too much away.

"It's rather a simple one really. My aircraft came down in the English Channel and while I was bobbing about in my life-raft I saw another aircraft crash into the sea near me. So I did the decent British thing and picked up the only survivor I could find. He was unconscious so I never got to chat to him to find out who he was. Then we found ourselves on the beach and you probably know more about the rest of the story than I do."

The little man's lips peeled back from his yellowing teeth as he snarled.

"So, where exactly had you been in your bomber before you crashed into the Ärmelkanal, what city did you annihilate last night and where is the rest of your crew?"

I pressed my lips together rather theatrically and stared at the little man. Naively, now that I was dressed and upright again I didn't feel quite so intimidated by Mr Angry. I perhaps should have been more wary.

"I don't suppose you would like to tell me about your squadron and what aircraft you flew in?"

I continued to stare at the man, but said nothing.

"Ah well, no matter. If I thought you were going to get back home safely I would have asked you to give my regards to your Wing Commander Fauquier, but I doubt that is going to happen now. How are things in 617 squadron at the moment anyway?"

He smirked with satisfaction as my eyes betrayed my surprise. Even though some of the stories I'd heard from the crew of N-Nuts suggested the Germans knew everything about us, I was still astounded. I wasn't too keen on his comments about me not getting home either. I should've smelled a rat then, but my unerring and often misguided belief in the basic goodness of my fellow man tripped me up once again.

The policeman appeared back in the doorway and resumed his vacant examination of the floor.

The little man glared at me and an unnerving grin spread across his disfigured face. Even though I remained sitting, his watery eyes were almost at the same level as mine.

"Now, I have a little something I want to show you, I think you'll be impressed. Sergeant, handcuff and escort the prisoner to the front of the jail for me."

The sergeant nodded and stepped into the room, still avoiding any eye contact with me.

"And please put your tunic and flying jacket back on, it's cold outside and we wouldn't want you catching your death would we?" he said as he marched from the room. His shrieking laugh hadn't improved any, it still grated on my nerves.

"Proper little comedian eh?" I said to the sergeant as I donned my tunic and flying jacket. I'm not sure whether he didn't understand English or simply chose to ignore me, but either way he made no comment and continued to stare at his feet as he removed a pair of solid looking handcuffs from his belt and secured my wrists together in front (thankfully) of my body. I followed him out of the cell and along the narrow corridor towards the bright sunlight at the far end.

The sergeant led us through a small reception area towards the ornately carved double front doors of what I now recognised to be a small provincial police station. The sergeant was almost certainly a local Dutchman following the orders of his German masters. The American and I had obviously drifted north after all and must have managed to land somewhere in the small part of Holland that still remained under occupation.

As an avid fan of 'Allo 'Allo' even I could work out that the little German's civilian suit and long black leather coat most likely made him an officer of the Gestapo. My stomach lurched at the thought, I knew I was in deep shit.

Speaking of my new American pal, I spotted him sitting in the small reception area, slumped between two uniformed German guards. His eyes were open and although he would have given his mother a fright, he looked a whole lot better than when I last saw him. He had a bloody white bandage around his forehead and his arm was tied up in a sling. His leather flight jacket was draped around his shoulders and the rest of his uniform appeared to have dried out. I wondered whether he had been subjected to the same heat treatment as I had.

He glanced up at me as we approached and smiled. He appeared to be a little older than I first thought, maybe in his late thirties or early forties? Underneath his flight jacket I spotted a well-tailored dress tunic in the colours of the US Army which appeared to be adorned with a whole host of brass pips. I assumed from that he was quite high ranking, but I found it hard to tell with the American officers, he might even be a general for all I knew. Under the circumstances I guess it didn't matter much out here.

The sergeant marched straight out through the open double doors and into the glaring sunshine. I wondered whether I had spent more than one night in the cell, I had no way of telling but I didn't think so. From the position of the sun sitting high in the cloudless blue sky I estimated it to be late morning.

Despite the sun, the temperature hadn't improved any and my breath condensed in front of me when it met with the icy air. A wonderful crisp winter's day, *a good day for a hanging* I thought (sorry I've also seen far too many westerns). As it turns out, it wasn't too far from the truth.

We stood in front of the local police station which was situated in one corner of a small town square. The square had an ancient, decorative stone fountain in the centre and the perimeter was lined with quaint two and three story houses, shops and cafes. No one sat out at the tables at this time of the year but it would've been easy to imagine the sights and sounds of people eating, drinking and soaking up the historic atmosphere on a warm summer afternoon in happier times.

On the opposite side of the square the somewhat predictable town church took pride of place, and that's where the townspeople were gathered. There must have been a hundred or so people crowded into the area directly in front of the white walls of the town's ancient house of worship. They all stood facing the church, none of them were smiling.

The two German soldiers half carried and half marched my new American comrade out through the police station doors and came to a halt next to me and the sergeant. Anticipation hung heavy in the air and something felt very wrong with the scene in the square. I feared the worst. I grinned at the American and he grinned back, but neither of us were laughing. I think he felt it too.

The nasty little Gestapo man seemed to appear from nowhere and beckoned us to follow him. He wore a beaming smile on his face as he strutted across the square, humming something tuneless. Whatever might be about to occur he was so obviously revelling in it. Little people often thrive on their limited moments of power - and I wasn't referring to his height.

He marched to the front of the crowd, stopped and spun around to face the gathered townspeople. I suspected none of them were there voluntarily. The American officer and I stood at the rear of the crowd with the police sergeant and the two soldiers guarding us. I also spotted about ten heavily armed German soldiers standing around the perimeter of the square with rifles at the ready. Two military vehicles and an open topped black limousine were parked along the far end of the square on the other side of the frozen over fountain.

The small Gestapo officer stood on the church steps with his legs apart and placed his hands behind his back. He drew himself up to his full five foot two stature and puffed out his chest, you could almost feel the self-importance emanating from him in waves. When he spoke, he did so in heavily accented English. I reasoned if he couldn't speak Dutch it was probably his best way of communicating with the people here.

"People of the town of Rockanje, you are gathered here today to witness justice being served. Justice as decreed by the Third Reich, and the justice of your masters. I want the events of this morning to be a stark reminder to you that we will not tolerate insurrection. We will not tolerate terrorism. We will not tolerate any resistance whatsoever. You may choose to believe that the Third Reich is finished, that the allies will soon be here to liberate you, but that is nonsense, remove that fantasy from your heads. Even now plans are afoot to strike back and the Third Reich will ultimately be victorious. You are under our control and will remain subject to our laws. Our laws are fair and just but we will come down hard on anyone who breaks those laws. All perpetrators will be dealt with and swift justice will be served. Don't forget people of Rockanje, I am the law here."

The little man's wild eyes surveyed the silent crowd.

"Does anyone here wish to speak out in defence of the perpetrators?"

I suspected they had been here before, to speak out against their occupiers would've been akin to signing their own death warrant. Whatever they were thinking, they kept it to themselves.

I glanced up at the sergeant and spotted tears glistening on both his cheeks. He dragged the back of his hand across his nose and shook his head almost imperceptibly at me before he resumed his focus on the cobblestones at his feet.

"Bring the airmen to the front!" shouted the little man. My stomach cramped and I thought for a second I was going to faint. My lips cracked, my throat was parched and I remembered I probably hadn't had any water or food for a few hours. At least I won't shit or piss myself when they shoot me I thought. It wasn't one of my most encouraging thoughts but it was probably the only positive one I could come up with at that moment. My mother always taught me to look for a silver lining in everything.

As it turns out we weren't the intended victims in the square that auspicious day. Our time would come soon enough, but at that moment our role was merely to be witnesses to the horror that unfolded.

My American friend and I were marched to the front of the crowd and only then did we fully grasp the enormity of what was about to happen. Five chairs had been positioned in a line in front of the church, and tied to those chairs were five young people, three men and two girls. The eldest would only have been in his mid-twenties and the youngest, a girl, appeared to be no more than sixteen years of age. A mere child in anyone's eyes.

Scanning the faces in the crowd I realised it wasn't only the police sergeant who cried. Many people wept openly as old men supported their wives and mothers supported their children. I for one was still struggling to comprehend and accept the reality of the scene before me when the little Gestapo officer pulled a Luger pistol from his pocket and stepped up to face the first man at the end of the row of chairs.

I glanced around the square and watched the German soldiers cocking and shouldering their rifles, ready for any trouble. If anyone in the crowd attempted anything there would be a massacre here this day, and everyone knew it.

The little man placed the muzzle of his revolver against the young man's forehead and without hesitation squeezed the trigger. The back of the man's head exploded in a shower of blood, bone and brains, and his body, along with the chair he remained tied to smashed backwards onto the shiny cobblestones in front of the church. A high-pitched scream rang out from somewhere in the crowd but nobody moved.

The Gestapo officer smiled at the townspeople. He was performing, enjoying his work. The acrid taste of bile was at the back of my throat and I wanted to vomit. *Are there really monsters like this in the world* I thought? Unfortunately, yes.

The little officer stood in front of the next victim in the line, placed his pistol against the man's head and pulled the trigger. A commotion ensued within the crowd and I closed my eyes as the soldiers in the square sighted their rifles and squeezed their trigger fingers. My back tensed, waiting for the impact of the expected bullets, but none came. It appeared someone in the crowd had fainted.

As I opened my eyes I spotted one of the German soldiers wiping the sweat from his forehead with his sleeve. It seemed as if it was only the little Gestapo man who enjoyed the thrill of the deadly tension, the excitement of being on the edge, the joy of killing.

As he moved towards his third victim, a young lady of about twenty, she shouted out in a perfect South London accent.

"You evil bastards. You've already lost the war, your pathetic Third Reich is finished and you can't even accept it. We've won! You're just upset because you'll now have to go back to being a pathetic insignificant little man again who can't get a hard on, like you were before the war!"

For a split second I thought the young lady might have been my agent from the drop. She looked similar with her blonde hair and her tatty brown coat and shoes, but no, it wasn't her, just another pretty young girl from back home, doing her duty and dying alone in a foreign land.

As she finished speaking her eyes sought out mine, a fellow countryman, and she smiled. I knew then I'd remember that smile for as long as I had breath in my body, which as things were turning out, might not be too long.

I clenched my fists against my legs. I was helpless, there was simply no way I could do anything to save her. It was obvious I'd be gunned down before I could move more than two paces and I'd most likely end up taking the rest of the townsfolk with me too. The only thing I could do was smile back, make a connection with her, and be there for her in her final moments. Our eyes locked together for what seemed like an eternity. There was a bond, a physical closeness in those final moments that I can't find the words to describe adequately, but it was there.

That bond was shattered when the first bullet struck that amazing woman. The little man spat and foamed at the mouth, and in his anger he'd lifted his pistol and fired before he'd properly aimed it and the bullet had smashed through the young girl's throat. She remained upright, staring in terror as a fountain of blood sprayed from her ripped open artery and arced towards the assembled crowd. The second shot in her temple finished it and her body smashed to the floor to join her two comrades. Her bright red blood trickled in rivulets between the shiny cobblestones in front of the church.

I felt physically sickened and couldn't bear any more. I closed my eyes tight as the last two shots rang out. When I forced them open again five bodies and five chairs were on the floor. The little man strutted backwards and forwards in front of the carnage, ranting on as he delivered more of his self-righteous drivel to the still captive audience. His face glowed crimson and his temples pulsed. I wanted to believe it was a result of the rather public verbal humiliation he had been subjected to by the defiant

English girl. This was his moment of power, of glory, and having one of his victims dare to abuse him obviously wasn't how he had visualised the scene, so now he was trying to make up for it. I stopped listening to him and concentrated on the memory of the brave young girl's last smile.

After the murder in the square the crowd were left to recover the mutilated bodies of their loved ones. I hoped that someone would look after the English girl and treat her with the love, care and respect she deserved. I knew they would, these were good ordinary folk simply surviving as best they could in extraordinary times.

The American airman and I were marched over to the small convoy of vehicles on the southern edge of the square and placed in the rear seat of the open limousine. My new friend sat on my left as the handcuff was removed from my right wrist and snapped onto his. We settled down into the plush hide covered seats, side by side and now shackled together. We had no idea where we were being taken and no way of escaping. I realised my life was once again in the lap of the Gods.

"I never got the chance to thank you for saving me," said my fellow prisoner as the little Gestapo man climbed into the passenger seat directly in front of me and the three vehicle convoy began to make its way out of the tiny Dutch seaside town of Rockanje. His accent came over as vaguely mid-western but with a little New York twang thrown in for good measure.

"Major Glenn Miller sir, I'm honoured to meet you," he said as he reached over and shook my free right hand with his left hand. "And who might I owe my life to?"

His perfect teeth sparkled white and I found his broad smile contagious. I hoped I was smiling back, but I think I only managed a sickly grin and a dribble out of one corner of my mouth. Glenn Miller, *THE Glenn Miller*? No way!

Wait till Bonnie hears about this. For a few wonderful seconds I was lost in the moment and completely forgot where I was, and of course the danger we were in. All I could imagine in my mind's eye was dancing close with Bonnie in the Bedford Corn Exchange and having Glenn, my new pal playing *THE* big band sound of the 40s just for us. I subconsciously slipped my hand inside my flight jacket to feel the reassuring lump of the silver locket that sat inside my tunic pocket.

My dream dissolved when I realised Glenn was staring at me with a frown creasing his forehead.

"Are you OK bud?"

I dribbled again and caught it this time with my right sleeve.

"Em...yes thank you. It's just that I've never met Glenn Miller...err you before. I mean..."

Glenn's face opened up with that broad smile again.

"And I've never met anyone who's saved my life before, so we're just about evens on that I'd say?"

We both grinned and the ice was broken. I wasn't sure I was completely over being star-struck, but we certainly had more important things to worry about for now. With the rushing of the wind across the open topped car I didn't think we could be overheard, but just in case I leaned closer and whispered into Glenn's ear.

"Did you tell shit-face up front who you were?"

"Yes, but he already knew. He'd read my dog tags while I was still out."

"Ah, how did he react? Did he know who you were?"

Glenn pondered that for a moment. "Nope, I don't think he realised who I was. Perhaps he's not into my type of music."

I glanced at the back of the little man's misshapen and balding head in the front seat. "I think you're probably right on that one, and I think we should keep it that way." I suggested.

Glenn nodded.

"Did he ask what you were doing flying over the channel?"

"Yes, and I told him I was returning to my unit after a spot of leave."

We grinned at each other like a pair of naughty schoolboys in the back of a parent's car.

"So what do you think they're going to do with us?" he asked.

My heart sank at Glen's question. I knew what they should do with us, but this guy was a loose cannon and making his own rules, or at least interpreting the rules his way, and I suspected we may well not be accorded the full rights of the Geneva Convention, or any of them in fact. I didn't want to accept it, but that was the reality of the situation. This little man was violent and insane, and at the present moment in time our lives were in his hands. Once again it didn't look too good.

I shrugged my shoulders in response. Glenn nodded. We both understood the very real danger we were in.

Leaving the outskirts of the small town behind us, we had been driving for only about ten minutes along a straight and deserted county road when the driver of our car leaned on his horn at a signal from the little man. The small army Kublewagon in front slowed to a halt at the side of the lane and we pulled up behind him. On our right hand side field after empty field filled the horizon, a flat, snow covered winter landscape. To our left a large copse of snow covered pine trees stood close to the road.

I glanced over my shoulder at the soldiers jumping down from the troop carrier that had pulled up directly behind us. When I turned back the little man was opening his door to climb out of the car.

"Why have we stopped?" I asked, already guessing the answer but not willing to face the obvious truth, just yet.

The Gestapo officer pulled the dull black Lugar pistol out of his pocket, pulled the top slide back and released it with a stomach churning click that was amplified in the icy still air. He pointed the gun at us.

"Get out of the car."

I knew instinctively what was coming. Stories of downed airman being summarily executed or strung up by civilian mobs were rife within Bomber Command and no one doubted they were true. The Germans were desperate and their command structure, perhaps even their entire society, was breaking down. People like our little man here were taking charge and doing things their own, often vicious way. After all, they knew they could get away with it, there was no one they needed to account to.

I tried to think on my feet, stalling for time.

"We can't get out, we're manacled together."

The little man stared at us, unspeaking. For a moment I though he was going to shoot both of us there and then in the back of the car, but instead he turned to the driver.

"Undo their handcuffs and get them out of the car, now!"

The Gestapo officer threw a small key ring over to the driver who caught it in one hand and leaned over the side of the car towards us. After a moment or two fiddling with the lock he had the handcuffs off us.

"OK, out now!" shouted the little man. "We're letting you go."

I knew that was a lie but at that moment I saw no other option other than to do as he said. I suspected he wouldn't have hesitated in putting a bullet in each of us there and then and getting the soldiers to drag our lifeless bodies out of the car, so clinging onto life for as long as possible seemed to be the most sensible option. There was always hope that something would come up, an opportunity might present itself, however unlikely.

I pulled myself out of the car and helped Glenn out while the little man kept his gun trained on us. He said something to the driver who then reached in to the front of the car and lifted out an evil looking machine pistol with a leather strap which he slung over his neck. The machine gun hung menacingly across his chest and he rested his finger on the trigger.

"Walk, that way," the little man said as he pointed the muzzle of his pistol into the woods. I stared over the little man's head at the German soldiers who now stood around their troop carrier lighting up cigarettes. Their greatcoat collars were turned up against the cold and they stamped their feet in the snow in an attempt at reviving their circulation after the freezing ride in the back of the open truck. They looked totally miserable and they paid no attention to the scene that was being played out behind them. I suspected they had been here many times before.

I glared down into the little man's cold grey, watery eyes.

"You are violating the laws of the Geneva convention. We are prisoners of war," I said in a raised voice, loud enough for the soldiers to hear. They took no notice. Perhaps they didn't understand me, or more likely they had simply heard it all before.

The little man's lips pulled back into that unique sneer of his which exposed his crooked, yellowing teeth and made him seem even more grotesque than normal.

"I am obeying the laws of the Third Reich Englander, they are the only laws that matter to you here. Now move!"

The German driver cocked his machine pistol. The sinister metallic click sent the swarm of butterflies in the pit of my stomach into a frenzy. Glenn and I glanced briefly at each other, we didn't need to say anything, we both acknowledged that time was running out.

I took a few faltering steps as my sheepskin flying boots sank into the soft pine needle and snow-covered floor of the small wood. Everything was still, silent. Nothing moved. My breath froze on the still, icy air. *Was this where I was going to die?* I wondered. It seemed ironic, I could easily have imagined myself dying in N-Nuts at any time as we dodged flak and fighters over Europe, I really thought I was going to die in the mangled wreck of the plane as it crashed into the English Channel, and I almost welcomed death during the freezing cold and exhausting hours in the life-raft, but I didn't see this coming. I wasn't destined to die with a bullet in my back in a cold desolate wood in the middle of nowhere. Was I?

The morning sunlight filtered in through the dense trees. Snowflakes swirled in the beams of light which cut through the darkness and painted stripes on the dark floor of the wood. I stumbled over a half buried branch and only just managed to regain my balance in time as we came to a large lichen covered tree trunk laying across our path.

"Halt!" shouted the little man.

We had only been walking for a few minutes but were far enough into the wood to have lost sight of the road and the other German soldiers. It was just the four of us and I knew this was it, the sand had finally run through my hourglass. We both turned to stare at our captors.

The need for action thumped relentlessly inside my head. I had to do something and had to do it now; if there was a time for action, it had definitely come. I clenched my sweating palms and tensed myself.

As if reading my thoughts the little man lifted his right arm and pointed the pistol directly at my head while the driver lifted his machine pistol and aimed it at Glenn. There was no way we could make the four or five steps it would take to reach either of them before we both went down in a hail of bullets.

A new stream of thoughts ran feverishly through my mind. I'm not sure at which precise moment I became aware I'd already accepted my inevitable death, but it surprised me that death no longer seemed my biggest concern. My anguish focussed on the manner of my death. Would I go down at least attempting to fight back or would I simply allow these two murderers to execute us. I wanted the first of course, but when the little man ordered us to turn around again and face the fallen log, for some reason I meekly complied.

For many years after those almost surreal events in the wood, I questioned my own actions in those final moments. I had long been fascinated as to why so many people apparently walked meekly into the Nazi gas chambers or dug their own mass graves, knowing they were about to die but simply allowing themselves to be executed without putting up at least a token fight. After all, they were going to die anyway so it wouldn't have made any difference to the outcome, other than showing a final act of defiance against their aggressors. I always thought if it were me in that position I would die fighting to the last, but when it came to it, I didn't either. I simply turned as instructed, tensed my muscles and waited for the inevitable smashing of the bullets into my back. I remember wondering briefly what it might feel like as the bullets ripped through my soft tissue and how much pain I might experience before my death. I hoped it would be quick.

When the shots came it wasn't as I had expected. There was no excruciating pain. Out of the corner of my eye I saw the German driver smash into the ground beside me, half of his head missing and his one bloody remaining eye staring, unseeing. I remember gazing down at the horrific sight but my mind couldn't comprehend what my eyes were seeing. I was still waiting for the pain but nothing came.

In a daze I turned and immediately spotted the little Gestapo officer lying on his back amongst the snow and pine needles. A hole had appeared in the lower part of his chest and blood bubbled out. A bright red stain spread across his crisp white shirt as he stared uncomprehendingly up at me.

As my mind raced to try and make some sense of what was going on a soft female voice drifted into my consciousness.

"Are you OK flight lieutenant?"

Even from those few words I instantly recognised the wonderful sing-song lilt of the accent. I turned to face the mysterious Welsh lady but found the heart-warming voice completely at odds with the vision before me. She was young and exceptionally attractive, that much was obvious, but the dirt covered face, the man's blue work overalls, the thick boots and the British made Sten gun hanging across her chest suggested she was anything but sweet and adorable.

"I said are you OK flight lieutenant?" she repeated, probably already starting to wonder if I was a complete idiot.

"Err...yes I think I am," was about all I could manage.

"Listen James...it is James isn't it? We don't have much time. The other Germans will come looking when the little man and his sidekick here don't return soon, and then they'll start shooting. We need to be ready.

As she spoke I watched as three other men dressed in similar blue work overalls appeared as if from nowhere. They were armed to the teeth with various Sten guns, pistols and knives.

"Gentlemen, meet Christiaan, Arnauld and Geert. Guys, this is flight lieutenant James Cunnion of the RAF and the famous Major Glen Miller of the US Army."

I felt a little like a spare prick at a wedding as the four young resistance fighters ignored me and turned to stare at Glenn, grinning inanely at my new American pal.

Glenn rose to the occasion and kissed the young lady on both blushing cheeks before hugging each of the three young men.

I'm not sure who heard the sound of boots crunching on snow and dried pine needles first, but almost as one we dived over the felled tree trunk in front of us and used its considerable bulk to hide ourselves from view.

The young girl immediately switched into leader mode and began issuing orders in Dutch. Two of the young men melted away in the half-light through the trees to our left and right whilst the third leaned over the tree trunk and grabbed the machine pistol the German driver had dropped. As he crouched back behind the trunk he offered the gun to Glenn.

Glenn beamed as he accepted the weapon and gazed down at it almost lovingly. He brushed away some of the snow from the burnished blue metal stock with his gloved hand.

"Have you ever fired a gun before?" I whispered to him.

Glenn glanced sideways at me and grinned. "Yep of course. My Pa bought me an old BB gun when I was a young-un."

I stared at him and shook my head, which made him grin even more. He almost caressed the smooth cold metal of the German made machine gun as he turned it in his hands.

"You know, it's so soft to the touch. The engineering and the finish is like my trombone, it's truly a thing of beauty." I did wonder whether he was in fact going to actually shoot it or try to play it.

I didn't have to wonder long when the first bullets cracked and ricocheted through the wood. A burst of machine gun fire stuttered into life a few yards away to my left and a blood chilling scream came from somewhere in front of us.

The Welsh girl shoved a big service revolver she'd produced from somewhere inside her overalls into my hands and smiled.

"Here, you may need this," she said.

A second machine gun fired someway off to our right and our Welsh leader and her Dutch comrade were suddenly up and firing their Sten guns over the top of the trunk. The noise was deafening but in the openness of the wood it certainly didn't seem as bad as the cannons in the confines of my gun turret.

Glenn and I glanced at each other. He shrugged his shoulders then eased his arm out of his sling, slipped his right index finger onto the trigger of his gun, raised himself up on one knee and joined the others firing over the top of the tree. I was the last to join in the battle of the tree trunk. As I peered over the top I spotted at least five Germans soldiers lying on the open ground in front of us. One of them arched his back and screamed in agony, the other four were silent with staring, already lifeless eyes.

Razor sharp shards of wood and bark flew into the air as the thud-thud-thud of bullets hammered into the tree in front of us. Perhaps more disconcertingly I sensed the rush of air in my ears as bullets whistled over our heads. Any one of them could have had my name on it.

A German soldier dashed out from behind a tree away to our right. He was level with our barricade and had a clear shot at us. In my position on the end, my body would have been the first to stop his bullets if Glenn hadn't swung his machine-pistol around in one fluid movement, as if he was swaying with his trombone, and downed the man with a stream of 9mm shells.

"Thanks," I shouted to him as the explosions from his machine gun still screeched and reverberated inside my now temporarily disabled eardrums.

The head of the young resistance fighter at the other end of the log suddenly snapped back and his body jerked violently backwards. He didn't scream and I wasn't sure whether that was good or bad.

I didn't have time to ponder it for too long as another German popped out from behind a tree over to our left and sighted his rifle on one of us. With my arm braced against the log I took aim and squeezed the trigger. The heavy revolver bucked in my hand and I almost dropped it, but miraculously the bullet slammed into the soldier's chest and he too followed his comrades to the ground.

Then, almost as soon as the battle had started, everything fell silent.

Well, almost silent. The soldier in front of us had thankfully stopped screaming but his body was going into spasms and his moaning echoed around the small clearing. Someone else coughed and the distinct sound of air rasping through ruined lungs made the hairs on the back of my neck stand up. It wasn't pretty.

Our Welsh leader knelt on the ground beside the body of her friend, holding his smashed head in her arms while she gently and lovingly closed his eyelids over his lifeless eyes. The two remaining resistance men returned and stood silently next to her, the three of them with their eyes closed. It was as if they were each taking a moment to say a silent prayer for their fallen comrade before they returned to their own perilous and potentially short lives again. There was no crying or wailing, simply a deep respect for what the brave young man had just given. The girl laid her friend's head gently down onto the snow and got up from her knees.

"Hi, I'm sorry I never got the chance to introduce myself properly before. I'm Amy. You've probably already guessed but I'm with S.O.E."

Glenn and I both nodded and smiled at her. I hadn't guessed but it made sense now she mentioned it. She seemed so young, so innocent, but at the same time so old and so wizened. She bore the full responsibility of leading this group of local resistance fighters on her own young shoulders. She was a bloody superwoman in my eyes.

The German soldier behind us started shrieking again and writhing around in the snow. Amy gave an almost imperceptible nod to one of the young men who immediately left our group and walked over to the dying German soldier. I didn't need to turn around to witness it, the single shot that rang out and the deathly silence afterwards told me all I needed to know.

"Christiaan, Arnauld, can you collect up all the German guns and ammo you can find, and anything else that's useful, and load them onto the German truck. Can you also gather our bicycles and load them too? When you're done, please place Geert onto the truck and we'll drop him off with Father Francois, then we'll hide the vehicles and guns in the old barn for now.

The two remaining resistance fighters nodded silently as Amy barked her orders and after they'd disappeared she turned to Glenn and me.

"And what are we going to do with you gentlemen?" she asked.

That was a good question and not something I'd considered until that moment. I suppose I'd got used to the idea I wasn't actually going to be leaving that wood, let alone concern myself with 'what next?' She didn't wait for a response.

"The options are limited, things are difficult here at the moment. The remaining Germans are retreating from the allies but they are still fighting. They're being squeezed slowly into a corner here in Holland and are becoming rather desperate. They're also making life extremely difficult for the local population, as you saw. We're doing the best we can to help the allied advance, but it's not without its risks." Amy glanced down briefly at the body of Geert before she continued.

"We'll never get you across the lines to the Allies, it's not safe. The best option is to hide both of you until the allies get here and it's all over, but we've no real idea whether that's going to be weeks or months. I hope it won't be years."

I noticed Glenn grimace and shake his head. It was obvious he wasn't going to be happy hanging around in a barn waiting to be rescued.

Amy stared at each of us in turn as she ran her fingers backwards and forwards over her lips.

"There's one other possible option if you want to get home quickly?"

"We'll take it!" said Glenn.

"You haven't heard what it is yet, it's a bit risky," said Amy.

"I don't care, we'll still take it," said Glenn.

Her broad smile lit up her entire face. It was easy to see that she admired a fellow adventurous spirit.

"OK, well if you're both sure?"

I wasn't at all sure I was as convinced as Glenn, but it didn't seem like I was getting a say in the matter.

"It's simple, there's a small airfield near here that the Germans have been using, and you're a pilot," she said as she nodded in my direction. "We go and steal an aircraft and you fly yourself home."

Any grinned and her eyes sparkled.

"Yes! I like it. Simple but effective," shouted Glenn as he punched the air in front of him with his good arm.

I wanted to say to them that I didn't like the idea at all. I wanted to say that I had no recollection as to how to fly an aeroplane despite the RAF wings sewn onto my uniform. I wanted to say it was too damn dangerous. I wanted to say it was a bloody stupid idea altogether, but I said nothing. I don't know why. Obviously I should have. The whole stupid plan relied on the fact that I could fly an aeroplane and I wasn't at all sure that I could.

"Well that's that then, we're going home bud," said Glenn as he slapped me on the back. "And you're going to let me and my band play for you and your good lady. It's the least I can do."

I guess deep down that was the real reason why I didn't speak out against the plan. I'd only just realised that more than anything I wanted to get home to Bonnie, to see her beautiful face, to hold her tight in my arms, and to never let her go again. Perhaps for that, I might even be able to fly an aeroplane."

The old tummy butterflies began to swarm again, but I was in far too deep now. The hare-brained escape plan was on.

Glenn hugged Amy and kissed her on both cheeks.

"And you young lady, I'm going to put on a whole concert for you in your honour when you get home," he said, eyes sparking and his infectious smile worked its charms again.

Amy smiled, she really smiled. She knew in her heart she was probably never going to make it home, the odds were stacked against her, but getting home was her favourite fantasy, and it had just got a whole lot better.

"OK, let's go and sort your ride home," she said as she turned to head back towards the road. She'd taken only one step when she stopped and stared down at the body of the little Gestapo man. I'd forgotten about him. I followed her gaze and my stomach lurched when I realised what had stopped her in her tracks. The little man was still alive and staring up at us, watching us with his cold grey watery eyes.

The front of his suit was soaked in blood and the redness had spread almost up to the collar of his white shirt.

I couldn't work out how he was still alive, but he was. He whispered something but I couldn't make out what he said. He stared directly at Amy, a little wide eyed now. I don't know whether he even knew we were there.

He opened his mouth to speak again.

"Help me." His voice rasped in his throat but it was unmistakable this time.

"Please help me."

Amy knelt down, picked up the little man's pistol that lay in the snow beside him and slid the barrel of the gun inside his open mouth.

"This is for Evelyn," she said.

The little man's eyes widened in terror as he realised what she was about to do.

She squeezed the trigger and almost simultaneously the back of his head exploded outwards, splattering the white snow with his blood, bone and brains. His lifeless eyes still stared up at Amy, fixed in horror. She smiled and threw the pistol back on the ground next to his body. That gun had seen enough killing, she didn't want it.

Amy's colleagues went off to deliver Geert to the local priest and hide the stolen vehicles and guns while Glenn and I clambered into the black limousine for the second time that day. Amy sat up front driving and Glenn rode shotgun next to her. I sunk back into the deep red leather seats in the back and closed my eyes.

So much had happened to me over the past few days I'd almost lost track of who and where I was. How I came to be living peacefully as a librarian's assistant in the year 2015 one moment, and then find myself tossed back into this nightmare world of December 1944 the next, was still unexplained. Everything suggested that this was my real life here in 1944 but I still didn't remember anything from before my arrival in the library three days ago. Yes, there were memories of a past life fleeting tantalisingly around the edges of my consciousness, but as yet I still hadn't been able to grasp onto them. They were becoming more frequent though, which I took perhaps to be a good sign.

And what about Bonnie? My heart told me I loved her deeply, but how could I when I'd only known her for three days? But then, perhaps not, was she part of a previous life I couldn't remember?

Whatever the reality, the one thing I was certain about was that I wanted to be with her more than anything else in the world. That above all else was driving me. I reached again for the reassuring lump the locket made in my breast pocket and smiled.

Amy flung the limousine around the narrow country lanes like a rally car and Glenn whooped at every corner. I kept my eyes firmly closed.

As she drove, Amy filled us in on how the police sergeant had got word to her of our arrival on the beach and subsequent incarceration in his cells. The resistance were aware that the little Gestapo man had used that particular wood just outside town for previous executions of captured allied POWs, so as soon as they received word from the sergeant that the Gestapo planned on leaving town with the two airman immediately after the executions in the town square, they had lain in wait for them. It was fortunate that the little Gestapo officer was a creature of habit and used the same spot for his crimes, otherwise I dread to think what might have happened.

After twenty minutes or so of sheer terror, Amy pulled the stolen car off the narrow lane and hid it in a small copse of trees.

"OK boys, this is where we get out and walk. The airfield is just the other side of this wood," she said, pointing through the trees. "It's not well guarded so we shouldn't need the guns, but we'll take them just in case."

Glen and I clambered out of the car and followed Amy as she marched off through the trees. After only a minute or two we reached the edge of the wood and stood peering through a six foot high wire perimeter fence. Across the airfield, about a quarter of a mile away a small drab grey airport tower and a couple of aircraft hangers with adjacent workshops were clearly visible. I spotted one or two vehicles and a few figures moving around the buildings but they were so far in the distance it was impossible to make out any details of uniforms or markings.

What interested us more though were the three aircraft parked up on a wide-open concrete apron area much closer to where we stood. The two larger ones were painted in a dark green camouflage that in my opinion was completely voided by the long bright yellow, almost luminous painted nose. They bristled with lethal looking cannon and had a sinister aura about them, like evil serpents waiting to pounce, which in a way I supposed they were. The third and closest aircraft was a much smaller machine that resembled something like a trainer aeroplane.

"There, that's your ride home boys," said Amy.

I stared at the aircraft. Painted in a uniform dark green with a thin yellow stripe around the engine cowling at the front, it was no bigger than a family car. There were black and white crosses painted on the tops of the wings and the side of the fuselage, and swastika decals were visible on the tail plane at the rear. After the monstrous Lancaster, this machine seemed tiny, frail and vulnerable.

Glenn whistled beside me as he stared up at the six foot high fence. I followed his gaze upwards and spotted the coils of razor sharp barbed wire running along the top.

"That's not gonna be easy," he said.

I had to agree with him on that. I didn't fancy my chances of getting over there unscathed, and I had one more useable arm than he did.

"Come on boys, let's not hang about," whispered Amy. She was on her hands and knees in the snow, snipping through the chain link fence with her wire cutters as if it were no more than paper.

"Like a girl guide, always come prepared," she said. What a girl. I swear she'd make some lucky guy a wonderful wife one day.

I watched her crawl through the hole she'd made and then stop dead in her tracks. Without standing she backed up through the fence again.

"OK, there's someone next to the aircraft, I think he's a mechanic or something. It's a good thing actually as I was wondering how we'd get hold of the keys for the aircraft if it was locked down. We don't have to worry about that now, he's your ticket home."

I didn't quite see how having to deal with a German mechanic was a good thing, but Amy seemed to be happy about it and that was good enough for me.

"You wait here for a few moments. I'll deal with him first then I'll call you over when the coast is clear. Look out for my signal."

Amy handed her Sten gun to me, unclipped the holster from her belt, removed her service revolver and handed the empty holster to Glenn. She tucked the pistol into the belt in the small of her back and turned to face us.

"How do I look?"

I stared at this beautiful, confident young lady standing before us. Wisps of blond hair partially covered her dirt streaked face. Her deep blue eyes sparkled with excitement and her naturally red lips spread wide across her face in a heart-melting smile.

Glenn chuckled next to me. "My dear, you look ready to take on the world."

"I'm just glad you're on our side," I added.

Amy chuckled with us, then without any further hesitation she crawled back through the hole in the fence and disappeared.

Glenn and I peered through the fence as Amy sauntered over to the aircraft. I swear I heard her whistling.

"Let's get through the fence and keep low on the other side. We'll get a better view and we'll be ready to go when Amy calls us," I whispered to Glenn.

My bulky flight jacket forced me to slither through on my stomach but we both managed to get through OK and sat on the snow covered grass on the other side. From our new position we were able to see the German mechanic Amy had mentioned sitting on the bonnet of a small tractor parked on the far side of the small aeroplane. Amy stood in front of him and they were chatting.

"She's a little close isn't she?" said Glenn. Her tactic was obvious, she was flirting heavily and the lad was doomed, even if he didn't know it yet. It was just a matter of time.

We both stared as Amy stepped forward and brushed her fingers against the mechanic's arm.

"He's done for," said Glenn.

After five minutes we spotted the mechanic step up onto the wing and pull open the Perspex canopy door on their side. He stepped inside and held Amy's hand as she joined him in the cockpit. We endured another tense few minutes as we waited for something to happen, unable to see anything inside the cockpit from our vantage point.

"Do you think she's OK?" whispered Glenn.

I immediately thought of the way she'd dispatched the little Gestapo officer.

"Would you want to be in there with her knowing how she operates?" I asked.

Glenn frowned for a moment before a wide grin spread across his face.

"Actually yes I would," he said.

We grinned at each other like a couple of virgin schoolboys.

Another five minutes passed before we spotted Amy again. She eventually stepped out onto the wing of the small aircraft as brazen as anything and waved us over.

"Whata girl," said Glenn as we dashed across the snow-covered grass. Amy stood on the wing and beckoned us up as we approached her.

"OK boys, get straight in, no time to waste,"

Glenn handed his machine pistol to Amy before he clambered into the tiny cockpit and settled himself down into the right hand seat. The cockpit was about the same size as a small family saloon car with two single leather covered seats up front and a double seat behind. As I stepped in I couldn't avoid spotting the young German mechanic lying on the rear seat. He had a trickle of fresh blood running across his forehead and his eyes were closed. Amy had also tied the seatbelt around him in a tight knot.

"Is he dead?" I asked.

She glanced down at the young man's body.

"No, but he's going to have a hell of a headache when he wakes up. Give him my apologies will you? He seemed like a nice guy, I didn't really want to hurt him."

"Are we taking him with us then?" asked Glenn.

"Of course, we can't leave him lying around here, he'd probably die of hypothermia, and anyway, if you get into any difficulties with the aeroplane it might be handy having an engineer on board?"

Amy smiled but I wasn't totally sure she was joking. My butterflies swarmed again and the knots in the pit of my stomach were so tight they were painful.

"Also, with him gone they might suspect he's the one who's stolen the plane. It might put them off your scent for a while, at least until they discover the hole in the fence that is," she added.

I glanced over at the two menacing looking fighter planes parked next to us.

"Don't you think they'll scramble those as soon as they see us take off? We'll be shot down in minutes," I said.

Amy grinned at us again.

"No, Karl here told me they have no fuel left, those planes haven't flown for weeks. The little bit of fuel they have they save for this aircraft to move officers and some supplies in and out. In fact it's just been serviced and refuelled this morning and there's water and snacks in the back, apparently they were planning on picking up someone this afternoon. Good timing eh? Anyway, Karl reckons this one has a range of over six hundred miles so you should be good to get home."

As I settled into the soft leather seat I handed Amy's Sten gun up to her.

"Thanks," she said, "here you take this, you may need it if he wakes up."

Amy handed me the heavy service revolver.

"Are you sure you won't need it?"

"No, we've got plenty of guns, it's the ammo we need."

I nodded and slipped the revolver into the side pocket of my flight jacket.

"I'm going to dash off now boys, I don't want to get caught hanging around here. Karl showed me the start button; see that black button in the middle of the control panel? Well that's it. He also said that's the runway right in front of us. You turn left onto it and then you're off. He told me the fighters were parked here for a quick getaway, apparently they could have them up within five minutes of the scramble signal, when they had fuel that is."

I stared down at the control panel's array of dials, switches and buttons, and then up at the runway in front of us. I didn't think I could do this.

"Oh, and I nearly forgot," Amy said as she pulled something out of her blue overalls and handed it to me. It was the small green silk bag the WAAFs had presented me with back in Tempsford. "I think it's your escape kit, it might come in handy. The police sergeant who took it from you managed to get it over to me as soon as he knew what we were planning. He's a good man in a very difficult position."

I had to agree with that, he certainly was, and we probably owed him our lives.

I opened the bag and pulled out the folded silk map and the tiny compass I'd used in the life-raft. The map was surprisingly detailed and would definitely be useful. I handed both items across to Glenn.

"OK boys, that's it, time to go. Hopefully I'll see you again one day back in Blighty when this lot's over. Oh, and Glen, don't forget that concert in my honour you promised?"

"You betcha, that's a promise Amy. You just get home safely," said Glenn. For once he wasn't smiling.

"I will," she said as she leaned into the cockpit and kissed each of us on the lips.

Amy pulled the cockpit canopy door over and slammed it shut. She gave us a wave from the wing before she jumped down and reappeared at the front of the aircraft holding up the wooden chocks from under the wheels. She threw them to one side, gave us a thumbs up, and was gone. Glenn and I stared after her for a few moments. Neither of us said anything but I'm sure we both experienced the same feeling of loss and vulnerability now that she was no longer with us.

"How can one so young be such a remarkable leader?" whispered Glenn.

I didn't want to answer in case my voice broke and betrayed my emotions, so I simply shrugged and began to scrutinise the controls in front of me as if I knew what I was doing. I'm not sure who I was fooling.

There was a tall metal control stick that came up from the floor in-between my legs. Glenn had a similar stick on his side. There were large pedals affixed to the floor in front of both of us, a wheel down on my left between the seat and the side of the cockpit, and a bewildering array of dials, switches and levers scattered all over the control panel in front of us. I stared at each dial in turn but had no idea what any of them might be for. There were labels affixed to each item, but just to make things more difficult they were all printed in German. My heart filled my mouth. I was certain I wasn't going to be able to do this. I couldn't fly us home.

"OK what are you waiting for James, take us home," Glenn quipped.

I leaned forward in my seat and covered my face with my hands.

"Glenn, I'm not sure how to tell you this, but I don't know how to fly this thing."

There was no response from Glenn so I turned to look at him. He stared at me, eyes wide.

"What do you mean you don't know how to fly this? Because it's a different type of aeroplane? Because everything is written in German? What do you mean?

I fiddled with the stick in front of me.

"No, because I don't know how to fly."

Glenn frowned. His confusion was obvious.

"But you're a pilot in the RAF, what do you mean you don't know how to fly?"

"OK, to put it more accurately then, I don't remember how to fly."

His frown deepened.

"What I mean is I think I've developed amnesia or something. I can't remember any of it. Something must have happened to me recently and I can't remember, I really can't."

I wasn't going to bother getting into an explanation of the library and my life in 2015. I didn't think that would help matters much. As it was, I imagined Glenn was probably going to burst a gasket any second now, knowing we'd got so far and were on the verge of escaping, only to be tripped up at the last moment by my incompetence.

But he didn't. He slapped me on the leg and laughed out loud.

"Ah is that all. I thought it was something really bad," he said.

I stared at him. Perhaps he hadn't heard me.

"Glenn, I said I can't remember how to fly. All these dials and levers, they mean nothing to me."

He glanced across the consul in front of us and then back at me again. A wide grin was plastered across his face.

"I know. I heard you. But you were a flyer right?"

I thought about that for a moment.

"Yes, everyone tells me I was, and perhaps even a pretty good one."

Glenn slapped me on the leg again. It was a little annoying.

"Even better then. So, you can do this, it's just that you've temporarily forgotten how to for whatever reason?"

I fiddled with the control stick. "Yes, I suppose that about sums it up."

Glenn rubbed his hands together and smiled.

"OK, that happens to me all the time. Let's get this baby started up, get the heater going and we'll be off." He reached across and pushed the black start button Amy had pointed out previously.

The engine coughed twice and a puff of black smoke escaped from beneath the engine cowling, but the single yellow tipped propeller didn't turn. Glenn pushed the button again and this time the engine coughed, fired, coughed again and the propeller rotated once.

"Third time lucky?" he said.

And it was. On the third press the engine fired, spat, and finally coughed into life. The propeller began to turn slowly and the vibrations ran through my seat and the control stick in front of me. It wasn't anything like the roaring of the four Merlin engines on the Lancaster, but in the tiny cockpit it was almost impossible to hear each other over the noise of the engine in that confined space. Glenn reached down between the seats and retrieved two flying helmets with earphones and intercoms attached. I pulled mine over my head and adjusted the strap to fit. The stale musty smell of the canvas made me want to gag.

Glenn's voice crackled through my earphones almost as soon as I'd put them on.

"Great, now let's sort you out," he said with a lot more confidence than I felt.

"I have that amnesia problem all the time when I'm playing. Time and time again I've stepped up onto the stage and frozen. For the life of me I couldn't play a flipping note on my trombone, couldn't remember how to, and watching the audience staring at me, waiting for the maestro to begin just made it ruddy worse."

"So what did you do?"

I closed my eyes, took some deep breaths, relaxed and let the old muscle memory take over."

"That's it?"

Yes, and it works."

"You mean you want me to close my eyes, take some deep breaths and fly this thing?"

"Yes."

"And with my eyes closed?"

"Yes, if you have to. Trust me, it'll work. Just relax."

I spotted a tractor emerging from one of the aircraft hangars in the distance. I needed to bloody well do something, and Glenn's suggestion was probably all we had right now, apart from ditching the aeroplane and trying to find Amy again. I didn't fancy doing that on foot in this weather, and I'm not sure I'd be able to face her anyway after all she'd done to get us here.

I wanted to go home. I think that's what finally made up my mind. So I rested my hands on the stick, placed my feet gently on the rudder bars and closed my eyes. I listened to the sound of the engine and felt the vibrations throbbing through the control stick. It was a familiar sensation, one I remembered so well. Somewhere in the hidden recesses of my mind something stirred.

I opened my eyes and grinned at Glenn.

"I remember something."

He seemed distracted, peering out of the cockpit window.

"Good, good, that's great, excellent, just close your eyes and do it again will you?" he said without looking at me. The slightly urgent tone in his voice wasn't lost on me. Something was happening out there and I probably didn't want to know what.

I closed my eyes and as soon as I began to feel the vibrations the memory stirred again. This time I kept my eyes closed and relaxed, breathing in, breathing out and concentrating on the feel of the little aeroplane. I reached forward with my right hand and pulled a lever on the control panel down one notch.

"Flaps down," I whispered to myself.

Reaching down with my left hand I found the top of the wheel next to my seat and made sure it was clicked into place at the top.

"Trim neutral," I whispered again. It almost seemed as if someone else was talking.

I reached forward again with my right hand and released the park break. The little aircraft jolted forward and started to roll. I opened my eyes and immediately applied some pressure to the peddle with my left foot. We eased around onto the main runway in front of us.

"Great work my boy, great work," came Glenn's whispered voice through my earphones. I wondered why he was whispering. "Let's not hang around, strike while the iron's hot as they say. Go for it."

I spotted the reason for Glenn's insistence we get a move on. A small Kublewagon with German markings raced across the grass towards us. I tried to ignore it as best I could and placed my right hand on the lever that stuck out from the middle of the control panel between our two seats. I sensed the power in the engine through that small lever as I eased it in.

The engine pitch changed and the propeller whirled faster and faster until it disappeared, leaving just the trace of a yellow arc visible around the nose of the tiny aeroplane. We began to move forward and pick up speed as we headed off down the long runway into the wind. I can only imagine the grin plastered over my face as I pushed the throttle lever in all the way and placed both hands back on the control stick.

"Yeeehaw!" shouted Glenn.

Yeeehaw indeed I thought as we raced past the Kublewagon that was attempting to intercept us on the runway. The dial in front of me said the engine was at 2,200 rpm when I pulled back on the control stick and the aircraft's nose eased up into the air. We were airborne.

Almost in recognition of that fact my earphones crackled into life again.

"Kontrollturm an B-F-einer-null-acht, Kontrollturm an B-F-einer-null-acht, bitte kommen. Bitte kommen. Was tun Sie?"

Glenn and I stared at each other.

"That'll be the Jerries getting all hot under the collar because we've nicked their aeroplane?" I said.

I saw his eyes crease up in what I imagined was a grin.

"Kontrollturm an B-Feiner-null-acht, Kontrollturm an B-F-einer-null-acht, bitte kommen. Karl, sind Sie das?...Karl?"

"I'm getting the distinct impression they think we're Karl?" Glenn said.

I glanced over my shoulder at the still unconscious mechanic in the back.

"Yep, poor bloody bastard."

Glenn peered out of his side cockpit window.

"Looks like we've started a bit of a commotion down there, people are running around everywhere. I bloody hope they don't take it out on the locals," he said.

I did too, but for now I had other things to occupy my mind, like trying to fly the damn plane and get us home safely before the Jerries sent someone after us.

I banged my left knee against a lever with a white knob on the end which reminded me I needed to pull the landing gear up. I eased the lever upwards and the mechanism of the landing gear whirred beneath our seats. I hoped there wasn't anything else I'd forgotten.

Now we just needed to be heading in the right direction.

"Glenn, we took off towards the west so we're going in roughly the right direction I think, but can you have a peek at that escape map of mine and try to work out a rough heading back to Bedford?"

"Yes sir!"

Glenn opened the silk map on his lap and scrutinised it for a moment. He placed the small compass on top of the map and squinted at the tiny face.

"My eyes aren't what they used to be, but I think it's around two-eight-zero."

"OK, let's take that and see if we can recognise anything," I said as I banked the aircraft slightly to port to bring the compass on the control panel in line with Glenn's heading. Even though I said so myself, flying felt like the most natural thing in the world. I was pretty impressed with myself, but probably more impressed with Glenn at that moment for making me trust myself.

The Dutch coastline disappeared behind us as we headed out over the Channel. I breathed an inward sigh of relief but I knew we weren't out of the fire yet.

"I'll keep us down at about 500 feet. That should keep us out of the radar on both sides of the channel and will hopefully also prevent any build-up of ice."

Glenn turned to stare at me. "Both sides?"

"Yes, we're in a bloody German plane with Nazi markings all over it remember. We're more likely to be shot down by our own side than the Germans now."

"I hadn't thought of that," he said.

As it turned out our flight across the Channel was thankfully uneventful. I can only imagine that no German fighters were available to give chase. *If they had, we wouldn't have stood a chance in this kite* I thought.

We flew over the English coast just north of the port of Felixstowe, which I realised was a big mistake as soon as the guns opened up on us. The now familiar puffs of black smoke appeared around us and even over the noise of the little Messerschmitt's engine I heard the rattle of the pieces of shell bouncing off the fuselage. Fortunately, as we were flying so low the guns hadn't ranged in on us and fired high.

"That's close!" shouted Glenn.

It was. I pushed the throttle in and pulled back on the stick, banking starboard. The little aircraft screamed in protest but we twisted and turned our way upwards, somehow managing to avoid all the exploding shells around us. At about 3,000 feet I glanced down and behind us. The enormous port of Felixstowe receded into the distance and its fierce ring of ack-ack guns fell silent once more.

"Phew!" said Glenn.

"Yep, bloody phew indeed," I whispered.

As our altitude increased I spotted a large city away to our left. Instinctively I knew it was Ipswich. I'd never been there but from somewhere deep in my memory I recognised it from up here as a marker, an old friend.

I banked to starboard again, deciding I wouldn't risk the city's air defences in this German plane.

"We'll keep to the countryside," I said. Glenn nodded, after the flak at Felixstowe I doubted he needed any further convincing.

For the next twenty minutes we flew over the patchwork of snow covered fields and hedgerows of the English Home Counties. The mid-winter afternoon sun hung low in the sky and the shadows lengthened across the myriad of little farms and villages beneath us as we made our way home. The familiar countryside stirred memories deep inside me. Good memories, wonderful memories in fact. I felt exhilarated, roaming free across the sky.

By either luck or design we found ourselves passing just south of Huntingdon and St. Neots and approaching Tempsford airdrome from the northeast. I recognised it immediately. From the air it appeared for all the world like a collection of old ruined farm buildings on a disused airfield. Unless you were aware of its existence and knew what landmarks to look out for you would never have spotted it, which was exactly the way the air ministry had planned it. Britain's most secretive airfield.

When the attack came I was almost paralysed by the violence of it. Bullets smashed through the Perspex canopy and thudded into the control panel in front of us, destroying most of the dials and switches in a mass of mangled steel and shattered glass. Large holes opened up along the flimsy fuselage of the tiny Messerschmitt and wisps of black smoke began to billow out from under the engine cowling.

The lone Hurricane with RAF roundels beneath its wings roared overhead and banked, obviously intending to turn and finish us off.

Like a rookie I'd been flying straight and level, lulled into a false sense of security over the familiar landscape and not scanning the skies. We were in a bloody German aircraft, what else should we have expected?

"Glenn, get a mayday out on that radio, and flipping quick!"

Glenn stared down at the German marked radio directly in front of him.

"Any idea what frequency we need?"

"117.9, standard RAF tower frequency, and try 118.1, that's the distress frequency." My mouth moved and it was definitely me talking, but I'd no idea where the information came from. I had no time to ponder the issue anyway as the Hurricane turned and lined up for his next run.

Glenn fiddled with the dial in front of him. "Mayday! Mayday!" He shouted into his mask.

I stared in horror as the Hurricane dived down at us. We were sitting ducks, but I waited, holding my breath. Just when I imagined the pilot's gloved thumb would be pressing down on the button to fire his cannon I corkscrewed the Messerschmitt down to port. The tracer fired over the top of us missing us by inches, and the Hurricane disappeared from view. But I knew he wasn't done with us yet.

As I struggled to pull the shattered aircraft up from its twisting dive a female voice crackled in my ears.

"Tempsford tower here, receiving your mayday. Who are you and what is your position?"

I flicked the microphone switch on my mask to talk.

"It's flight lieutenant James Cunnion of 617 squadron. We're in a stolen Messerschmitt 108 and there's a bloody Hurricane trying to blow us out of the sky. Call him off!"

There was no response for a few seconds. I managed to pull the tiny machine out of its dive and levelled off at about a thousand feet. I peered down at the landscape and even under its blanket of snow I could make out the detail of the now familiar airfield below us.

"What's your location flight lieutenant?"

"Right above you and you're going to get our burning remains on top of your bloody tower in the next few seconds if you don't do something."

Silence again.

"OK flight lieutenant. Making contact with the Hurricane now."

I glanced over my left shoulder and spotted the Hurricane already screaming down onto us like an avenging bird of prey. There was nothing else I could do, nowhere to go. I tensed and waited for the impact of the bullets which would undoubtedly end both our lives.

The Hurricane roared overhead but didn't fire. As it levelled in front of us it dipped its wings and then banked again for a turn. I remember breathing a sigh of relief when I realised he'd been contacted in the nick of time. Glenn turned in his seat and stared at me. The part of his face that was visible above the mask looked ashen. I suspected mine might have been a similar colour too.

Glancing down I saw half a dozen figures running out from the control tower and peering up at us while a fire truck emerged from the old hangar and raced around the perimeter track towards the runway.

Thick black smoke billowed out from the engine and poured into the cockpit through the smashed canopy. It was obvious the aircraft wasn't going to remain aloft for much longer and we had no parachutes on board, so I had to get it down, and quickly.

The Hurricane eased alongside our smashed machine and the pilot gave a wave. For a moment I considered giving him the finger, but managed to stop myself and waved back. It wasn't his fault, I guess I would've done the same in his position.

As I banked the struggling aircraft around to approach the airfield, the Hurricane circled above us. He could have left but I suspect he didn't want to miss the show. I hoped that maybe he felt just a little guilty.

I pushed the flaps down a couple of notches and lowered the landing gear as I lined the aircraft up with the runway. No sooner had we began our descent to safety the engine coughed, banged and coughed again before it finally expired in a belch of black smoke and flame. The propellers ground to a halt and we were gliding in.

The runway rushed up to meet us and my stomach gave a lurch when I thought we were going to drop short. At the last moment I pulled the nose up and our wheels skidded onto the smooth concrete. The light dusting of snow on the runway caused us to slip and sway for a bit before we finally slipped off the side of the runway and nosedived into a bank of snow.

Glenn knocked his head on the smashed canopy, which opened up the barely healed gash across his forehead. Bright red blood ran down his face as he tore off his mask and grinned at me.

"Well done son, well done. I knew you could do it."

The nose of the little aircraft was buried deep in the snow drift and any flames there might have been were out now for sure. Lumps of snow dropped into the cockpit through the smashed canopy as we hung in our seats, suspended by our harnesses. I turned and grinned back at my new pal. We'd made it. We were home safe and sound. Well almost.

It didn't take long for the fire crew to prize open what remained of the canopy and manhandle us out of the cockpit. As soon as we were out and standing trembling on the runway a short stocky mechanic sergeant I recognised immediately stepped over and shook both our hands.

"Hello Percy, how are you?" I said.

"Hello sir, more to the point how are you? That was some ruddy entrance," he said, glancing up at the Hurricane still circling above and then staring down at the wrecked German aircraft.

I peered up at the Hurricane and waved both my arms in the air. The pilot waggled his wings in response, banked his thoroughbred machine and roared off into the distance.

The rescue team seemed quite concerned about the gash on Glenn's head and insisted we get into the fire truck. The driver and Percy accompanied us back to the Gibraltar House building for debriefing while the rest of the crew set about examining the downed enemy aircraft.

The first thing I noticed as we jumped down from the fire truck cab was my snow covered Norton still parked outside the officer's mess. The second was the welcome committee waiting for us outside the CO's office.

"James! James! Christ man, you made it!" shouted the grey whiskered officer as he strode towards us with his arms outstretched. I was a little surprised when he hugged me like a prodigal son. Behind him stood about twenty uniformed aircrew, WAAFs and ground crew. I scanned the group and my heart sank when I didn't spot Bonnie. A beaming Jackie was easy to spot though, standing at the front just behind the CO.

"Err...let me introduce my friend, Glenn...Glenn Miller," I said as I untangled myself from the CO.

I glanced at my new buddy. "Glen, this is Group Captain Fielding, our CO."

The CO stared up at Glenn, mouth agape. It might have been the still bleeding gash across his forehead, but somehow I didn't think so.

"Glen...Glen Miller...*the* Glen Miller?"

Glen wiped the blood away from his eyes and grinned. "Yep, the one and only."

"But...you've been missing since the 15th. Where've you been and how did you meet up with James here?" The CO stared at me and a frown creased his forehead.

"And...James...what happened to you? We thought you went down over the channel. Larry says he didn't see you get out, he didn't see your chute."

"Larry? Did he make it, is he here?" I asked.

The CO smiled. "No, but I've spoken with him on the telephone from a field hospital in Bruges. His leg was shot up and broken but they said they'll have him back here in time for Christmas."

Of course I desperately wanted to know what had happened to the rest of the crew of N-Nuts, but as the CO hadn't offered the information I sensed this wasn't an appropriate time or place for it to be discussed. The question was left unspoken and as the CO's moist eyes met with mine he smiled and gave an almost imperceptible shake of his head. The moisture evaporated from my mouth and bile rose in my throat. It seemed the rest of them hadn't made it.

"Major Miller, I'm so terribly sorry. Let's get you to the medic to have a look at that head before we do any more talking."

He turned to face the group behind him. "Will one of you accompany the flight lieutenant and major Miller to the sick bay please?"

Jackie stepped forward before anyone else could even think about it. She grabbed Glenn by the hand and smiled up at him. It was a little unprofessional but he didn't seem to mind.

"Come this way Major Miller, let's get you fixed."

As we followed Jackie the CO called after us.

"I'll join you both there soon for a debrief?"

I didn't respond, I had absolutely no intention whatsoever of going to the sick bay.

"Jackie, where is Bonnie?" I asked, not knowing whether I wanted to hear the answer or not.

Jackie stopped walking and turned towards me. She wasn't smiling, but neither did she appear angry. A frown creased her forehead.

"James, she thinks you're dead. She was in a bit of a state and the CO gave her a few days off. I know she's not on the base but I don't know where she'll have gone? I believe her family live over in Berkhampsted, that's not too far. Perhaps she's gone there?"

I could have cried with joy. The sense of despair I'd been carrying around in the pit of my stomach ever since that tiff with Bonnie now turned into elation which threatened to burst from my chest. I needed to get to her.

Jackie stared at me but a beautiful smile now spread across her face. She still held onto Glenn's hand.

Glenn grinned.

"Well, what are you waiting for boy?" he said.

I grinned back at him for the briefest of moments before I dashed across to my snow covered motorbike, hoping and praying it would start after all this time.

Chapter Ten - Bedford Dec 16th 1944

I needn't have worried, the old Norton started on the first kick. My goggles and gloves were still in the saddlebag where I'd left them, was it only three days ago now? The gloves were frozen solid but I managed to force them on.

The ride through the dark snow covered lanes was a bit hair-raising and I nearly came a cropper at a few corners. Thankfully I still had on my sheepskin lined flight jacket and boots and I'd endured a lot more cold than that over the past few days, I was almost immune to it. I was back in England, safe and on my way to Bonnie, which was all that really mattered.

I knew where I'd find her too, the one place where she felt truly relaxed, surrounded by the books she loved. The library. I somehow sensed it was right too, I was being drawn back to that library for some reason.

The clock on the tower of the Church of St Paul showed five o'clock as I sped past the darkened square and roared up a still busy Harper Street, full of people making their way home from their daily toil. I left the Norton, engine hot and ticking in its usual place around the side of the old library and raced up the slush covered stone steps. The double doors were still open.

I was still running when I emerged into the dimly lit library and careered into the front desk.

"James," shouted the girl seated behind the front desk.

"Hi Sarah," I responded. "Have you seen..."

"Bonnie!" she screeched before I even had time to finish the sentence.

"Bonnie!"

There were a few people in the library and they were all now staring at the commotion at the front desk.

"What is it Sarah?" asked Bonnie as she emerged from the cupboard doorway behind the front desk.

She was wearing the same cotton floral dress I had seen her in the last time I was in the library, but this time she had a baggy, drab grey coloured woollen cardigan on over the top. Her red hair still hung in those wonderful ringlets around her shoulders and she looked as stunning as ever, but even her tortoiseshell glasses couldn't hide the tired, lifeless look in those deep emerald coloured eyes. Her pale lips parted as her eyes tried to accept the ghost standing before her.

"James? James!"

She very nearly vaulted over the desk in her attempt to reach me. The books piled on the edge of the desk crashed to the floor as Bonnie swept past and flung her arms around my neck, pressing her face into my chest.

"Oh James," she said again as she leaned back to stare into my eyes. Warm tears flowed freely down both of her cheeks and I smiled as I attempted to straighten her fogged glasses.

We held hands and gazed at each other. There was no need for words and I wasn't at all sure I was going to be able to speak anyway without betraying my emotions to the small crowd of library users who had gathered around us.

We hugged and kissed, smiled and cried in each other's arms and I don't believe there was a dry eye in the library. No one explained what had happened to the gathered crowd, no one needed to. A young airman back from the dead and a young lady in his arms could really only tell one story.

Eventually Sarah had to usher the reluctant people out and close up the main doors.

I sank down into the worn soft leather folds of an old Chesterfield sofa and Bonnie eased herself down onto my lap, arms still around my neck. It didn't look like she was going to let me go anytime soon, and I wasn't complaining. We still hadn't spoken a word to each other.

445

"I'm just going to pop the kettle on and make you two a nice cuppa, then I'm going to need to get off, I've got my dressmaking class in half an hour," said Sarah as she left the two grinning idiots on the sofa.

The tea duly arrived and Sarah left. I don't think either Bonnie or I really noticed.

It was some time before I spotted the elderly little man in the dark Crombie coat and the black felt Homburg hat sitting in the armchair facing us. His wide beaming smile lit up his entire face and I'd say his expression had smug and satisfied written all over it.

I kissed Bonnie's forehead and gently tapped her shoulder.

"We have a guest my love."

Bonnie glanced up at me and then turned to stare at the stranger in the chair opposite.

"Ah, hello Mr Albright, I'm terribly sorry but the library is actually closed now," she said.

The old man continued smiling at us.

"I know Bonnie, I hate to interrupt your moment together but I needed a word with you and James here."

His voice wasn't strange or sinister; in fact it had an almost comforting sort of sing-song Norfolk lilt to it. Bonnie slid off my lap and sunk down on the sofa next to me, still grasping my hand in hers.

"Who are you?" I asked.

"Benjamin, Benjamin Albright at your service," he answered, as if that somehow explained everything.

The old man removed the ill-fitting hat from his small head and placed it on the thick leather arm of the chair next to him. His slicked back hair was still almost blue-black in colour whilst his complexion was a stark white in contrast. He was obviously a man who had spent most of his life indoors, away from the sun.

"But who are you really," I asked again.

447

Benjamin Albright smiled and placed the tips of his delicate white fingers together in his lap, as if he were about to pray.

"Ah, yes, straight to the nub of the matter eh James? No fannying about, I like that."

He leaned forward and picked up one of the delicate china cups off the small table in front of us.

"Would you mind awfully if I stole one of your cups of tea? I hate to see a good cup of tea go cold and my throat is parched."

I had forgotten all about the tea Sarah had left for us.

"Yes please go ahead Mr Albright, be my guest," said Bonnie, smiling at the old man who was obviously no stranger to her. He sipped his tea and sank back even deeper into the comfortable old armchair.

"I so love a nice cup of Earl Grey don't you?" he said. He was old, maybe in his seventies, and yes he was certainly a little eccentric, but his eyes betrayed a sharpness most people didn't possess, even at a much younger age. He was staring at both of us, thinking, analysing.

I nodded but didn't say anything. I was still waiting for an answer.

The old man's eyes locked onto mine and he smiled. "Yes James, I do believe you deserve an explanation."

Bonnie turned to stare at me, a frown creasing the soft skin of her forehead.

"What explanation James, what are you two talking about?"

I squeezed her warm hand. "I'm not too sure either Bonnie but I'm hoping we're going to find out a few things from Mr Albright here."

Bonnie turned to stare at the old man, her frown still in place.

"Yes Bonnie, James is correct. I do have a story to tell both of you."

Bonnie flicked a questioning glance at me and then stared back at the old man. He had our full attention.

His smile disappeared as he laced his long white fingers together in his lap. "I'm a time guardian."

"You're a what?" I asked, not sure I had heard right.

"I'm a time guardian," he repeated. "That's my job, that's what I am."

His alert eyes darted from one to the other and back again, searching for a reaction.

"Go on," I said.

I stared as the old man took a deep breath and heard a deep sigh as he exhaled. He seemed as if he was about to recite a story he had told many times before.

"I don't wish to sound too grand but to explain what I do and why this involves you I need to explain a little about the workings of the universe. But first let me ask, do you understand anything of Einstein's theorems of time and space?"

Bonnie shook her head.

"A little," I said, "but only from what I've read in books and magazines, I'm certainly no expert."

The old man nodded before continuing.

"This whole story concerns the apparent flow of time. The best way to describe this to you is if you can imagine the flow of time as an infinitely long river meandering through a valley. The river twists and turns naturally here and there and loops back on itself in many places. Like time, the river is always running or flowing in one direction, sometimes it seems to speed up and sometimes it slows down, just as time does from different viewpoints, but it is always flowing in one direction. Now, it's the loops that are our main interest."

I didn't see yet how any of this related to my recent experiences but the old man was obviously trying to explain an extremely complex theory in very simple terms. I suspected all would be revealed soon enough.

"When the flow of time loops back on itself, sometimes connections are made between one loop and the next one. We call these connections between the loops wormholes, and there are lots and lots of them. You see, the fabric of space and time is rather like a sponge with a myriad of holes and tunnels running through it, and whenever the flow of time loops back on itself these sponge like holes form wormholes from one point in time to another. Are you following me so far?"

I thought I understood it, but still wasn't quite ready to accept I believed it.

Bonnie nodded. "And these wormholes are large enough for a human to walk through?" she asked.

The old man placed the tips of his fingers together again in his lap.

"Not all of them no," he said. "Many are too small to even see, but quite a few are large enough to step through, although there is no real sense of walking through a tunnel or anything like that, it's more like a porthole, or a hole in the fabric of time you step through. One moment you are in one time and in the next instant you are in another period of time, or in another section of the river of time if you like."

"But wait a minute, are you really saying you've found these wormholes or portals or whatever you call them and actually stepped through, to another time?" Bonnie asked.

I turned to face Bonnie. "Yes he is," I said. "And I have too."

Bonnie's mouth opened a little as her eyes flicked between the old man and me. That frown had returned too.

"Yes Bonnie, James is correct. I've stepped through many hundreds of time wormholes in my life and James has experienced it twice so far."

The old man glanced at me and I nodded.

"So, if there are so many of them, why don't more people see these holes and step through them constantly? Why haven't I seen one?" asked Bonnie.

The old man smiled and sat up a little in his chair. He was enjoying himself now.

"Well Bonnie, there are good reasons for that. You see, these holes linking one point in time with another have existed since our universe was formed a little under fourteen billion years ago. As the flow of time meanders and bends so more wormholes are created, and just like a river, sometimes the flow of time straightens and wormholes disappear. There are holes all over the universe right now linking one point in time with another. Similarly, there are holes all over this marvellous planet of ours. They were there before the Earth was formed and probably most will still be there long after the planet has gone. Remember, they exist in the very fabric of time, regardless of whatever else gets in the way."

"But that still doesn't answer why no one, apart from you, sees them?" said Bonnie.

The old man leaned forward and placed his empty cup back on the table in front of him.

"Ah yes. That's a very good question Bonnie, and not one to which we really have an answer. The holes exist everywhere; there are literally hundreds across the United Kingdom alone, but for some reason not everyone can see them. In actual fact let me correct that, no one can actually see them, but a very few people - me included - can sense them when we come close. We don't yet understand why some people can and most can't, that's just the way it seems to be."

I thought back to the strange fizzing sensation I experienced in my head whenever I got close to the stockroom doorway back in 2015, before the old man pushed me back through to 1944.

"The wormholes have been known about for centuries. Throughout history, many cultures from all over the world have made mention of these mysterious places where people disappear or reappear with strange supernatural tales of gods or mysterious animals and peoples. These events caused superstition and unrest amongst the local populations so most leaders began to protect and guard their local wormholes; mostly to prevent people who couldn't sense them from stumbling through, but also to protect and keep for themselves whatever powers and mysteries they believed they could gain from the holes. You see they knew there was tremendous power there but they didn't understand what the holes were. Well, not until Einstein came along that is."

"So what about the wormhole in this library?" I asked.

Bonnie turned and stared at me and then back at the old man.

"This library?" she said. "There's one in this library?"

The old man leaned forward.

"There certainly is Bonnie. In fact there is likely to be one in almost every library in the land."

Bonnie and I stared at the old man who tilted his head back and laughed out loud.

"Let me explain. Over the centuries the various wormholes across the British Isles were documented and guarded by successive Kings, noblemen and latterly politicians. A system of guardianship was developed using the skills of those rare people who could sense the holes, time guardians, like me, although they didn't call them time guardians back then of course. They were more likely to be priests, alchemists or wizards."

The old man sank back in his chair and beamed.

"Where populations grew up around the various holes it was decided to incorporate them in the planning of the villages, towns and cities and hide them within buildings so that they couldn't be easily found and could be better protected."

"That makes sense," I said.

"Yes it does, and as a result, there are wormholes hidden deep within most ancient castles, churches, cathedrals, palaces and even the Houses of Parliament. After Einstein enlightened the world as to the true nature of time and space - and incidentally he himself was able to sense the holes and travelled through many in his time - we began to understand what the holes really were and of course the inherent dangers of allowing people to travel backwards and forwards in time willy-nilly. Should someone stumble through and inadvertently alter something in history, the whole world could change in an instant, and that would be just the accidental ones. When we contemplated what some people with personal gain or evil intent in mind could actually achieve, we knew the wormholes had to be protected at all costs. In fact, most nations came to the same conclusion and decided to act. In 1908 a global body was set up to manage and protect the wormholes to ensure no one nation could act unilaterally. That body is the International Alliance of Time Guardians, the IATG."

"And you work for the IATG?" Bonnie asked.

"Yes, I joined in 1960 and have been protecting the world ever since." He beamed at us again, obviously proud of his long history in such a responsible role."

"Now, my throat's a little dry with all this talking. Are there any other refreshments?"

"Oh I'm so sorry Mr Albright, how rude of me. More tea?" said Bonnie.

The old man screwed up his nose and shrugged his shoulders. "Well, if that's all you have. Something a little stronger would've been nice," he said, a sheepish grin spreading across his face.

Bonnie rubbed her finger against her chin.

"Well, I do have something, but it was to be James's Christmas present," she said, finally.

"My Christmas present?" I asked.

"Yes, I've had it for weeks. It's a single malt I know you love. I was going to wrap it up but when you went missing I put it at the back of the store cupboard. I wasn't going to get rid of it but I couldn't face looking at it, the pain was too much, so I hid the bottle." Tears welled up in Bonnie's beautiful green eyes again.

I brushed her damp cheek with my fingertips. "Thank you Bonnie. I love you and no one was ever going to keep me away from you."

Her mouth quivered as she smiled at me.

"Em...em," coughed the old man. "I do love a whisky."

I grinned at Bonnie. "Then maybe we should all have a little glass to celebrate?" I suggested.

"Celebrate what?" asked Bonnie.

"Well, celebrate me getting home alive, celebrate you and I being in love, and celebrate the fact that Mr Benjamin Albright here is about to tell us what the bloody hell is going on."

Bonnie slapped my leg hard. "I've told you before about that mouth of yours James. No swearing! But yes, I agree, all of those are worth a celebration. I'll get the whisky."

Bonnie pulled herself up from the sofa, straightened her floral dress and smiled at both her admirers before she rushed off to the store cupboard.

"She's a lovely lady James, I wish I were forty five years younger."

"Yes she is, thank you Mr Albright."

"Please James, call me Benjamin."

"OK, thank you. Is there a Mrs Albright, Benjamin?"

461

The old man tented his fingers together again as if in prayer.

"No I'm sad to say there never was James. You see I got involved with this work shortly before my twentieth birthday and unfortunately the nature of it doesn't lend itself much to building a stable relationship with anyone."

"What do you mean Benjamin, why is that?"

"Because of the nature of the time holes. Let's imagine I had a girlfriend for six months here, now, in this time. If I stepped through the time hole and back again I would arrive back on the first day I had arrived, I would be right back at the start. There would've been no six months, I would have to meet the young lady again for the first time, in her eyes at least. As I said previously, each wormhole is attached to a fixed place in time, to the same exact second of the day, it never moves."

As I was trying to get my head around that mind blowing conundrum Bonnie arrived with a silver tray of cut glass tumblers, a small jug of water and a bottle of Johnnie Walker Gold Label, complete with a red ribbon tied around the neck. She set the tray down on the small table in front of us and turned to me.

"Happy Christmas my love," she said, before blowing me a kiss.

"Thank you my darling. Oh and that reminds me, while we're on the subject of gifts."

I had remembered Bonnie's family heirloom, the locket. I pulled it out of my tunic pocket and held the treasured necklace out to her. Bonnie stared unblinking at the locket for a moment.

"No James, you keep it for now. You can give it back to me on our wedding day and I'll wear it forever." Her eyes found mine and she wasn't smiling, it was a question.

It was also a question that didn't require any time to consider.

"OK, perfect," I said. "Let's make it soon then."

We grinned childishly at each other, and we might have stayed that way for God knows how long if the old man hadn't interrupted us.

"Well James, it's your present, are you going to do the honours? Mine's a half and half with water, and I must say Bonnie your choice in whisky is superb. That particular one is a lovely smooth drink."

Bonnie picked up the bottle and handed it to me.

"Actually I understand nothing about whisky. All I know is it's my Uncle Willy's favourite brand and he loves his whisky. It's been a little hard to get though with the war on."

I pulled the cork stopper and poured a measure into each of the tumblers, added the water and handed the glasses out.

"Cheers," I said as I held out my glass. We clinked glasses and uttered the appropriate salutations before settling back in our seats.

"So, back to the wormholes," I said. "You say these things exist everywhere?"

"Yes James, there are thousands in all locations around the planet. To the best of our knowledge there are four hundred and forty seven recorded wormholes across the United Kingdom."

A worrying thought struck me. "So there will be wormholes in Germany or Japan?"

The old man smiled again. "Yes of course, and I understand your concern. If a rogue government decided to, it could potentially send someone back in time to change events to suit their own plans. Fortunately that is where the work of the IATG comes in. Since 1908 the IATG has kept the exact locations of each wormhole extremely secret and we do not share much of the detail with anyone, including politicians, monarchs, presidents and particularly not despotic rulers. Most leaders and politicians around the world know nothing of the wormholes or the work the IATG does, although some trusted ones do.

Of course there are legends, and rumours abound, but we do what we can to throw people off the scent with our own versions of those legends and rumours. We also constantly monitor the political situation in each country. If there is a potential troubling event, such as the rise of the Nazi party, then we lock down entirely in those regions. Oh, certainly some people try. Heinrich Himmler believed the legends and spent many years searching for the wormholes within Germany, but I am pleased to say he's been frustrated at every turn."

"That's a spot of luck then," said Bonnie.

"Yes, well not quite luck. You need to remember that unless you have the ability to sense the wormholes you're never going to locate them, unless you possess a map of course, which to the best of my knowledge none exist outside of the IATG. And to add to that, almost everyone who has the ability to sense the wormholes either works within or is in some way attached to the IATG. If it hadn't been for the IATG the world could most definitely have been a much different place."

Something the old man had said earlier was nagging at me. "So how come there happens to be a wormhole in each library up and down the country?"

The old man took a sip from the golden coloured liquid in his glass.

"Ah, that's an easy one," he answered. "In fact it's not that there happens to be a wormhole in each library, it was designed that way. In this country in the early part of the 19th century, when our various scientists began to realise these holes were not something supernatural that led to other worlds or fantasy lands, but were in fact portals that led to another time, we understood we needed a way of monitoring events to make sure no one had in fact stumbled through a wormhole and inadvertently changed time. The people who monitored the wormholes at that time found the easiest way of keeping a track on any changes in the world was to simply review the encyclopaedias of the day."

"So as they passed from one time to another they would always appear within a library and would have instant access to a whole range of encyclopaedias and text books to make sure nothing significant had changed in the world?" I asked.

The old man nodded and smiled. "Yes, exactly, and when the IATG was eventually formed in 1908 the time guardians like me continued this practice. In fact the structure of the IATG around the world now is based almost entirely on that early structure introduced within this country."

I took a sip of the whisky and felt the smooth liquid warm my throat and chest as it slid down. Aside from the fact that during the past hour the old man had revealed a whole breath-taking new world to us that we never even knew existed, everything he said seemed to make sense. Apart from one thing.

"So how do I fit into all this, how did I end up living in 2015, and why are you telling us all of this if it's so secretive?"

Bonnie's head snapped around.

"Living in 2015, what are you talking about James?"

"Yes, I did promise you an explanation didn't I? I think your memory has at last started to come back hasn't it James?"

"Yes, a little, but mostly it's still flitting around the edges, just out of reach."

"Memory, what memory? What are you two talking about?" asked Bonnie, her eyes darting from one to the other of us.

"Sorry Bonnie, please listen, there are some things you're not aware of yet, but all will become clear, I hope. So James, I'm no doctor and I'm unable to help you much with the medical side of what's happening inside your brain I'm afraid, but it does sound as if things are gradually coming back. I feel sure you realise enough by now to understand that you're back in the right time, your time, don't you?"

The conversations with my parents, Bonnie, the CO, Larry and the rest of the crew flicked through my mind.

"Yes."

"I feel sure your parents, Bonnie here and your friends will all be better placed to fill you in on your history more than I ever could, but suffice it to say you are a war hero. In fact one of the best and most experienced bomber pilots in the RAF at this moment in time, and you are in 617 squadron. Does that mean anything to you?"

"No, not really."

"James, you were a pilot on the dam buster's raid back in '43, you flew with Guy Gibson."

Another fleeting memory tantalised me, but as always it was just out of reach.

"Did I?"

"James?" Bonnie's frown was back. I glanced at her and shrugged.

"You've flown over seventy missions and are one of the most decorated fliers in the RAF James. As I said, you're a hero."

I didn't feel much like one. "So what happened to me, why don't I remember?"

Now the old man's face creased in a frown.

"James, on your last mission to the Ruhr at the beginning of December your aircraft was hit by one of the Luftwaffe's latest weapons; an Me262 jet night fighter equipped with an upwards firing cannon. You didn't stand a chance, he was on you before you could have even known he was there and fired upwards directly into your fully loaded bomb bay. Everyone believes your aircraft disintegrated in mid-air."

I swallowed hard. A vivid memory of an intense burning followed by instant coldness and a feeling of falling through space flooded into my mind, and this time stayed with me.

"What happened to everyone?"

"As the skipper, you were the only member of the crew with a parachute strapped to you, in fact you were sitting on it. No one else survived James. You were picked up by American troops just east of Antwerp; lucky for you they spotted your parachute coming down. You were unconscious, bleeding and bruised but amazingly enough you had no life threatening injuries. You were back in Tempsford within a couple of weeks, but it was obvious to everyone you had changed."

Bonnie grasped my hand and squeezed.

"Yes, I remember, you seemed to be in a daze for a few days after you got back. It was perfectly understandable of course, everyone was aware of what had happened which is why we all gave you some room. The CO refused to allow you to go on ops and you were here in the library almost every day after that. The CO asked me to spend a little more time here and keep an eye on you. You would come here in the morning and sit reading until we closed at five thirty each day, you were distant James, you barely even spoke to me."

The tears welled up in Bonnie's eyes again and it was my turn to give her hand a squeeze.

"I'm sorry my love. I don't remember any of it."

Bonnie smiled and wiped the back of her hand across her cheek.

"That's OK James, I understood the reason, and it must have been horrific for you. Then on Wednesday, after you came in I hadn't seen you all day, I was doing my last

473

walk around the shelves just before closing time when I spotted you and Mr Albright here over at the far wall. You were still distant, but I remember thinking you seemed and looked different somehow. Do you remember that, we went to Rosie's tea shop for some cake?"

"How could I forget?" I said, grinning. "That's when I had just returned from the library in 2015."

Bonnie's eyes widened but she said nothing.

I turned to the old man. "So what did happen to me, how did I end up in the year 2015?"

"Well James, I believe during those days in this library after the death of your crew, you sensed something, sensed the wormhole and went to investigate. You inadvertently stepped through the portal and arrived in the same location, but in 2015. You obviously had no idea then what had happened to you but you would have realised you were in a different place, a place where there was no war and where no one knew who you were and there was no one to remind you of what had happened to you. I suspect you were trying to get away from your memories so you decided to stay and do just that."

"Do what?"

"Hide from you memories, erase them from your mind and remain in this new safer world you found yourself in."

I nodded. Yes, that all made some sense, why wouldn't I?

"So how did you find me and what was all that with the messages in the books? That was you wasn't it Benjamin?"

The old man took another sip of his whisky and sat back to enjoy the warming sensations in his throat and chest before he responded.

"Yes it was James. I have to admit I knew nothing of you or your career before all of this happened. The first time I became aware of the issue was when I was alerted to the fact a change had happened up-time, a large change that had significantly impacted on the course of history. I was sent to investigate and after a few months of painstaking research I managed to pinpoint the source of the change to this particular wormhole at this point in time."

Our eyes were glued to the old man.

"So what was this large change I apparently caused?"

The old man swilled the remaining whisky around in his glass while he considered his response.

"It is rather what you didn't do that caused the problem. When you left December 1944 and remained in 2015 you didn't go on the last mission you were supposed to have been on, and the knock on effect was that you didn't save Major Glenn Miller from a watery grave as was supposed to happen. That resulted in some serious shifts in the course of time further upstream."

Recent memories of watching Glenn cartwheeling out of his destroyed aircraft, dragging him onto my life raft, patching up his wounds, escaping from the Gestapo and flying him home rolled through my head like an old adventure movie.

"You mean Glenn Miller isn't missing?" asked Bonnie, who swallowed the rest of her whisky in one go and only just managed to stop herself from coughing it straight back up again.

The old man grinned at her. "No, your future husband here saved the great bandsman."

Bonnie turned to me and stared. Was that a look of awe in her eyes? I hoped so.

"So apart from the obvious point of saving his life, what else changed?" I asked.

The old man laughed out loud. "What else? Well just about everything. In the true course of history Glenn and his band went on to support the allies through the last months of the war in Europe and Japan with regular concerts for the troops in the front lines. After the war he

477

continued on for several years playing concerts in the USA and Europe to help raise money for the homeless and starving war refugees. He departed the army as a Colonel and his career then took a new turn in the late forties and early fifties when he moved to Los Angeles and got into the movies. He had varying degrees of success with that before he made a switch back into the music business and took a few up and coming rock and roll stars under his wing and managed their careers. Two of his biggest stars were Buddy Holly and Ritchie Valens."

"Yes, I've heard of them," I said. "I read about them when I was in 2015. They died young didn't they?"

The old man smiled. "Yes, and that's the point, they shouldn't have. After the war Glenn never flew in another aeroplane again and he also had a strict rule with the artists he managed, no airplane rides for them either. Buddy Holly and Ritchie Valens never boarded that doomed aeroplane with the Big Bopper on the night of 3rd February 1959 and they went on to become two of the most prolific and successful stars the world has ever seen. Ritchie eventually teamed up with Elvis Presley in Las Vegas in 1975 and began an incredibly successful song writing and performing partnership until Elvis's unfortunate death in 1994 due to cancer."

Bonnie leaned forward and grabbed the bottle of whisky from the table. She splashed a large measure into her tumbler and downed it in one go.

"You're talking as if all this has already happened. You're both mad, the war isn't even over yet." Her eyes were wide and her lips were trembling. She looked as if she was going to burst into tears at any moment.

"Bonnie," I said as I took her hand and squeezed it. "I realise how hard this is to get your head around, and from where we're sitting right now of course none of this has happened yet, but I've been there, to the year 2015, to the future, and like Benjamin here I know it will happen. It's going to take both of us a bit of getting used to, but Benjamin is telling the truth."

The old man sat forward in his chair. "Bonnie, James is right, this will take a little adjusting to but everything I've told you is the truth, it's how things really are. It's just that most people don't get to see it for real. It's nothing to be afraid of, if we're careful with the past."

I finished my own glass of whisky, placed the glass on the table in front of me and stared at the old man.

"So, is everything back to how it should be then?"

The old man sank back in his chair and rubbed his chin for a moment before he spoke.

"Yes, I think so, but a little more research will be needed to confirm that."

I nodded.

"So, what was all that with the messages in the books, why didn't you just come and get me, and take me back?"

"Well James, I realised it was best to give you some time to deal with the trauma. There was simply no point in me arriving out of the blue in 2015 and trying to explain to you that you were a time traveller and I had to get you back to December 1944 so you could go on a bombing mission to Europe and save Major Glenn Miller's life. You'd have assumed, rightly, that I was completely stark raving bonkers. I also didn't have any specific deadline to work to as I knew when I returned you to your time it would be at the exact same moment you left, so no time at all would have passed in 1944. The only problem would be of course that you and I were still ageing in 2015 and after too long you would have returned looking much older, which might have been difficult to explain away. So when I thought the time was right, I used the messages in the boxes to stimulate your brain to begin to question why things were as they were, and hopefully make you more accepting of the change when I bundled you back through the wormhole. It was the only plan I managed to come up with, so I apologise if it was a little mysterious. I also needed to make sure everything was back on track here, so under the authority of the Air Chief Marshall himself I went and discussed the forthcoming mission with your CO. As dangerous as it was, I knew you had to go on that mission and I had to make sure you did. "

Everything the old man said made sense now. At least it did once I had managed to accept the principle that time travel was indeed possible. But a few things still didn't add up for me.

"I do have a couple more questions that for some reason hadn't occurred to me before?" I said.

"Fire away," said the old man.

"OK, I'm a little confused about how I sensed the wormhole here in the library. The pain I received in my head in 2015 was almost unbearable, and because of that I know I would never have come back through without you pushing me, yet I didn't seem to have that pain here in 1944, which is possibly why I stumbled through in the first place. Why is that?"

"Ah James, a good question. That's another one of those things we can't fully explain. It seems that moving through a wormhole upstream, in the same direction time is flowing is relatively easy and painless, however trying to go back against the flow of time is much harder for all of us and can get quite painful. As I say, we don't know why, it just seems to be that way."

I nodded, and thought about the next question that was troubling me.

"OK, got that. So, during that year I was in 2015, how did I manage to live and rent a flat? I know I didn't own a car or a mobile phone or anything like that, but the library must have needed a copy of my birth certificate to pay me and my landlady would have wanted a deposit wouldn't she? I don't understand how that all came about."

The old man gave a wet snort as he chuckled.

"Oh I'm sorry, how rude of me. I say, Bonnie dear, may I have some more of that fine whisky?"

Bonnie leaned forward to pour another measure into the old man's and my glasses. I noticed she didn't take any more herself.

"Thank you Bonnie, now where was I? Ah yes, your job at the library. I needed you there so I could keep a close eye on you in 2015. I simply explained to the town council that you were to work at the library temporarily as part of your rehabilitation and I provided them with all the necessary paperwork. With the backing and influence of the IATG at your disposal these things are fairly easy."

"And my apartment?"

"Ah yes, your lodgings. Well that's easy, you see, the attic room you rented is owned by the IATG. In fact the entire building is, and the landlady Mrs King is in our employ too. By the way the other young lady I believe you met at the premises, a Miss Buxley, is also one of our agents. She's from 2135 and was investigating an occurrence in 2015 while you were there."

I stared at the old man again. I hadn't even contemplated there might be people from the future flitting about the corridors of time too.

"You mean there are IATG agents from the future too?"

"Well of course there are. In fact most of the gadgets and gizmos we use nowadays for research and communicating with each other come from the future."

"How far in the future?" Bonnie asked.

"Well, here's another slightly mysterious part of the science of time travel we simply don't understand as yet. Each wormhole seems to be limited to a maximum of a 100 years jump at a time. To move about further in time we need to go from one wormhole to another. As you'd imagine, having maps of each wormhole and where it leads

485

to are pretty essential pieces of our toolkit as it all gets a little complicated. However, even moving about using different wormholes we still can't seem to be able to get back past say, around 1490 AD. The wormholes appear to decrease in number the further we go back in time until there's none left that we know of. At the moment our limit to the past seems to be the 1490 AD line. Likewise, in the future the wormholes peter-out around 2520 AD. As time moves on we find we lose a few more wormholes in the past, bringing our boundary forward in time and to balance that we usually discover a few more wormholes in the future which extend in that direction. This keeps our limit of travel forwards or backwards pretty constant, but it does all creep forward slowly down that time stream I mentioned. As I said, no one understands for sure why this is, it's probably one of the fundamental principles of the universe but as yet we're pretty much in the dark as to why."

I had to admit it was all getting a little above my head at that point and after a full-on day escaping certain death from the hands of the Gestapo, stealing an aeroplane from the Luftwaffe and getting shot up by a Hurricane, all this time-travel stuff was just a bit too much.

I put my arm around Bonnie's waist and pulled her close to me. She rested her head on my shoulder and closed her eyes.

"I'm sorry but I think we're done for the day Benjamin. I'll need to get Bonnie back to her billet at the base and I'll need to hit the sack too."

"Are you seriously thinking of taking Bonnie to the base on the back of your motorbike, in this weather?"

I hadn't actually given that much thought.

"Bonnie, how were you planning on getting back to the base?" I asked.

"Mmmmm...what?"

"I said how were you getting back to the base?"

"Mmm, by bus. The last one's at six thirty in the winter," she said. The whisky was working its magic, she was almost asleep.

The old man pulled his gold fob watch out of his waistcoat pocket.

"It's seven forty now, it's too late and you've missed it."

I glanced down at Bonnie, snoring gently against my shoulder and was just contemplating making her comfortable for a night on the sofa when the old man dropped the remaining bombshell on me.

"James, I want you to listen to me carefully now, I am going to put something to you. I don't need an answer right away but I think you should take this very seriously, very seriously indeed."

"Go on," I said, the tiredness forgotten for the moment.

"James, I am seventy five years of age and I can't go on for much longer. I want to go back home and spend my final years in a place and time I feel comfortable in. I can't do this any longer, I'm too tired. I've been searching for years to find someone else with the sense, someone who can take over from me, and I think I've found that person."

My stomach churned. Those damn butterflies were back.

"You mean me?" There wasn't anyone else in the library but I needed to be sure.

"Yes James, I mean you. You are young, fit and courageous beyond belief, and you possess a strong sense of duty as well as having the all-important sense of time."

I stared at the old man. I'm sure I was dribbling but to be truthful I didn't care.

"I'm an officer in the RAF Benjamin. I know we both know the war in Europe will be over in five months, but I still have a job to do."

The old man smiled again and raised his glass to me.

"You see, that's what I meant about your sense of duty. James, you've already completed seventy two missions. A normal expected tour of duty in Bomber Command is thirty missions. With an average loss rate of five percent it is mathematically impossible for anyone to survive, but they of course do, and history will record only around twenty five percent of crews survived their first tour of thirty missions. Most crews went voluntarily onto a second tour of twenty missions but the chances of surviving that were almost zero. You've done three complete tours James and you're now operating fully on borrowed time. You've done more than your fair share in this war and it's time to move on. You're needed elsewhere now, undertaking something which is arguably much more beneficial for the future of mankind."

"Yes Benjamin, I see that, but I'm an officer in the RAF, I'm not going to be able to simply walk away."

The old man took a sip of the golden nectar in his tumbler and grinned sheepishly.

"Ah...yes...well, I've already taken the liberty of raising this with your CO, Air Chief Marshall Harris and the commander in chief himself, Winston."

"You mean you've already discussed this with Bomber Harris and Winston Churchill?"

"Yes, and they are both supportive of it. They understand the critical nature of the work we do in keeping the world safe. You have been offered a promotion to wing commander if you accept your new post in the IATG."

The old man stared at me. He wasn't laughing anymore.

"Let me get this right Benjamin, and forgive me if I'm a bit naive with all this time travel business, but if I accept I will be expected to travel into various times, solving any hiccups in the normal flow of time as and when they occur?"

"Yes."

"And if I were to come back through this wormhole into my own time I would always return on Wednesday 13th December 1944?"

"Yes."

"And I would be right back where I started and none of this would have happened?"

"Ah yes, well...of course there are paradoxes in time travel. You are able to move around through the various wormholes, backwards and forwards into other times and your disappearances and appearances are somehow allowed under the rules of our universe, but we do tend to avoid ever coming back through the original wormhole into the exact same place we started from. That never seems to end happily."

Not end happily? That was a bloody understatement. I was beginning to see the downside in all this.

"So let me get this right, if I take this on and begin time travelling, I'll never be able to return here to see my own parents again?"

"No, that's not correct. I said you shouldn't come back here to this exact place and time. There are a vast number of wormholes where you can pop back to visit your parents whenever you like at any time during their natural lifetimes. You'll just have to make sure you get the timings roughly right so they don't notice you looking too old or too young at any given time."

"OK, I get that." At least I thought I did. "But what about Bonnie?"

"Ah yes, Bonnie." The old man glanced down at my sleeping beauty.

I didn't like the sound of that at all.

"You never had a wife or a family did you Benjamin?"

"No."

"Because it's too difficult when you're time travelling most of your life?"

"Yes." The old man clasped his hands together in his lap and stared down at them.

We sat without another word for a few awkward moments, with neither of us willing to make eye contact. I finally broke the silence.

"OK, then I'll do it."

The old man's head shot up and he stared at me.

"You will?"

"Yes." I grinned. "But only on one condition."

"And what's that?"

"That Bonnie comes along as my permanent sidekick."

The old man sat in silence with a deep frown etched across his face for at least five long minutes. He was obviously churning all the permutations, potential conflicts and opportunities around in his mind. Eventually he spoke.

"It's highly irregular. In fact to the best of my knowledge it's never been done before."

"But...?"

"But...I agree. Why not? It's a marvellous idea."

The old man slapped his hand against his knee and laughed out loud. "Let's drink to it," he said as he reached forward and poured out another two good measures.

"Whoa," I said. "I've still got to get Bonnie sorted and back to the base myself. I'm not one hundred percent on that old Norton yet you know, especially in this weather."

The old man laughed out loud again.

"You don't have to worry about that," he said as he leaned back and fiddled for something in his waistcoat pocket which he eventually found and threw at me. I caught the shiny silver object and peered down at my hand. It was a single silver key.

"What's this?"

A grin spread across the old man's face. "It's the key to your new house. You'll know it well, you used to live there in 2015, only now the ground floor apartments are all yours. There are a few rooms on the first floor we keep ready for other IATG agents should they need to stay, but otherwise it's all yours. All you need to do is walk your lovely lady over the bridge and make yourselves comfortable. I suggest you leave your motorbike here."

I stared at the key in my hand.

"But that's where you live isn't it?" I asked.

The old man was still smiling. He was like one of those bloody clowns with the permanently painted on grin.

"No, I moved up into the old attic two days ago. I'll be happy there for the next couple of months while I hand over to you. Besides, I can do with the additional exercise."

I had a sneaking suspicion that my decision had been a foregone conclusion all along, but as I glanced down at the beautiful red haired girl asleep in my arms and imagined our cosy apartment I decided not to complain too much.

"So, shall we have a final nightcap to seal things?" the old man suggested.

I glanced down at the half empty bottle of Johnnie Walker in front of us.

"Yes, OK, just one."

The old man had just leaned forward to lift the bottle when a loud buzzing sound came from inside his jacket. He sat back in his chair and pulled out a small silver tablet, about the same size as a mini iPad but amazingly wafer thin, like a single sheet of paper. A frown creased his forehead.

"Oh no," was all he said.

"What's up?" I asked, sitting forward in my chair, staring across at him.

"It's a message from up-time. Lee Harvey Oswald just missed the president. Kennedy survived."

Chapter Eleven - Epilogue

Bonnie never got to package the books up that New Year's Eve after the library was damaged by the V2 bomb, as she was otherwise engaged.

Wing Commander James Cunnion and Bonnie Ohain were married on the 31st December 1944 in the church of St Paul, St Paul's square, Bedford town centre. Larry accepted the honour of being James's best man and Bonnie's proud father, Karl Von Ohain was there to give her away. The CO, wanting to play his part, met James's parents in Glasgow and personally flew them down to Bedford for the occasion in a Lancaster bomber from RAF Prestwick.

The reception was held in the Bedford Corn Exchange that final New Year's Eve of the war and Glenn kept his promise, the Glenn Miller Band played the entire evening. It was a sell out and unsurprisingly not a single guest turned down an invite. A surprise wedding guest that evening was Winston Churchill, accompanied by his wife Clemmie, who had come to honour one of the famous Dambusters.

James and Bonnie *'officially'* moved into their new apartments in Bedford the following day, 1st January 1945.

Larry Knight was promoted to Flight Lieutenant and completed his final tour of operations in March 1945. He married Jackie in May 1945 and they celebrated their honeymoon in style on VE day. Larry left the RAF in 1947 but volunteered for duty during the Berlin Airlift between June 1948 and May 1949 and went on to establish his own highly successful cargo airline he and Jackie named *Knight's Riders*.

Of the rest of the crew of N-Nuts:

Dicky the flight engineer was listed as missing during Bomber Command's last mission of the war on 3rd May 1945. His body was never recovered.

Ricky the wireless operator recovered from his wounds received over Essen and was repatriated back to Australia. He opened a crocodile farm in Queensland in 1946.

The body of Eddie the bomb aimer lost over Essen was never found. His name is listed on the RAF memorials along with the other 55,572 of those heroic men of Bomber Command who lost their lives during World War 2.

Frankie the rear gunner never made it back to his family business and his cello in Banff. Despite the valiant efforts of James and Dicky he succumbed to his wounds and is now buried in the Canadian war cemetery at Grosbeek, Holland.

Alky the navigator survived the war and left the RAF in 1946. He was charged with horse rustling in County Clare in 1947 and contracted malaria and died whilst bringing food aid to the people of Tigray, Ethiopia during the famine of 1958.

Amy the SOE agent got that concert she was promised. Glenn Miller and his band put on a show in her honour in the Albert Hall, London on the 1st August 1945.

After three months working with James, Benjamin Albright retired to spend his final years in his old family cottage in the quaint Dorset seaside town of Lyme Regis. The date, 1st May 1898.

As for James and Bonnie, did they live happily ever after? Only time will tell.

A thank you from the author

Time is the most valuable commodity we humans possess. None of us know how long we have left, it may be years or it may be months, but whatever it is there is one thing that we can all be certain of, we never have enough time. That is why I want to personally thank you from the bottom of my heart for the amount of your highly valued time you have already invested in reading this book. Thank you.

In common with all new independent authors, my stories will either live or die depending on the amount of feedback they receive. It is a fact in this on-line digital age we now live in, that without feedback many products simply won't be purchased and books won't be bought without adequate on-line feedback. So, before you go, can I ask you please to invest just a little bit more of your time and write a short review for this book on Amazon? Just a few sentences is all that is required and your comments will add to the story. Please, this really matters.

You can also drop me an email at info@michael-stewart.net and I will be happy to respond, or you can visit my website at www.michael-stewart.net

Thank you most sincerely and I hope to see you again in another story.

About the author

Michael Stewart was born in London, England in 1959 and is married with five children and two grandchildren. Following a lifetime in business within the aviation industry, travelling and living in various parts of the world, Michael has now settled on the West Coast of Scotland to follow his passion of writing.

Michael's debut novel *The Angel of Time*, a fascinating tale set during the First World War with a thrilling time travel twist was published in October 2014 and is available now on Amazon in Kindle and Paperback versions.

The Search for Excalibur is Michael's second novel and his first venture into the Young Adult genre. If you enjoy tales of mystery, magic and adventure, this is the one for you. Available now on Amazon in Kindle and Paperback versions.

Please review these and Michael's other short stories on www.michael-stewart.net

Printed in Great Britain
by Amazon